Accidental Series

ACCIDENTAL BABIES

SAIYIDAH RAHMAN

type
writer
pub

To Wattpad readers who have supported me from the beginning

Typewriter Pub, an imprint of Blvnp Incorporated
A Nevada Corporation
1887 Whitney Mesa DR #2002
Henderson, NV 89014
www.typewriterpub.com/info@typewriterpub.com

ISBN: 978-1-68030-998-0

DISCLAIMER
This book is a work of fiction. The characters, incidents, and dialogue are drawn from the author's imagination and are not to be construed as real. While references might be made to actual historical events or existing locations, the names, characters, places, and incidents are either products of the author's imagination or are used fictitiously, and any resemblance to actual persons living or dead, business establishments, events or locales is entirely coincidental.

FREE DOWNLOAD

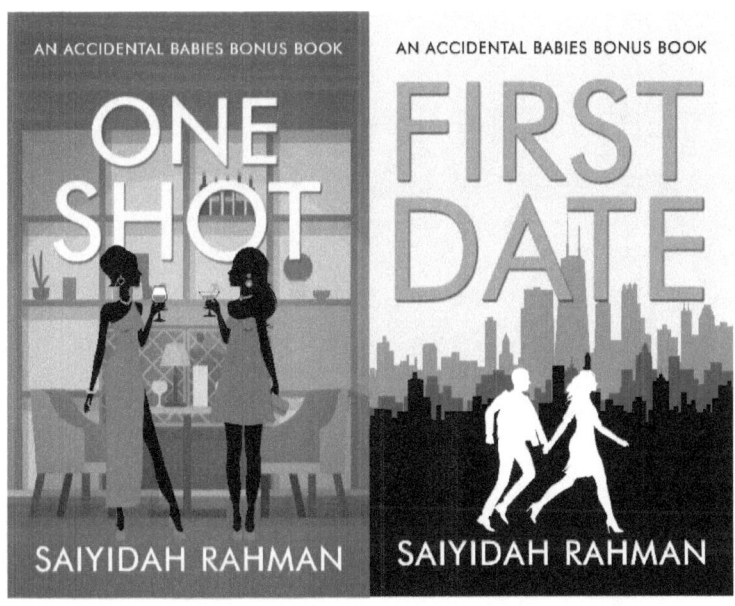

Get these freebies and more when you sign up for the author's mailing list!

saiyidah-rahman.awesomeauthors.org

CHAPTER 1

Jason Halloway leaned back into his chair, stretching slightly. He was happy that he managed to accomplish and clear his workload for the day. Clearly, his decision to leave the twins in his assistant's hands was a sound one. They hadn't bothered or called for him at any point of the day—well, aside from the first hour—but that had been expected as they were in a new environment. Yes, it was a good day. Now, he just had to bring them home, hopefully have an uneventful bath, dinner, and a fuss-free bedtime.

"Janice, please get the twins ready. I'll be going off in ten minutes," he said into the intercom as he packed. Silence greeted him. He frowned. Janice, his assistant, was always prompt in acknowledging him. "Janice?"

"Ah, Mr. Halloway," she finally said, but her voice was extremely strained. "A few more minutes, please. I have to, um, change them."

"Do you need any help with them? They can be quite a handful,' he offered, wanting to feel them in his arms. It was a surprise to find that he was missing them even though he had only had them for a few weeks. He was, then, shocked when Janice sputtered in response. A frown furrowing his brows, he knew he had a reputation for being cold and stern but they were his children, and he'd found out that he liked being a hands-on father, entirely different from his parents.

"N-no need for that, sir. I, um, have to go now. I'll bring them to you in a minute," she said hurriedly and disconnected. A sense of foreboding started in his chest, but he waited. Janice had assured him that she would be able to take care of them. He could trust her. She hadn't proved him wrong in the past. Surely his children were in good hands.

~

It had been thirty minutes, and his patience was starting to fray. Actually, it had frayed within ten minutes, and now, he was ready to snap. He was second-guessing his assistant. Even if the twins were being difficult, it shouldn't take that long to change them. Deciding to get to the bottom of this, he left his office and was greeted with an empty desk. Not surprised, he continued to the main office and was greeted with chaos.

All of his employees were on their hands and knees, looking under chairs and tables. It would have been amusing but not worth commenting if they weren't calling his children's names. Were they *looking* for them? Processing that implication, he naturally came to the following conclusion: they were missing.

"M-Mr. Halloway," one of the female workers cried loudly. Everyone stopped and looked at him with arrested expressions. One that morphed into guilt. All of them hurriedly stood and rushed to their desks, contriving to look busy.

"Mr. Halloway, I, um, we—*I*—can explain," Janice said, running toward him. Her beautiful face was red, and her dark grey eyes were darting about, never settling on him. His sense of foreboding grew.

"Where are my children? And how long have they been missing?" he asked coldly. He knew bringing them to work had been a bad idea, but there was no one else available and he trusted his assistant. He didn't want to leave them with someone he hadn't vetted either. His blood ran cold. Did their mother take them?

Surely not. She had dropped them into his arms like hot potatoes and left with no explanation three months ago. She'd even signed the contract stating she gives up her parental rights. The last he had heard of her, she was in Paris, and that was three hours ago. She wouldn't have had time to arrange a kidnapping in such a short time. So, it definitely wasn't her. Which just left his incompetent assistant.

"Actually, sir, it's my fault," one of the female workers said nervously, joining Janice. He recognized her. She was one of Janice's best friends in the office. Another joined them. Still another of Janice's friends. "Janice had to photocopy and mail an important document and left the babies with Aubrey and me which was about two hours ago. We have neighboring cubicles so we thought it'd be easier for us to look after them than Janice. Since, you know, two are better than one and all that."

"That still doesn't answer the question," he said slowly, his anger reaching a boiling point. They didn't appear to be responsible enough to take on the care of his children. Slim and beautiful, yes. But not responsible.

"As Karen was saying, we thought it'd be easier, but I thought she was keeping an eye on them and she thought I was keeping an eye on them. We got absorbed with work and when we next turned to look at them, they were, um, already gone," the other woman, Aubrey, said anxiously.

"What?!" he roared. The entire office jumped. He didn't care who witnessed his anger. This should serve them a lesson. "When did you realize they were missing? Have you searched the entire office? The entire floor? How about the entire building? Did you consult with the security guards and the cameras?"

"We-we were about to but—"

Suddenly, baby voices were heard, interrupting Janice. Relief coursed through him when he recognized them as his

3

children's. Everyone turned to where they heard their voices. It seemed like they were heading towards him, but he couldn't see them. Probably because of all the cubicles and the fact that they would be crawling. Impatient and disgusted with the lack of action from his employees, he was about to head for them himself when *they* rounded the corner.

More accurately, they rounded the corner within the arms of a tall, overweight, disheveled auburn-haired woman—someone who definitely didn't work for him. And, yet, they looked quite happy and content to be in her arms. They looked even happier when they saw him. Bouncing about in her arms, they stretched their arms toward him.

Still puzzled, he grabbed them from her. He didn't exactly snatch them away, but he wasn't gentle either. While he nodded absently at the baby talk from his twins and jostled them slightly when they became restless, his eyes fixed on the unknown woman. She was fidgeting uncomfortably under the eyes of the entire office on her but under his penetrating glare, she withered.

"Who are you?" he demanded, his voice as frosty as ice.

"I-I'm April Saunders. I am—was—here for an interview when I saw them crawling along the hallway. I, ah, picked them up after I realized they were unattended," she said softly, her eyes taking an interest at the burgundy carpet. He shot a glare at the three women before focusing on his twins' new caretaker.

"When was this?" he asked. He was curious to how long they'd been with her and how long his twins had been alone.

"About two hours ago, approximately? I had been trying to find their parent or nanny when they suddenly decided to take a nap. That was about an hour and a half ago. I mean, it was hard enough to carry them when they were awake but they became deadweight when they slept," she said with a small tremulous smile that withered away when he didn't return the sentiment. "They just woke up fifteen minutes ago and sent me on a wild goose chase," she said with another smile. This smile was more genuine and directed at the bundles in his arms. Jason was slightly distracted by that smile. It transformed an otherwise plain face into a pretty one. The warmth in her obsidian eyes made her even more attractive. He was also relieved his children hadn't been roaming alone for long before they were found by this woman. Suddenly, his son Tanner, reached for her. She looked to him for permission. He hesitated but, at Tanner's insistence, he relented.

Tanner looked awfully comfortable with her. And he was the fussier of the twins. His daughter, Daphne, had also looked comfortable in her arms before. His twins always had a difficult time adjusting to the changes in their lives. They'd disapproved all the nannies and caretakers he'd hired, crying relentlessly, throwing their toys around, and refusing to sleep. He was continually worried about them. He'd consulted child psychologists who, instead of helping, just gave him empty platitudes that were worth less than shit. He had tried to seek help from his aunt, which had worked for a while, but she had her own life. Furthermore, he hadn't been entirely comfortable dumping the twins on her. He'd been at his wits' end when he brought them to the office.

But it seemed that the twins didn't need him to find a nanny for them anymore. They'd found one all on their own. He just hoped he didn't have to send her away.

CHAPTER 2

April shifted in the chair uncomfortably. She hadn't known that those babies she'd taken care of were the Halloway Corporation CEO's children. None of the people she'd encountered had said anything. Hell, they didn't even look at her. They just bumped into her and walked away without a by-your-leave even though she'd been carrying the twins then. Surely, they'd recognized their own boss's kids?

Now she was in Jason Halloway's office probably to be punished for taking his children without permission. He could be thinking that she was really trying to kidnap them. Or sell them away on the black market. He could even be calling the cops right at this moment.

Logic tried to intrude, reminding her that she didn't know anyone on the black market and of the fact that she was not going there in the first place. Shoving logic out of the way, she let her other thoughts run wild and unchecked. It didn't help that she was alone in the office. She tried to distract herself by shifting her attention to the decor. The floor was all hardwood and there was a group of sofas placed across one end of the room, the exact material of which she couldn't quite put her finger on, but she guessed it was most likely made from expensive leather. It was in a modern design—all white and uncomfortable-looking. In the middle of the room, there was a long table with a grouping of eight chairs around it, probably to hold meetings for the upper echelon of the company. And at the other end, where she was sitting and waiting, was the main desk. It was quite a large desk containing all his stationeries, stacks of work, and even a few family photos.

She studied some and noticed a few of them featured Mr. Halloway with quite a handsome man who had blond hair and grey eyes. Not that Mr. Halloway couldn't hold a candle to this man—where his handsomeness was refined, the other man had an air of savagery. There was another man with them. He had dark hair and piercing very light blue eyes. Just looking at his pictures made her uncomfortable. There were some pictures where he had a light air to him—he was smiling widely, showing two dimples, one on each cheek. But as the pictures showed their progressive growth and maturity, his face had an equally progressing darker air about him. His smiles grew smaller and his eyes colder. She wouldn't want to meet him in a dark alley.

Mr. Halloway's chiseled features fit his heart-shaped face perfectly, and his eyes—even though they had been hard on her—were in a beautiful soft shade of olive green. His mouth, though, was the most sensual of his features. Even as he'd glared into her soul, her eyes hadn't been able to stay away from those lips. His thin upper lip was a perfect complement to his plumper and eminently nibble-worthy lower lip. Before she decided if making out with the picture was a good idea, she put the frame down and stepped away.

From the resemblance in the pictures, she could tell they were related—brothers or maybe cousins. They seemed close from the way their arms slung around each other as seen in some candid photos of them goofing off. She noticed one frame for the twins. But it was just the one when they were probably seven months old. *Why didn't he have any photos of them from much earlier? And where was their mother?*

"I'm sorry to keep you waiting, Miss Saunders," he said, suddenly coming into the room. April jumped slightly. It would have been good if he had announced his presence, but this was his office anyway. She made a motion to stand up but was waved away by Mr. Halloway. "I had to retrieve your résumé from the HR department. It seemed like they were almost going to throw it away when you didn't show up for the interview. May I know what position you were applying for?" he asked her while settling in his chair behind his desk.

"Receptionist, sir," she told him, shocked that he went to get her résumé. Whatever for? She knew she'd blown the interview when she decided to go after the twins. "May I know why, Sir?"

Mr. Halloway looked at April, one eyebrow arched high in confusion. April looked to him then to her resume in his hands and said, "Um, my résumé, Sir...why did you—"

"Why I retrieved your résumé? So that I can determine your suitability as a nanny for my children," he told her absently, studying the document. "You wrote here that you've only one relevant experience and all other experience basically amounts to waiting tables. Why the switch?"

"I, um, I wanted a change of pace. Frankly, I'm getting too old for it. The long hours. Unreasonable customers. Plus, I've just graduated. So, I wanted a job that's somewhat relevant to my qualifications," she told him, puzzled. *Nanny to his twins? Of course not.* She must have heard it wrong.

"Yes, it's listed here that you have a degree for Business Administration. So why a receptionist?" he asked, looking at her over steepled hands. She frowned.

"Excuse me, but may I know exactly why you are asking me all of that? I know it was bad of me just to pick up the twins, but I do not think it warrants all these questions," she said softly, trying to ask for a clarification in case she hadn't heard properly.

8

"Ah, my apologies. It seems that I've forgotten to tell you about the nature of our meeting here. Seeing how my children have behaved with you earlier, I would like to offer you the position as their live-in nanny. Accommodations will be provided for, as will transport and food. Your only job is to take care of the twins. My housekeeper will take care of the house, including the laundry and meals. However, as she's on her holidays for the next two weeks or so right now, you'll have to fend for yourself until her return."

"Nanny? That's not even relevant to my education," she cried, her mind unable to wrap itself around the idea. *Nanny?* She had only taken care of them for, at most, one hour so she didn't see how she could possibly be a good nanny to them. She could barely take care of herself. And he wanted to entrust them to *her?*

"Well, it's the only position I am willing to offer you," he said, his eyes as hard as granite. She was happy she had the wide expanse of the table between them.

"What about the receptionist role?" she asked, disappointed. She'd hoped to move up the ranks if she got the position.

"I do not like to repeat myself," he hissed. She flinched and ducked her head down, using her hair as a barrier from those eyes.

"But why me as a nanny? Surely there're more qualified people," she said softly. His lips twisted wryly.

"Well, my children have chased away 'qualified people' in the field, leaving you. The children miraculously slept with you. Do you know how difficult it took all those qualified people to achieve in a day what you did only within half an hour of meeting them? That immediately convinced me that you're suitable for the role," he said firmly.

"But don't you want to check my background? What if I'm some serial killer who's just good with babies? What if I have a fetish for them? You can't decide on this just based on our two-hour interaction," she argued, ignoring her inner voice who told her to just take up the position without any hassle. But these were babies they were talking about. She had little to no experience with them. She didn't want to compromise their general well-being with her lack of knowledge.

"That's why you'll be having a one-month trial period. If, within that month, there is anything that I'm not satisfied with, I'll terminate your role as a nanny and offer you a different position within the company that is suitable to your qualification," he offered. She saw a hint of smugness in his eyes. He was so sure she wouldn't be able to resist his offer and—damn him—he was right. She only needed to spend time with those adorable twins and, if it didn't work out, she'd still have a job. It was a win-win situation.

"Well, Ms. Saunders?"

"I'll take you up on your offer, Mr. Halloway. I hope we will both benefit from this arrangement," she said stiffly.

"Then, here is my address, Ms. Saunders. Please be at my door by 7 am sharp with all your luggage. You'll be expected to live with us within a month. And if things go well, we'll discuss future accommodations after the trial period is over. Do you have any more questions?" he asked softly. She shook her head, giddy that she'd secured a job and also sick with worry about her lack of knowledge with babies. "Good. I'll see you tomorrow then. Good day."

She didn't know what she said to him as a farewell. All she was thinking about was calling her mother up to consult with her about the care of babies. Hopefully, she won't be yelled at again.

CHAPTER 3

Jason smiled in satisfaction when he heard the doorbell. He knew there was a possibility that she wouldn't show up but that was a small percentage. He straightened his cuffs and went to answer the door. She looked even scruffier in her worn sweater and faded jeans when surrounded by the opulence of the hallway. Since he hadn't specified the appropriate attire, he didn't bother pointing it out. Surprisingly, she had one small suitcase with her. He wondered. Weren't women always travelling with at least three to five pieces of luggage?

He let her in and proceeded to outline her various roles. "Thank you for showing up, Ms. Saunders. Let me brief you on what is expected of you. Since I used to hire live-out nannies, I'm the person who bathes the children in the morning. But, in your case, as you'll be living *in*, that'll fall under your jurisdiction. I'll come in when they become too rowdy. Their usual breakfast includes milk and some baby food; you'll find that with the instructions on the fridge. After that, their activities are up to your discretion. Here is a list of approved activities, vetted by some of their earlier nannies. You may take them anywhere you want, but please be back by six. I'll try to be home by then, but if I'm not back, please bathe and feed them. Do you have any question? As I have said, my housekeeper is away for two weeks, but she has prepared food for me. You are welcome to get some food as well but generally, you don't have to worry about cooking for us."

She looked faintly overwhelmed by all that he had thrown at her but he saw her recover. "If I have any question, may I contact you, Sir? Just in case. And is there any emergency contact?" she asked, looking up at him. He felt himself drowning in those deep dark blue eyes. *Why was he so fascinated with her eyes? Maybe because it's her most pleasant feature? But her smile was quite a contender. And her hair as well.*

A shrill scream broke him out of his reverie. He sent April a dry smile. "My daughter. She's an early riser and is never content to let anyone sleep in. In a few moments, you'll be hearing my son as well." And, true to his words, Tanner's cries were heard a few seconds later. "Shall we?"

"Um, may I inquire about their mother, Sir?" she asked hesitantly. Jason felt himself stiffen involuntarily. He didn't like talking about their mother. In his mind, they didn't have a mother. They just had a surrogate who decided that having children did not suit her image and then dumped them on their unsuspecting father. However, he knew he had to warn April about her. She was vindictive and might even try to take them away if she thought it might benefit her, even when she'd signed away all her rights to them in a legally binding contract.

They paused outside the twins' nursery. The twins had settled down slightly, probably entertaining each other. April looked uncertainly up at him and he was struck with the fact that she didn't have far to look up. She must be quite tall for a woman because he was 6'5" and she already reached his shoulder.

"You don't have to talk about her if you don't want to." He knew she was willing to let it go but he didn't want her to be caught unaware.

"You are never to leave them alone with their mother. Ever. This is the one rule that you have to follow to the letter. Do not even deviate in the slightest," he told her. He couldn't have stressed the importance more. She nodded in understanding, but he could see she was puzzled by his instruction. "Their mother is a public figure and if having the kids would help her, she'd do anything to do so. She's Carrie Carter."

"The supermodel? The one who had to be dropped by her label because of some fight or something?" she asked with a gasp. Amusement filled him. This was the first time someone had mentioned that fight in a long time. Usually, people would mention her career or her tabloid exploits. Shaking the amusement, he was gratified when she took the threat seriously. "I understand and will never, ever let that woman near them."

"Good. Now let's take care of my children." He didn't know why he believed her; he'd never trusted any of his managers so implicitly before. But he trusted that this woman—this tall, frumpy, overweight woman—would guard his most prized treasures with her life. And what more could he ask for?

~

April dropped onto the sofa wearily. The twins were very active and liked to crawl into every nook and cranny they could find. Her entire morning up until their nap in the afternoon was spent chasing them around the apartment, no, penthouse. And like all penthouses, it was a big one with its decors professionally done. When she first entered, she wondered whether she'd just entered a photo shoot for a home decor magazine. It was beautiful.

There were five other huge bedrooms that the twins had not wandered into. The office and kitchen were off limits. She steered them away whenever they tried to go there. Luckily, they liked to go everywhere together so keeping an eye on both of them was easy. Plus, they always made sure she was within sight. If she was slow, they would stop, and then continue when they saw her again.

Now that she had time to actually think, as opposed to just impulsively react to what antics the babies would think of, she wondered what they should do during the afternoon. Most of the specified activities looked dull and unlikely to capture the attention of two active 9-month-olds. Visit the museum, *blehck*. Who would ever want to do that? Actually, she would love to but not with the twins in tow.

Looking out of the window, April was entranced by the clear sky and big puffy clouds, and it brought an idea to mind. Since the weather was still relatively warm and there was no forecast of rain, it would be a lovely day for a walk. *Maybe to the office building and back?* That would be a good distance for her to get some exercise and for the twins to enjoy the fresh air.

Relieved that she has decided on what to do, she began to get ready for their afternoon out. Diapers and formulas are important of course. She also made sure to pack baby wipes, a change of clothes, an *extra* change of clothes, emergency formulas. A thermos of hot water to make their milk; toys to entertain themselves; extra toys in case they get bored with the first batch of toys; and blankets in case they get cold.

The stroller looked full to bursting when she was done. She hoped she didn't miss anything. And hopefully, the twins wouldn't give her a hard time.

She heard a cry and that was her cue to get ready.

~

An hour later, the three of them enjoyed the relatively fresh air as they basked in the park. Being in the city, the air was not exactly *that* fresh what with the emissions from the vehicles and all. Even so, they were enjoying being outdoors. The twins looked up at all the buildings and windows in wonder, gesturing to April excitedly, while she was just glad that they were having a peaceful outing. Sometimes, people—mostly women—would stop and remark about their cuteness. The twins would just smile up at them, showing their deep dimples before looking up at April, as if signaling the time for admiring them was over. Daphne liked the attention so, more often than not, it was Tanner doing the signaling. April laughed at how disgruntled Tanner would sometimes look when they had to stop. He sure doesn't like it.

Finally, they saw the building which Mr. Halloway owned and where he worked. She breathed a small sigh of relief. They were halfway through their outing. The café further down the street should give her time to recharge and possibly refresh the twins. The twins started bouncing when they saw the building, saying, 'Da Da,' happily. She smiled down at them, reveling in their enthusiasm, when a drop of water fell on her head. Startled, she looked up and was dismayed. The once languid, puffy white clouds had turned into roiling black angry ones.

She started pushing the stroller faster, surprising the twins with the sudden speed, and entered the only shelter in sight: Mr. Halloway's building.

CHAPTER 4

"What's that ruckus over there?"

Jason looked up from the files he had been reviewing and looked in the direction his cousin, Cameron Ballard, indicated. A tall woman was arguing with one of the security guards. She was standing protectively in front of a stroller with two seats, gesturing to the pouring rain outside. Suddenly, a ball shot from the stroller and fell to the floor. The woman paused their argument and picked the toy up, returning it to the child inside.

The woman looked very familiar. As did the stroller. Without thinking, he walked toward them. His suspicions were confirmed when he saw Daphne and Tanner in the stroller, brows furrowed, looking at the security guard. April and the security guard had stopped arguing when he was within sight but April's expression was livid. The twins hadn't caught sight of him yet and he saw Daphne throwing her doll in the direction of the guard but, alas, it fell short. He felt amusement bloom in his chest, even as his heart melted at her show of loyalty. He realized he made a good choice in hiring April.

"May I know what is going on here?" he asked placidly. The guard looked unexpectedly smug. "Mr. Worden?"

"This woman and her children," he said, spitting out the last two words, "will not leave the building, Mr. Halloway. I've tried to force them out but she won't budge. And these monsters keep attacking me with their toys."

"But clearly, it's raining quite heavily. Why would you do so?" he asked, perplexed at the guard's attitude. April looked ready to argue but he shot her a chiding look. She stepped back, picking up Daphne's doll, and shot him a fulminating look which took him aback.

"Because you hate children," the guard said a-matter-of-factly. Jason felt his jaw drop. He might not like children in the past but he has certainly changed his opinion of them with the advent of his own. And he had *never* hated them. "You fired one of your managers because he brought his wild kids here. And you've always glared at any child you find in the lobby."

"Really? You did that?" April asked disappointedly. He didn't know why but he didn't like disappointing her. He felt a wild need to reassure her of his good character.

"Da," Tanner suddenly cried, waving his arms at him, asking to be picked up. He felt a smile tug on his lips as he unbuckled Tanner and drew him into his arms. Daphne asked to be picked up too so he unbuckled her as well.

"Are you attacking unsuspecting security guards, Tanner? Not good of you to do so, little man." Tanner just sent him a drooling smile and laid his head on his shoulder. He pressed a kiss on Daphne's head when she threw her arms around him. "You too, princess?"

"See, he can't possibly hate children," April told the stupefied security guard.

"Th-they're yours?" he croaked. Jason shot him a cold glare even as he nodded.

"Yes. Now, please pack your things. I don't need someone who abhors children working for me," he said frostily, struggling to avoid the twins' outstretched hands. April took Daphne from him, her brows slightly furrowed.

17

"Surely you don't have to fire him? The job market is so difficult right now. I don't want his unemployment to rest on my head," she said, looking beseechingly up at him.

"But he insulted you. And the twins," he sputtered, surprised by her plea. He'd thought she'd be happy, vindicated even.

"Oh, the twins don't know what he's talking about. They were just angry at him because he was shouting at me. Right, baby girl?" She directed the last sentence to Daphne while rubbing her cheek against Daphne's. Daphne smiled and continued playing with her doll. "See, they're fine. If you need to satisfy your manly pride and all that, you can get him to do the graveyard shift for, like, a month or so."

"My manly pride?" he asked in disbelief.

She nodded absently. Realizing that they'd gathered an audience, he let the guard go but his gaze told the man they'd have a reckoning at a later date. His sharp glare dispersed the audience, leaving only his cousin who was looking very amused. Jason cleared his face and prepared to introduce them. "April, this is my cousin, Cameron Ballard. Cam, this is my nanny, April Saunders."

"Hello," April said, handling a raucous Daphne. She wanted to be put down but April managed to appease her with a biscuit. Her voice had an unsettled edge that made Jason look at her in concern. She started. "The two of you are very good-looking. You must have had your share of women in the past. Well, until you got married that is. I heard that you already have three children; your wife must love you very much. Wait. Is it four? She's pregnant with another one, right? I mean not to pry but you and your family are always in the news. Your kids are so cute. Do you really bring your boys with you when you're scouting in another city? Sounds like a lot of work. And how does your wife do it with so many kids? I mean, I am already a mess taking care of just these two. I hope she can give me some pointers because I'm very much new at this. But I do like the twins. They're very likable. Even when they latched on to me when we first met, they did it with such a charming smile. Who could resist them?"

"April," Jason said sharply, cutting her off. Tanner had grown interested in his tie so that it was now loose enough not to choke him. She looked up at him guiltily.

"I'm blabbering, aren't I?" At his befuddled nod, she let out a deep sigh. "It's just that I'm a bit high-strung. I've never been in an argument before. Obviously, I'm a person who avoids confrontation but the guard... well, he was just unreasonable. Wanting to throw the twins out while it's still raining. I thought others would have helped if your distaste for children but your own had been known."

"Well, I'm glad the issue has been resolved," he said comfortingly, adding a silent, "for now." He still had to educate the guard on the proper ways to treat children. All children. "Now, let me drop the three of you home. And it looks like I have to change as well."

"Oh, you don't have to do that. The rain has stopped and I'm sure the twins would like a walk back. They had been very excited on the way here," April said earnestly. "From the way they acted on the way here, I gathered they hadn't been out a lot. So, this will be a good start. Maybe when we are back at your apartment, we can discuss where exactly I can bring the twins so that they can enjoy the air and probably play as well."

Jason was startled by her observation but couldn't refute it. His children were more energetic and happier, even after the debacle with the security guard. He was glad April had noticed that and was working to rectify it. He didn't want his children to have the childhood he had and, he now learned, April was a good start to prevent it.

"That's a good idea, Ms. Saunders," he said, noticing how her cheeks flushed and her eyes lit up at his praise. It made her look very sweet. And delectable. And her eyes brightened to look like the sky just before dawn. He wanted to praise her more just to get that look. Maybe kiss her?

"How about *we* walk you back, April?" Cameron said, bringing him out of his reverie. "I need a place to rest and Jason needs to change. It would be a win-win."

"Considering that you live barely half an hour outside of the city, it does not entitle you a resting stop at my house," Jason said drily even as he fought to suppress his anger at Cameron for suggesting. *Why would he want to spend time with an attractive woman? He was a married man, for goodness sake. Surely, he wouldn't be coming onto April?* And why did a burst of flame explode from his chest at the very thought? Surely, he wasn't jealous? Or angry that Cameron was hogging all her attention?

No, Jason wasn't attracted to April. She wasn't his type. He liked them petite and slim, not tall and voluptuous. So, he shouldn't care that she was sending all her genuine smiles Cameron's way but only looked politely at him. She wasn't his type. And he shouldn't care that she'd spoken with Cameron more than she had ever spoken to him. Even if this was her first day. She wasn't his type.

"So, let us all walk back. I have a meeting later at five and Tanner has utterly ruined my suit," he said abruptly. Ignoring April's surprise and Cameron's amusement, he placed Tanner back into his seat, buckled his children in and started to push the stroller out, inclining his head to anyone who passed, even when they were gaping at him.

Even as his chest burned with a feeling he was not willing to identify, he reminded himself that *she* was not his type.

~

Mr. Halloway was acting strange, April thought as she prepared the twins' dinner. Since it only required opening a jar of baby food, it didn't take long. Her thoughts returned to Mr. Halloway as she walked out to the dining room, where she had left the twins. He would not leave Mr. Ballard alone with her. When he had to change, he asked his cousin to look for some document. She had been busy taking the twins out of their coverings so she hadn't noticed. He'd also stayed close to her when Mr. Ballard said goodbye. Not noticeably close but closer than was appropriate for an employer and an employee. She did notice the amused glint in Mr. Ballard's eyes but hadn't known the reason why. She *still* didn't know why.

She was glad that the twins were still occupied with their toys. She noticed that as long as she didn't leave them alone for any longer than ten minutes, they wouldn't make a fuss. Putting their bibs on them, she proceeded to feed them. Only to have all their dinner over her a few minutes later.

"Don't you guys like your food?" she inquired, puzzled. They didn't answer her but just avoided the spoon. She looked at the bottle, thinking she got the wrong flavor Mr. Halloway had specified for each meal of the day, but it was chicken and rice. It shouldn't be that objectionable.

But when she took a whiff of it, she gagged. "What the hel- heck is this? People actually feed this to babies? Why am I feeding this to you? This is an outrage! I shouldn't feed this to you. But what are you guys going to have for dinner? Maybe there are recipes suitable for peeps your age. Hold tight, little guys, while I go and look up homemade baby food."

She went to take her smartphone, still stunned by the awful taste of that baby food. How did it even get past quality control? Knowing there were some websites dedicated to making baby food, she looked them up, giving the twins half a banana each to occupy them.

After deciding on a recipe, she lugged the twins to the kitchen, knowing it would take at least half an hour and started preparing the dish. She decided on a chicken and apple dish, since that was what they were scheduled to eat anyway. She also decided on keeping to the "four-day rule" advised by the website, as this was the first pure chicken that they will eat. The chicken in the baby food jar did not count. Luckily, the kitchen was well-stocked. She didn't want to make any changes to the recipe since it was her first time using it. And on babies too.

The twins were fascinated. They were raptly watching her chopping and cooking. As luck would have it, she'd cooked rice for her dinner so the twins didn't have to wait any longer for theirs. She felt bad enough about delaying their dinner as it was but she could not, in good conscience, feed them that successfully commercialized nuclear waste.

She allowed them a taste of the chicken along with some sauce to see if they liked it. She watched them chew with their currently present teeth. Since she'd made sure the chicken was in extra small pieces, they were able to get through it quite fast. From their faces, she saw that they liked it. Pleased, she prepared to bring them back to the dining room but Tanner demanded another spoonful. Then Daphne.

In the end, she fed them in the kitchen. And that was where Mr. Halloway found them when he returned.

CHAPTER 5

Jason was stunned. When he thought of home, his nanny feeding his children in the kitchen did not come to mind. But that was what greeted him when he went to get a drink after work. His children were happy to see him, waving their hands up but his nanny was less so.

He didn't know what to feel. They were Halloways, and Halloways never ate in the kitchen. In fact, he'd never seen his mother ever enter the kitchen. So, he should feel indignant and angry. However, he saw how happy his twins were. They beamed up at him, melting his heart, but once their mouthful had been swallowed, they turned back to April and demanded more. She obliged but sent him a nervous look.

"Can you explain?" he finally asked.

"I was feeding the twins their dinner but they didn't like it. They spat it out the moment it entered their mouth. So, out of curiosity, I tasted it, and it was awful!" she cried, scrunching her face to show her displeasure. He felt his lips curve up but pushed it down. He hadn't decided how he felt about the scene in front of him.

"I can't possibly feed them that horrible concoction so I decided to look up homemade baby food and came up with this." She showed him the food as she fed Tanner some of it. "I brought the twins into the kitchen since it was going to take a while for me to get their food ready. I did plan to feed them in the dining room but I made the mistake of letting them taste some here. They didn't want me to move them; they insisted on being fed the moment their mouth was open. I'm so sorry, Mr. Halloway. It won't happen again," she finished in a rush.

He sighed. He wasn't angry but he didn't like the thought of his children eating in the kitchen. On the other hand, he liked that April thought of a way to resolve his children's eating issue instead of forcing it down their throats. And the twins didn't look any worse off. Instead, they seemed to be enjoying the food despite their surroundings. So, he didn't have much ground to stand on if he objected to her method. He would still have a talk with her about using the kitchen. His housekeeper was very particular about who used it.

"It's alright, Ms. Saunders. The twins look like they like it anyway. Why don't you get them ready for bed and come see me after? We'll talk about your first day," he said with a tired smile. She nodded bashfully, but he saw the pleased twinkle in her eyes. It made him feel three times bigger. It made him uncomfortable too, at how much pleasure he took in pleasing her so he was harsher than he had intended to when he said, "I'll be in my office."

~

April tried, for the hundredth time, to suppress the grin that was creeping into her face as she headed to his office. She didn't have a strong sense of approval in her life. Her mother tried to uplift her self-esteem but when continually faced with everyone else putting her down, it's tough to keep that lone light in mind. She didn't know why, but Mr. Halloway's approval meant the world to her.

Mr. Halloway was on the phone when she entered. He waved her to a chair but continued talking. She studied the interior of the office. It was totally different from his work office. There was a warm homey feel to it, different from the cold, intimidating atmosphere from work. The theme was a mixture of dark red, mossy green, and mahogany that worked well. As usual, he had a huge table that dominated half the room and was situated right in front of a floor-to-ceiling window. The mossy green carpet on the floor was so thick, she could literally sleep in it. His walls were a dark red but the white trimmings stopped it from being too overpowering. She felt surprisingly comfortable in the room.

"Thank you for waiting, Ms. Saunders. Work will not wait for a man like me," Mr. Halloway finally said after twenty minutes. She sent him a smile and waited for him to continue. She knew he was planning a hostile takeover so he was understandably busy during this period. "So, how was your day with the twins?"

"It was fine. They are full of energy and liked to explore. They went through the entire house this morning before their nap. Luckily, they waited for me to catch up before they scrambled away again. After the nap, we went for a walk, as you already know. And then, we bathed and had dinner," she told him with a bright smile. He nodded with a blank expression. "Um, would it be overstepping my boundaries if I asked for a few changes in the house?"

"Please go on, Miss Saunders," he just said, neither agreeing nor disagreeing. She felt her lips twist a little in indecision.

"Could I put away some of the fragile and more valuable items in some rooms so that we could buy a walker for the twins? They express interest in walking but it seems that they have not had much practice with it. They wobble precariously on their feet. I do not want them to hurt themselves or accidentally break something," she mumbled, finding great interest in the carpet.

"And how about the walker?" he asked.

"I was thinking the twins and I could go to a store and grab one. It'll be a great adventure," she said, her voice expressing her enthusiasm for it. She was looking forward to looking at all the cute baby stuff and it'd be great fun for the twins.

"How are you going to bring the walkers back, then?"

"We'll call a cab. Or the store could have a delivery service. I'll look it up."

Mr. Halloway was silent, making April very nervous. She looked up at him and was caught in his intense green eyes. The feelings they evoked disconcerted her so she looked down again.

"Will the day after tomorrow be a good time?" he finally said.

"Um, sure. It'll give me time to look things up."

"Good. I'll get Janice to rearrange my schedule and we'll go after their nap."

"Wait. 'We'? You want to come along?" she asked incredulously.

"Yes, Ms. Saunders. I want to be a part of my children's upbringing. Every aspect of it," he said in a tone that dared her to argue. However, she was amazed.

"That's a great plan. Most parents have a bad time managing their work and children. I hope you can enjoy every step of their lives with them," she said. She hoped it didn't sound so much like praise. It's not like she was somebody. She was just his nanny, but she could, at the very least, applaud his efforts. She hoped she could do the same thing when she had children.

"Lovely. From what I have seen, Ms. Saunders, I am very pleased with your first day. The twins like you and are not giving you much trouble. In return, you anticipate their needs and give them a good environment to grow up in. I hope you will continue after the trial period."

April didn't know what they talked about after that. Something about being careful to put the utensils back where she found them after use and his housekeeper. She was just basking in his approval. This was the second time in four hours he'd praised her. She was walking on air. She wished she knew of a way to repay him.

Wait, she forgot. Had he even eaten dinner?

CHAPTER 6

Stepping into the baby store was like being hit with a bomb of bright colors and cute music. It was disconcerting, alarming, and loud. April and the twins were unfazed but Jason had to pause for a moment to orient himself. Everywhere he looked were brightly colored baby and toddler toys and apparel. He was getting dizzy just looking at them.

"Do you know what you're looking for?" he asked April, his only anchor in the storm of baby-related items.

"Well, I looked up online and there were a few websites saying that walkers were not effective when it comes to teaching toddlers the art of walking which is rather alarming. I mean, I used a walker and I walk alright. Maybe less than alright but I'm upright, right? But, anyway, they did recommend this contraption called an exersaucer so we could go from there," she said, looking up at him for approval. He nodded even though he had no idea what she was talking about. *Exersaucer? What, in fucking creations, was that?*

"Hi. Can I help you and your wife?" a male store attendant asked brightly. His nametag shows 'Brendan.'

"Oh, we're not married. I'm his nanny," April corrected in a rush, flustered. Jason didn't like her denial or the speed in which it came. However, he didn't like the predatory gleam in Brendan's eyes more when he heard that. Much, much more. "I'm looking for exersaucers. These two munchkins are showing great interest in walking and I thought those will help them." She looked up at him

28

after she took the toy away from Tanner. Both twins were extremely happy to be surrounded by toys and wanted to grab all of them.

"If you would follow me," Brendan said, leading the way but Jason had seen his eyes glance to April's bountiful chest, which had pressed against her sweater when she'd bent down to retrieve the toy. He didn't know why but he felt the familiar burning sensation in his chest. He didn't like the way that man was looking at her as well as the fact that April is causing this feeling inside him. Why wouldn't it go away?

"These are some of our models. Some parents have expressed worry about it, saying it is similar to a walker and will have the disadvantages of walkers. So, I would suggest you use it for limited periods of time. Use it when you're cooking, cleaning, or taking a rest," he said with a bright smile at April. Jason saw her cheeks turn red and the burning sensation worsened. He tried to alleviate it by reminding himself that she wasn't his type but it wasn't working.

"Oh yeah, I've read that too," April said absently, looking over the different types. "What do you think, Mr. Halloway? Which ones do you like? I was thinking maybe we should go for the ones with the most features. I read this could help with their sensory development." April and that man continued talking about the toys, the different features, which toy was good for which stage of the development. The twins were, surprisingly, well-behaved. They didn't fuss when the stroller stopped moving. They didn't cry out for toys. He was amazed. However, he didn't like the rapport building between April and Brendan. It made him want to toss the man away. He had to do something.

"That's a good idea. Why don't we look over for some other models? Is there a place where my children can test out the toy?" he asked coldly. Brendan, seeing that his commission was almost in the bag, went to find his manager so that they could set up a room for him. He did send a look of promise to April, who didn't see it as she was tending to Daphne. Disgruntled, he went on his way.

"You know there's no place where you can test the toys out, right?" April asked hesitantly. He could see the puzzlement in her eyes. She was looking for an explanation.

"I know," he simply said. He didn't explain he couldn't stand the burning sensation in his chest for much longer. He didn't explain that he wanted the man to leave or he wouldn't be accountable for his actions. He didn't explain that he only wanted to be with his children and her and didn't want any store assistant breathing down his neck. He didn't explain any of that but he did bask in the sense of satisfaction and triumph now that the pesky fly was gone. Now, he could have her all to himself.

~

The twins loved their new toys. There were a lot of buttons and toys and noises to be explored. So much so that April wanted to rip the saucers apart. She was going crazy. Don't misunderstand. She didn't mind the dangly toys or the colorful light-up buttons. However, the noisy buttons were killing her.

This was only the second day. April did follow the suggestions of the store assistant but the twins kept crawling to their exersaucers. They'd stand—using the exersaucer as support—and press all the buttons. Many, many, many, many times. Of course, she'd be behind them to catch them in case they fell. She'd also placed the exersaucers close together so she'd have an easier time keeping an eye on them.

It was during one of those times when Mr. Halloway called her on the cellphone he provided.

"Hello?" she greeted, placing the phone between her ear and shoulder.

30

"Ms. Saunders, are you busy right now?" Mr. Halloway asked without preamble. He sounded very harried and stressed out.

"Um, not really. I'm just watching the twins play. Can I help you, Sir?"

"Yes. Can you go to the computer in my office? I need a file today and I forgot to make a copy on my flash drive."

"I'll be happy to help you but I hope you understand that it'll take me a while to actually get to your office. I'll have to bring the twins and their toys there. Well, I say toys but I mean their exersaucers."

"Are they still playing with that?" Mr. Halloway asked with a smile in his voice. He was also starting to sound more relaxed. "I thought they'd be bored with it by now." She let out a small laugh.

"They're still playing with it, and it looks like they're not going to stop anytime soon."

"Are they still pressing the musical buttons?"

"Unfortunately, yes. Frankly, I'm regretting this purchase. I don't think I can handle any more of this. I believe I may have to tender my resignation soon." She had been partially serious but hearing his laughter coming through made her spirits fly.

"And leave me to listen to that horrendous music? You're not getting away that easily, Ms. Saunders. And who was it that convinced me to purchase those infernal things? Who was it that did all the research? Who was it that recommended that contraption?" April didn't know whether to feel outraged or sheepish. She wanted to berate him in turn but managed to control herself. He seemed to take her silence as defeat so he continued, "So I put all the responsibility onto you. You have not paid enough penance as of yet so no, I will not accept the resignation," he said sternly but she heard the teasing note in his voice. As much as she wanted to remain indignant, a snicker escaped her lips. "Are you laughing at me? I assure you— yes, Janice?"

April was having such a good time talking with him that she didn't feel like hanging up but his conversation with Janice burst that bubble. She realized the importance of that file. He wouldn't have asked this of her if it wasn't. "I'll call you again once I have reached your office," she told him when he returned to the line.

"Yeah," he sighed wearily. She felt concern bubbling inside her. He was pushing himself too hard, barely sleeping four hours every day, even on weekends. He goes straight to his office when he returns, giving the twins a tired smile and sometimes forgetting to eat. This was not healthy and she wouldn't be surprised if, one of these days, he'd fell sick. "Talk to you later?"

"Sure. Goodbye," she said hesitantly.

He stayed on the line for a few more seconds before hanging up. She looked down on the phone. She knew she shouldn't be developing feelings for him but this conversation showed a different side of him. And she didn't know if she could suppress her feelings for the playful Mr. Halloway.

CHAPTER 7

It felt like a boulder was lifted from his shoulders. Finally, the takeover was completed. Jason kept the triumphant grin to himself until he reached his office. He felt like jumping with joy which was unlike him. He also felt like calling April and sharing the good news with her. He suppressed the impulse and walked with measured steps to his desk.

Once he was seated, he realized there was still a lot of work to be done. There were reports to be done and meetings on restructuring the newly merged companies. He felt a bit of that weight returning and a headache was coalescing at the top of his head. His nose was starting to run as well.

All he wanted to do was go home and play with his children. He'd been neglecting them with all the reports and files he had to compile in preparation for the meeting that day. He didn't feel right putting his work aside but he'd made a promise to himself to be a more hands-on father. So, with great reluctance and willpower, he switched off his laptop, told Janice to rearrange his schedule for the day, and left.

~

"Good morning," Jason croaked to April as he shuffled to the kitchen for breakfast. He had a hard time waking up this morning. He'd overslept and missed his workout. As it was, he had to take a quick shower, which had surprisingly taken longer than usual, and had a small breakfast. He didn't like skipping breakfast. His staff was just going to have deal with his bad mood.

"Are you alright, Mr. Halloway?" April asked, concern in her voice. She'd been feeding the twins their breakfast but paused when he entered.

"Of course, Ms. Saunders," he said imperiously. Well, he tried to but a wracking cough interrupted him. April fed the twins a bite and went up to him. He felt her cool hand on his forehead and saw the worry in her eyes.

"You're feeling quite hot," she murmured.

"I have a lot of things to do, Ms. Saunders. I don't have time to be sick," he snapped. Her eyes snapped angrily up at him.

"Mr. Halloway, you are sick. You have to rest and recuperate. What will happen to the twins if anything happened to you? At least let the doctor look you over," she tried to cajole. He was getting mesmerized by her sweet, mellow voice. He almost nodded but found his mind at the last moment.

"Are you trying to manipulate me? Because you won't succeed. I've been in the company of some of the most deceitful women in the world and have come on top," he said through a cough. April had to support him as this cough shook his entire body. His chest hurt, his face hurt, everywhere hurt. He didn't know if he had the energy to stand; the cough had sapped whatever energy he could chalk up from the moment he got out of bed. However, even through his coughing fit, he couldn't help but enjoy leaning against her. She felt soft and warm, unlike his previous dates. They were all stick thin and uncomfortable.

"Would I do that? I'm just thinking about the twins. What if this is contagious? You did spend quite some time with them yesterday. Maybe they'll catch whatever bug you're having. The doctor will know better. Please, Mr. Halloway?"

He hesitated. He looked to the twins. They looked fine to him, playing with whatever toy April allowed them on their high chairs, laughing and smiling with each other. However, he couldn't risk it. They were still young after all. He started to nod when his world started to turn.

He didn't know how it happened but he found himself in bed with his shirt and boxers, under the covers with April putting a damp cloth on his forehead. The twins could be heard in the room across his. They sounded content, and he felt so comfortable. His eyelids drooped and his mind drifted off to dreamland.

~

April looked down at Mr. Halloway, worried. The family doctor had just left. Mr. Halloway had barely woken up during the visit but even with his minimal involvement, the doctor—a dignified middle-aged man—was able to figure out that it was mainly exhaustion and stress that struck him down.

Of course, she knew that but had to play the twins card to get him into bed. The male sex was notoriously stubborn when it came to admitting any illness or weakness. Luckily, he was more worried about the twins and conceded. Or so she thought. He had almost fainted in the dining room when she saw him lift his head in what looked to be a nod. It was good enough for her.

She had a hard time getting him back to bed. He did help by staying on his feet and taking a few staggering steps in the right direction. After dropping him onto his bed, she noticed he was wearing his suit and it looked very uncomfortable. Initially, she'd decided to take off his belt, shoes and socks, but when she saw he was wearing boxers, she took off his pants as well. She removed his tie and blazer and unbuttoned the first few buttons of his dress shirt.

Even though she'd worried about the twins the entire time she was attending to him, she couldn't help admiring his male physique. Luckily, he was unconscious or he would have fired her. *It would be worth it though*, she thought with a dreamy sigh. That was the first time she had been close to a fine specimen of the male sex. And Mr. Halloway was oh so fine. He had strong arms and thighs and had a wide, defined chest, his chest hair peering out from the shirt. Only when Daphne started crying did she snap out of her perusal.

She settled the twins in the room across Mr. Halloway's. The room was intentionally built there so she could see into it from inside his room. In case anything happened, she'd know right away. They seemed content to play with the toys inside, though. And she had a video playing for them on a tablet. Luckily, the music didn't disturb Mr. Halloway's rest.

She had to call Janice to request for the doctor's number. It hadn't been pleasant. And she, the queen of nice, had to be rude and just plain nasty.

"Look, Mr. Halloway will not be coming into the office regardless of whatever you say. Apart from the fact that I don't want him to go, he's currently unconscious and unresponsive. So, you better move his appointments around or get someone to replace him," she snapped into the phone. She felt very satisfied and empowered, acting tough and all, but hearing Tanner cry burst that bubble.

The twins were becoming fussier and clingier afterwards. They wouldn't let her out of their sight. Because of this, she had a difficult time putting them down for their nap. They'd wake up at the slightest sound, and when one woke up, the other soon followed. So, receiving frequent calls from Janice was not welcome.

"No, Janice. I'm not able to help you with that. I don't know anything about the situation. I don't have a clue about who or what you're talking about. Didn't Mr. Halloway hire you because of your self-reliance?" April was getting frazzled. Both the twins were crying their lungs out, and nothing she did helped. She was currently bouncing both of them on her hips with the phone on her shoulder.

"Well, yeah but he didn't give me specific instructions and—can you please put those heathens down?" Janice snapped over the phone.

"Well, you can put your attitude where the sun doesn't shine," she snarled.

"If you hadn't done something to Mr. Halloway, I wouldn't be in this fucked up position right now. So, you can stuff your own problems up your ass and help me solve mine. Clearly, mine are more important, seeing as it involves a lot more people than those two bastards," Janice shot back loudly. April felt her blood boil.

"Listen here, you crazy, dumb Barbie doll. Obviously, Mr. Halloway hired you because of your skillset. Supposedly, you are the best candidate for the job. But, seeing as I have seen no evidence of this, I believe I should feedback to Mr. Halloway that he'd hired an incompetent, mindless person to help handle his work and he should just find another one. And the twins aren't bastards!!" April was surprised to feel the phone slipping away from her grasp. Wait, it was slipping *up* and... to the *back*? Looking behind her, she was confronted with the wonder that was Mr. Halloway's shirtless chest.

"Let me talk to Janice," he said, his voice still rough with sleep. At that, she stepped back, shaking her head. The twins had quietened down when they saw their father. Daphne was sucking her fist while Tanner had taken hold of her hair and pushed it into his mouth. Their chest still heaved faintly from all the crying, but they looked less stressed than before. She was happy about that even as she was trying to think of a way to get her phone back.

"No, Mr. Halloway. You'll just use it for work."

"I promise I'll just give her some instructions that will take care of the office for the next day or two. Go to my room," he said gently. And that was when she was reminded of her job. Wow, she was certainly showcasing her capabilities. She hesitated. "I promise it won't be longer than ten minutes."

After deliberating for a few moments, she nodded and he began talking to Janice. Looking at him, she was glad that he looked better. The five-hour rest had done him good. Plus, she had a nutritious chicken soup bubbling away for him. Hopefully, he'd get much better before the day was over.

The twins were finally settling down for their nap. Their heads were settling into the crooks of her neck and they had difficulty keeping their eyes open. They must have been worrying about their dad. Clearly, seeing him almost faint had had an adverse effect on them. *Darling babies*, she thought, smiling down on them.

"April, lay them on my bed. I'll join the three of you shortly." She nodded, still looking at the twins, and made her way to his room.

It was only when she was almost to his room when she realized he'd called her by her first name.

CHAPTER 8

Jason sighed, leaning against the wall outside his room. He was still weak and listless, but at least he had more energy now than this morning. That was a plus. However, dealing with Janice had sapped most of his recovered energy away. He hadn't known his assistant was so inflexible and incompetent when it came to dealing with unexpected fuck ups.

He knew he had never been ill before, but he was still human. Anyway, he could very well not come in if he didn't feel like it. Even though that had never happened before, she should have been able to adapt to changes and not trouble him with more problems. However, when he had taken the phone from April, she inundated him with all the issues that had cropped up. To him, most of them were easily solved by turning to his vice-president but apparently, the man was missing. If that was how the higher ups in his company were behaving without him, he had to do some restructuring when he went back. He managed to resolve all the problems and leave instructions that should cover the next day or two. However, it took him more than the ten minutes he promised April. Hopefully, she wasn't mad at him.

Walking into his room, he stopped short when he saw the sight that greeted him. April was lying on the bed with the twins on either side of her. Both of them were snuggled close to her side, eyes closed, looking like they weren't willing to let go. She had her arms around them, and her face was relaxed in repose.

He didn't know why but his chest felt lighter, and a smile grew on his face. He wanted to join them, putting the twins in between him and April. Such a domesticated thought had never entered his mind before now. Before the twins, he hadn't thought much about children and what they entailed. And once he had them, his main focus was juggling their care with his work. Never had he thought to sleep with them. Now, with April, the thought was very appealing.

"Mr. Halloway?" April said, her voice thick with sleep. She moved to stand but the twins cried out, so she just laid back down. "Sorry for falling asleep. I didn't know I was so tired." A yawn engulfed the last few words. "And sorry for taking your bed. It seems the twins are not going to release me anytime soon."

"It's alright," he said, sitting beside Daphne and within sight of April. He ran his hand over Daphne's hair, finding the silkiness of her hair soothing. "Thank you for taking care of Janice when I was out of it. She mentioned that you called the doctor. So, what did he say?"

"Well, you have an incurable disease that they are still working to identify. They'll be bringing you to quarantine soon. In fact, I have to keep the children away from you," she said gravely, her face set in serious lines. He knew she was joking. Knowing he should feel offended, he arranged his face into a scowl.

"Are you sure? Because, in my opinion, exhaustion is not a new disease," he said. It was comical watching her face change. She knew she was caught and sent him a shy smile, making it difficult for him to maintain his scowl.

"You heard what the doctor said?" she asked meekly, bringing Tanner to Daphne's side, and laid on her side, making it easier for them to converse. Tanner only shifted once before falling back into a deep sleep. April shook her newly-freed arm with a slight grimace. "Dang, my arm hurts. Didn't expect that. Wha—

</>

Mr. Halloway, you don't need to do that." He was currently massaging her arm over the twins' heads. He sent her a determined look when she tried to take it away. She rolled her eyes at him and left it in his care. He felt a warm satisfaction, knowing he could bring her some comfort.

"No. But I just guessed. And, if you'd thought I was jeopardizing the twins, you wouldn't have brought them anywhere near me." Her face lit up at his comment but he was serious. He knew she took the twins' well-being seriously, and he respected that. He couldn't have asked for a better nanny.

"Well, I hope you'll take care of your health then. Unless you've updated your will in case you keel over and die. That way the twins will always be taken care off." She made it sound like a joke but there was a bite to her words. He liked the way she took care of him, so he relented.

"I'll rest as much as possible but I can only spare one more day before things go ape shit in the office."

"Language!" she hissed, looking pointedly at the twins. He didn't know how to feel, being taken up to task, but he mouthed his apology. "I guess that's the best you can give, then. But, please, don't do this again: work until you basically collapse. The twins were very clingy and fractious. They kept fussing over everything, and nothing comforted them. They didn't want to go down for their nap, that is, until they saw you. They fell asleep soon after seeing you back on your feet."

Looking down on the relaxed faces of his children, he felt warmth and guilt build up in him. "I'm still adjusting to being a dad. My parents weren't good examples; they only focused on their work. I guess I followed in their footsteps until I was given these two brats. I floundered those first few nights. They kept crying, and nothing but being in my arms helped. Luckily, I had my aunt to help. She is a fantastic person, and the twins grew to love her, but

41

they wouldn't let me leave for extended periods of time. Some people recommended a nanny, but, as you can see, they didn't help."

"I believe they have a definite idea of who they like. Look at me, for example. They immediately latched on to me when we first met but when I tried to pass them off to someone else, they wouldn't let me go," April related with a laugh. Jason smiled, the heavy feeling of guilt lightening.

"Being a dad is harder than being a CEO. Sometimes, I look at them and wonder whether I'm doing the right thing."

"I don't think you'll ever be sure. People are ever-changing. When you think you've got it down to pat, they'll show another side and you'll have to readjust. I think that you're doing a fine job as it is. From the way they behave, it's like you've known each other since they were born. I have to admit, they were quite clingy and dependent on normal days but I'm sure they'll grow out of it the longer they're exposed in a secure, loving environment. I don't even want to think about how their mother must have treated them. From what I've been reading, they must not have received the loving attention they needed."

"From the way they initially acted, I wouldn't be surprised. I hope we can help them replace all those bad memories," he said before realizing his slip. He knew she caught it; her eyes had grown almost double their size. "Um, you know. We as in…um…anyone who is involved in their upbringing."

"Oh. Yes, that makes more sense," she murmured, pulling her arm from his hand and covering a part of her face with her hair. His hand moved to take it back, but he stopped himself.

The tension and awkwardness grew in intensity. He didn't know what to say to break it, and nothing came to mind. He had had no practice with being in this situation. Suddenly, his stomach let out a loud and rather obnoxious grumble. His face went red with embarrassment, while April tried to hide her smile.

"There's a pot of chicken soup for you in the kitchen," she said, her hidden smile evident in her voice. He sent her a mock glare.

"I see that my job here is to provide you entertainment. Please excuse me while I fuel up for future acts," he joked haughtily. A giggle escaped her. He felt something inside him soften. As always, he was experiencing new things around her, but this scared him. He didn't know why but instinctively, he shied away from it. Not knowing what else to do, he immediately left the room.

These feelings had to stop.

~

The next morning, the twins were acting weird. They kept going to Jason's room and asking for him. April told them he'd gone to work but they seemed to be unsatisfied with the answer. They kept crawling around the house, shouting, 'Da Da' here and there.

She tried calling Jason on his personal phone, but he wasn't picking up. She was starting to get worried. They eventually settled down for their naps but it was a fitful rest. She decided another outing was called for.

~

The twins looked happy to be out. The Chicago weather was cooperating with them and clear skies could be seen all around. Women, and some men, cooed to the twins when they stopped at a traffic light, and they absorbed all of the attention. Finally, Jason's building came into view. The twins became even more excited. The words 'Da Da' and 'wek' kept spilling out of their lips. She laughed at their antics and they showed her their three-toothed smile.

Their entry into the office area was unhindered this time. The receptionist and guards let them in instantly. However, the only issue was when Daphne threw her toy at the guard near the elevator. She wouldn't stop frowning up at him. April tried to explain that he wasn't the guard from before, but she was resolute. Laughing softly at her stubbornness, she sent a look of apology to the guard. He just shook his head and sent her a charming smile. Her cheeks reddened when she realized just how attractive he was and immediately looked away. Attractive men and she just didn't mix.

The office was as bustling as ever and April felt a pang that she couldn't work the same scope as them. She really wanted to put her education to good use. In her opinion, why go through four years of college and not use the piece of paper? It's practically wasteful.

Comforting herself with the twins, she continued to the CEO's office. Janice let them through with a nod and April sent her a thankful smile. However, seeing as he hadn't answered any of her calls, she could only think that he was busy in a meeting. She then decided to see whether the coast was clear, so she parked the twins beside the door and entered alone.

And immediately came back out.

CHAPTER 9

Hearing the door slam close, Jason lifted his head up from the couch. He furrowed his brows. He had specifically told Janice not to let anyone in so no one would disturb him. He thought he heard Tanner shout belligerently, 'Da Da.' Thinking it was a figment of his imagination, he dropped back down the sofa, but shot up when he heard April say, "Da Da is busy, Tanner. We'll wait for him at home, alright? Here's a biscuit."

"Jason," the naked woman beside him moaned sleepily. "What's going on?"

Jason shot up and looked down at the woman in horror. *Had April seen her?* Of course, she had. She'd have to be blind not to. Their clothes were everywhere and the couch was within sight of the door. Panic grew in his chest. *Oh god, what was he going to do?* He didn't want April to think that this was the only thing he did at work, that he was a playboy. He didn't know why, but he didn't want her to think that. What if she decided to quit? He couldn't have that.

He hastened to dress and told Janice not to let April leave and to make sure she wouldn't see the woman leaving. Getting the woman to leave was a harder task. She was still there when he returned from his personal bathroom to wash up. He didn't even know who this woman was, but she was acting like he had betrayed her. She whined and tried to stall. Finally, having to threaten her with security, he had the office to himself. Regaining his

45

composure, he told Janice to bring them—April and the twins—to the office.

Janice confidently opened the door to Jason's office to let April in, but she stayed behind and peeked in from the door. Once assured that everything was back to normal, she pushed the stroller in. The twins began jumping in their seats when they caught sight of him. Their pleasure at seeing him lightened the load of panic in his chest and he bent down to release both of them. They gave him a kiss before wondering about the office.

"Um, I'm sorry for walking in earlier," April mumbled softly. He was kneeling beside the stroller, watching his children be happy and free. When he looked up, he saw her face was flushed red and her eyes were darting everywhere except him. When they briefly landed on him, he saw a tinge of pain in them. He didn't know why but his heart fluttered with pleasure. And guilt too, but his pleasure far outweighed that. God, his emotions were everywhere when it comes to her.

"Who told you that you can enter? I told Janice that I wasn't to be disturbed until I revoked that command," he asked curiously. Her eyes stopped moving and her brows furrowed cutely down at him. *Cute? When had he ever used that as a description for a woman? Never, that's when!* So that word did not just come into his mind.

"Janice told me I can enter," she said slowly. Now, his own brows were drawn together. Why had Janice willfully disobeyed him? She might not be the most independent assistant, but she always followed his directions to the tee. Any direction.

Suddenly April shot to his desk. Tanner had somehow found his way onto his office chair and was standing up, using the table as support. Luckily, April caught him before the chair moved too far away. He liked the way Tanner turned to her and smiled, showing his single tooth and one growing stump. He also liked the

46

way April reacted with a smile, tickling his chin. So much so that he felt a stirring in his heart.

That immediately wiped the smile off his face. Why was he still affected by her? He'd thought the interlude with that woman would have helped keep this attraction away. Because wasn't it due to the fact that he hadn't had a woman for so long? A month was long right? He knew he had been busy with the twins so he didn't have as much time as he usually did. But why was his dick stirring again?

"I'm, um, so sorry for coming uninvited," April suddenly said nervously. She was currently on the floor with Tanner in her lap. He caught her sending him a guarded look and realized she'd misinterpreted his scowl. Before he could say anything, she rushed in and said, "I tried calling but you didn't pick up. I thought that you were in a meeting, so I decided to drop by for a quick visit. I didn't think that it was a *personal* meeting. Next time, I'll wait until you give me the green light before I make my way here."

The discomfort she was exhibiting made him feel ashamed of the pleasure he felt. He didn't want her to feel uncomfortable— and especially not pain—in his presence. Walking over and dropping down beside her, he slung an arm over her shoulder and faced her, wanting to comfort her. Initially, she became stiff.

"Don't beat yourself up over this. It's not all your fault," he said. Her eyes were trained resolutely on the floor. "I shouldn't have neglected my phone. You wouldn't have been able to reach me if anything had happened to the twins. I promise I'll pick up all your calls from now on."

She'd looked up during the middle of his speech. Somehow, both of their heads had moved closer to each other so that his last word was whispered on to her lips. He felt himself getting caught in those dark eyes of hers and becoming entangled in their mesmerizing depth. Her eyes darted down to his lips and back up to his eyes. He saw the struggle in her eyes: to let him kiss her or not. Just as he saw her beginning to lean into his lips, Daphne suddenly let out a happy squeal.

April's head whipped to where his daughter was and a horrified gasp escaped her. She immediately shot to his daughter, taking the pen out of her hand. Her arms and legs were full of her scribbles and she didn't want to let the pen go.

As April carried his unrepentant daughter into his personal restroom, he let out a half-amazed, half-incredulous laugh. Settling on the floor, he saw Tanner crawling into his lap, deciding to have a rest. His mind turned to what just happened, gently stroking his son's hair. Cock-blocked by his own daughter. He guessed that's what all parents had to deal with.

He'd just have to manage around it.

~

April let out a heavy sigh as she left the building. She had a hard time convincing Mr. Halloway that she could return on her own. He'd insisted that it wasn't safe for her to be out alone, citing the crime rate in the city and even the paparazzi. Fortunately, she wasn't troubled by either of them so she dismissed his concern. However, he'd almost succeeded in sending them back until she pointed out all the work he had to do which was counterproductive to his healing and that she wanted—no, needed—time and space to deal and process what she'd walked in on earlier.

She knew Mr. Halloway was a man and had urges. She even accepted that his name would always be linked to prominent, beautiful women and that he'd eventually wed someone from his class. *So why did she feel a hollow and faint throbbing in her chest? Why did it feel so difficult to breathe?* Even though she tried to will them away, they always returned twofold.

"Hey, aren't you the nanny?"

48

A male voice broke her out of her thoughts. Realizing they were at a traffic light, she looked to the voice and saw the guard from before. Only now, he was out of his uniform and was in a black tank top with dark worn blue jeans. He had a duffel bag slung over his shoulder, highlighting his bulging biceps. Her eyes were stuck on those big biceps. *Would he let her touch it?* Finding his glittering light blue eyes on her, she immediately turned to the road.

"You haven't answered my question." *Question? What question?* His biceps had effectively wiped all thoughts out of her head. "But with that stroller and those twins, I think it's pretty self-explanatory. What's your name, then, beautiful?"

Her cheeks flushed and she felt a smile tug on her lips. "Does that line always work for you? 'What's your name, beautiful?' Maybe with some flexing and a sexier drawl, but that line definitely doesn't work on me," she told him with a laugh. His astonishment was such that his mouth hung open even after the light turned green. "Aren't you going to cross?"

"What? Oh, yeah. And I don't go around using that line alone. I have other lines. But, anyway, I'm Connor, Connor Johnson. Now that I've introduced myself, manners dictate that you return the favor. What would your mother say? She spent all those times instilling those lessons in you and you're to just throw it out the window? Tsk."

"Well, I don't want to let my mother down, so here goes nothing. I'm April Saunders and yes, I'm *the* nanny. In the stroller are Daphne and Tanner. But I don't know you so you're not allowed to hold them," she said firmly. He let out a laugh, but she didn't see what was so funny. She didn't know the guy. He could be a pedophile for all she knew. Or a hired man. As handsome and charming as he was, she was not going to take that risk.

"Hey, wanna grab a cup of coffee? This can also be a chance for you to get to know me better. I know *I* want to get to know you better," he invited with a smile. She hesitated. She hadn't gone for a personal outing since she started taking care of the twins. But it didn't seem right, especially when she was currently out with the twins. Regardless of how handsome the outing was.

"Maybe another time? I really need to get back and prepare the twins' dinner," she offered. He looked taken aback. It must be the first time a woman turned him down. "Let me give you my number and we'll arrange a time."

"Sure. Here's my phone." He gave her his iPhone and she put in her personal number. Of course, she wouldn't use the one Mr. Halloway gave her. That was purely for twins-related issues. "Alright. Let's meet again soon, then. Bye, babies."

The twins waved, surprising her. She didn't know they could do that on demand but she smiled nevertheless. Her heart fluttered slightly and her face turned pink when he sent her a wink. She blamed it on the fact that he's a charmer, seeing as there's a lack of that in her life, but she dismissed it.

Continuing on their journey home, her mind returned to the afternoon. The smile immediately dropped from her face and her heart felt so much heavier. She didn't want to admit it but she knew she'd developed some feelings for Mr. Halloway. Romantic feelings. Maybe bordering on love—

She shook her head vigorously. No, she couldn't have fallen in love with him. One reason being he was so far out of her league. She might as well be in the mud while he's a prince in a glorious castle. And another reason would be his reputation. He's a consummate professional but his private life was littered with models, actresses, debutantes, and even a princess—all beautiful, poised, confident women. April, on the other hand, was borderline pretty, embarrassed herself on a regular basis, and barely had the courage to talk to Connor, regardless of the fact that he initiated the conversation. So, she had no business developing a crush on him.

She had to get over this crush and behave in a professional manner with him. Hopefully, she could hide her feelings from him while she worked on getting over him, which was unlikely, but hope springs eternal.

They'd finally reached the penthouse and she released the twins from the stroller. She had already barricaded the entrance to the hall and kitchen so they could only roam around in the living room. With that, she went back to keeping their stroller and putting away their toys, jackets, blankets, and everything else she packed for their outing.

With her hands full, she was unprepared for the arm which suddenly wrapped around her waist, the stiff body which crowded her back, and the words whispered in her ears.

"Who was that man?"

CHAPTER 10

Jason was furious. His vision was a sea of red. He felt like tearing someone apart, preferably that blond bastard who tried to hit on her. He tightened his arm around her and asked her again.

"Who is that man?" She sent a puzzled look up at him. He noted absently again that she didn't have to look up far. He liked that. He also liked that she was a warm, sort armful almost to the point of forgetting that man. Almost. "That man who walked with you to the coffee shop."

"Oh. That was Connor. He's a security guard at your building. He wanted to stop for coffee," she said with a hint of wistfulness in her voice, "but I reminded him about my responsibilities so we're just going to arrange for another time."

"You're not going out with him," he told her harshly. She frowned at him. He scrambled to think of a reason that would explain his decree and he found one that was fairly acceptable. "Employees are not allowed to fraternize. So, you are not allowed to see him again. Ever."

"But we're only going out for coffee! It's not like we're meeting for a rendezvous," she protested with a scowl, turning in his arms. He had to loosen his hold to accommodate the load in her arms. He almost smiled at her outrage but didn't because he knew it wouldn't help his cause.

"Regardless, I do not and will not condone any further contact with him. If you disobey me in this, I will have a bodyguard trail you. Don't fight with me on this," he snapped fiercely. He knew she wasn't happy with his dictate, but she treasured her anonymity. The twins' even more. With a grumble, she nodded.

"That's a silly rule to have," she mumbled as she tore out of his arms. "I didn't read about this when I prepared for the interview. Stupid rule."

Jason felt an unexpected surge of relief. He tried to play it off as protecting his naive nanny, but he could never lie to himself.

He had rushed through work so that he could surprise her while she was on her way back and even cancelled meetings and forced it down his executive's throats just so he could clear his afternoon. He looked out for her as he drove along the path she took and almost crashed his second-most prized possession when he'd seen her with *Connor*. He'd almost stomped out of his car and dragged the woman away from *that man*.

'Almost' being the key word here. Before he could act on his impulse, he decided to continue home and talk to her about it, like the rational adult he was and not the overbearing, possessive male that he was becoming toward April. Only, she'd taken an inordinately long time to return. Every minute that passed, his mind thought of all the sexual positions those two might have engaged in and his anger flamed to new heights. He forgot about the twins being with her and how they might be a damper to any sexual overtures. All his mind could focus on was them. In bed. Together.

When he'd finally heard them enter, his anger exploded into this animalistic fury. He had to make sure that man hadn't touched her, hadn't touched what was *his*. He had to make her stay away from him. In the state of mind he was in, he didn't pay attention to what he thought. Verification was all he could focus on.

He avoided the twins—knowing they'd give away his presence—and hid in the kitchen, knowing she had to pass it to reach the twins. Once she passed by the entrance to the kitchen, he struck. He was immediately hit with her own scent of baby powder with a hint of marigold underneath. With no male scent interlaced with hers, he relaxed, only to stiffen again when she expressed interest in *that man*.

Now that he'd made sure she wouldn't go near *that man* again, through an admittedly fictitious rule, he knew he couldn't hide from his feelings anymore. The raw intensity and anger he'd just expressed were not typical of an employer-employee relationship. It indicated that he wanted a deeper and more intimate relationship.

But with what she'd walked into this afternoon, would she want to develop their bond further?

~

April was in a bad mood for the rest of the day. She had been looking forward to having a male friend. Or just a friend, period. With her life as it was, it was difficult maintaining friendships. She'd lost contact with all of her high school and college friends even though she'd graduated barely two months ago. And most of them had been mere acquaintances. Well, all of them actually.

She'd hoped to develop more meaningful friendships in the workplace. But, seeing as her workplace involved infants and an unreachable boss, there goes that plan. She sighed. Friendship just wasn't in her cards.

She was in her room, musing over her lack of luck in finding and keeping friends. Truthfully, she believed she was going to be a cat lady. She just needed her own place, a kitten to start off and she'd be good to go. Smiling at her own morbid thoughts, she shook it off and started to get ready for bed.

Suddenly, her phone beeped, indicating that there was a notification. That was unusual. She only received texts from her mother and calls from telemarketers. With her near-homeless state a few weeks ago, she rarely answered calls. Furthermore, her mother only texted her every few weeks just to make sure she was still alive and well. She'd sometimes call her mother for a more in-depth update but that was the extent of her phone usage. So, receiving a notification was an abnormality.

Cautiously approaching her phone, she picked it up and saw that she had a text from an unknown number. The number was from the area but she didn't recognize it. Opening it, a smile suddenly lit her face. It was Connor. He was arranging a time for them to meet. Her smile turned bittersweet as she recalled that she had to stop all contact with him.

Hey. Connor here. Just wondering if you're free to meet up.

Taking her time to compose her answer, she made sure she was alone before answering. Luckily, she'd settled the twins down for the night. And they only wake up once or twice in the night. So that's one task done. She could focus all her attention on Connor now.

I'm sorry but I have to decline. Mr. H says employees are not allowed to fraternise >:(Hope you're not too disappointed :)

I didn't know we had that rule. Let me check it and get back to you =) Hahaha. I'm sure we'll run into each other when you come and visit him. Just don't be too surprised by what you walk into. Or learn to hide it. The entire building is talking about how fast you hightailed it out of there.

April frowned. *Everyone knew? How?* She asked Connor about it.

Janice set you up. She wanted to scandalize you. Everyone thinks it's because you made Mr. H stay away from the office. I think she has a crush on him and wants to clear the field of any competitors.

Competitor? Me? As if. I'm not pretty enough to get his attention.

We're on a fishing expedition, aren't we? ;)

Fishing expedition? What was he talking about? Has it been that long since she'd texted? Was she so out of the texting lingo? God, just how old was she? Deciding to bury her pride, she asked him about it and immediately sent a refusal when he explained.

What? No!!!! I'm just stating the truth. Anyway, thanks for the offer but…I need this job.

Hey, don't mention it. And I totally understand. With the job market as it is, we need any job that comes around. See you around then =)

See you :)

April put her phone down. She couldn't stop smiling. Maybe this could be the start of a beautiful new friendship.

CHAPTER 11

"Mr. Hall—"

"Jason," Jason corrected April. He heard her sigh on the other line and stifled a grin. "Why are you calling me, April?"

"Well, Jason, there's this woman here who claims to be your housekeeper."

"What does she look like?" he cut in, the urge to hide his grin a thing of the past when he heard her huff of annoyance.

"Plump, petite, and matronly. Salt and pepper hair. Grey eyes. Take-no-prisoner attitude. Ring a bell?" she recited sassily.

"Yes, I believe so. And I also believe that I told you she's returning in two weeks. I admit Mrs. Salvador's early by a few days but I don't think that would be an issue."

"Well, no. The twins seem to know her and are playing with her now. She's surprisingly gentle with them. And I think she's taking over the making of their meals, which is more than fine with me. But the thing is, she's banned me from the kitchen!" she wailed/hissed.

He winced. He knew how much she liked his kitchen. If he didn't know any better, he'd think he had hired a chef because she kept cooking for him. And since Mrs. Salvador had already left him a freezer full of dinner, he had a hard time finishing them all. He would be hard-pressed to decide whose cooking he liked better, though.

Suddenly, a movement from his peripheral vision returned his attention to his surroundings. He was in his favorite restaurant with his closest friends and cousins. They'd decided to meet up since one of them had finally graced the East Coast. And usually, they do not allow phone calls to cut through their meal, but this was April. It could have been about the twins. Or, in this case, a conflict between his nanny and housekeeper. Plus, she'd been acting distant since *that* day. He tried to lighten the air between them, talking and joking with her more often, but there's always seem to be a barrier between them. And he didn't know how to push it away. So, he'd always entertain any voluntary contact from her. Always.

Seeing his cousin looking extremely pissed off, he decided to end the call. "We'll talk about it when I get back," he promised her. Laughing at her second huff of annoyance, he left kisses for the twins and returned to his cousins.

"I didn't know we allowed phone calls at the table," his cousin, Harry Reynolds, said coldly. Jason shot a glare at him as he took a seat. "And what's with the happy look and smiles? You look like you've just arranged a hook up."

"That was my nanny—"

"Is there anything wrong with the twins? Sharon can come down for a look if you want," Cameron offered, cutting in. Taking in a deep breath for patience, Jason waited a while before replying.

"No. Mrs. Salvador has returned and apparently banned April from the kitchen," he explained. Cameron barked out a laugh while Harry's lips twisted into a sneer.

"Why do you need to care so much about your nanny? Why does it matter if she gets banned? As long as she's doing her job, whatever happens in her life should no longer matter," Harry said dismissively. Jason took a while to take a good look at his cousin. His mahogany hair was stylishly cut and his suit was immaculate. He was a consummate businessman, but he had an air of detachment around him. Like he wasn't touched by his surroundings.

Jason felt his heart sink. This wasn't the man he'd grown up with. This man was cold and callous. He had no heart. Whatever had happened to him that changed him, well, Jason had no idea and he certainly doesn't know how to relate to this man anymore. And to think he'd have agreed with his remark a few months ago— before the twins, and later April, came into his life.

"Well, seeing as she prepares the twins' meals, I guess it's an issue for me," he fibbed, getting annoyed with his pompous attitude. Cameron, sensing the tension growing, started to change the subject.

"So, Sharon's throwing a party for Mom's birthday and she wants all of you to come. It's next Saturday," he said as he sliced into his steak. Harry started to refuse but Cameron cut in. "Did I say I want you to? She demands your presence. Work is not a reasonable excuse. If you try that, she's going to have your balls on a platter. She'll hound you for the rest of the year if you're not there."

"I don't know why you accede to these women's ridiculous demands," Harry said, his voice Arctic cold. A fact about him was that the more irritated he gets, the colder he becomes. Cameron and Jason shared a look and decided to ignore his comment.

"So, where will you be staying? And how long will you be here?" Jason asked, abruptly changing the subject.

"I'll be staying at my usual hotel and I'll be going back tomorrow. Do you want to hit the clubs tonight?" he asked Jason. When he hesitated, Harry scowled. "Come on. It's been so long since we got together. I'd actually like to do something fun."

"Yeah, alright," Jason said, giving in. It was not often that Harry felt like having fun so he should accommodate him this once. "Let me inform April about this. Excuse me."

Ignoring Harry's overcritical look and Cameron's amused one, he left the restaurant and made the call. It rang a few times before April picked up, sounding all breathless. His mind immediately took him to all the reasons she could possibly sound breathless, the only reasons he could only think of being sexual reasons, which made him miss her greeting.

"Hello? Mr. Halloway?" he heard her ask. His phone was right beside his ear but she sounded very far away. "Hello? Shh, shh."

"Jason. Call me Jason," he answered absently as he returned to reality. He heard Tanner's babble nearby and concluded that she was carrying him. "Is everything alright? Why isn't Tanner down for his nap?"

"He's very active this morning; he refuses to lie down. Luckily, Daphne's down or I won't know what I'll do," April told him, responding to Tanner's babble with *hmms* and *yeahs*. "So, why are you calling?"

"I'll be home late tonight. My cousin is in town and he wants to go to the clubs," he told her. The silence at the other line was making him antsy. He didn't know why but he felt like reassuring her. "I promise I won't bring any woman back and I'll definitely be home by midnight."

"So, you're Cinderella now. Glad to know. Tell me again, when was your sex change? And where's the fairy godmother?" she teased.

"Hahaha," he deadpanned, to which she giggled. He had to smile at that. It was joined with Tanner's own giggle and it only needed Daphne's laugh to complete the picture.

"Oh," she said excitedly, stopping suddenly. "I'm now allowed back into the kitchen."

"How? What did you do? Promise to sell your future newborn?" he asked lightly, taking a seat at one of the benches that were always in the hallways of the country club. He heard her snort and Tanner laugh. "It was a valid question because Mrs. Salvador does not ever allow anyone into her kitchen. She has a strict No Entry policy. She even barely allows me to move around in there. And that's only when she leaves."

"Well, the twins weren't eating and I tried to entice them by eating some to show that it's delicious and accidentally ate the entire bowl. I know Mrs. Salvador made some extras so I went for a refill and they began to eat. Then, she said, in her husky voice, 'You can come in', and just left. I didn't want to ask for a clarification so I just took it that I'm back in!" she finished excitedly but softly. From the *shh* and humming here and there, he knew Tanner was finally settling down for his nap.

"That's good. I have to go now. Give the twins a kiss for me," he said softly. Once she acknowledged, he ended the call and was surprised to find his cousins beside the chair.

"What are you guys doing here?"

"Did you have a nice call?" Cameron asked with a big smile.

"Yeah. How are the twins, Casanova?" Harry came in lightly. Jason was confused and didn't know what they were talking about.

"This brings me back to those days where I'll just talk for hours with my girlfriend. High school, middle school," Cameron sighed wistfully. Jason caught his gist and felt his face heat up.

"Luckily, you now have a wife," he said sharply. He saw the way Harry and Cameron looked at each other before they burst out in laughter. This reminded him of all the times the both of them teased him mercilessly during their childhood. Being two years younger than them, he always took the brunt of their teasing. As much as he didn't like it, he enjoyed the way Harry's eyes lit up. It wasn't as cold and distant. And, for that, he didn't mind being laughed at.

~

Feeding the twins breakfast was a tall order. They didn't like the texture of the porridge and she often had to deal with spit ups. She was on her way to make the twins' breakfast when she noticed an unfamiliar man sitting at the dining room table. Startled, she paused and studied the man warily.

He looked familiar but she could not, for the life of her, figure out where she'd seen him before. He was very attractive. Like model attractive. Meaning hot but cold. Unattainable. Someone who one just sighed over before returning to reality. She had never met this paragon but Mr. Halloway came close.

Suddenly, he turned his piercing blue eyes on her. She subconsciously took a step back. This guy was really cold. Like freezing. She didn't know how she hadn't formed icicles yet. She wouldn't be surprised if he admitted to be a robot. Trying her hardest to ignore the intensity of his gaze, she skirted him and went to the kitchen.

She finally remembered where she'd seen him: the photographs on Mr. Halloway's desk. He'd been in a number of them but in the photos, he'd looked more approachable than this cyborg before her. She was being mean now. If he was a cyborg, then Mr. Halloway was not in any way real as well. And that would be a waste.

"I want three eggs, sunny side up; two wholemeal toast; and coffee. Black. No sugar," he suddenly said. It was so unexpected that she almost dropped the twins' breakfast. Seriously?

The first time they conversed and that's what he says? Rude. But he was her employer's friend. She should just entertain him.

After making his breakfast, she went to fetch the twins. They got up late that day. As much as she liked the extra few minutes of peace, she knew it would adversely affect their day. Just as she was going to enter their nursery, she heard a groan from Mr. Halloway's bedroom.

Curious and slightly alarmed, she went to the doorway and was instantly hit by the smell of alcohol. *Oh God, how much did he drink?* she thought, waving her hand before her to at least disperse the smell. Hoping to dispel the scent from the room, she went to draw the curtains apart and opened the window.

"No. Don't," Mr. Halloway barked weakly from his bed. Ignoring him, she went to all the windows and opened them. "April. I'm a vampire. I don't like sunlight." Standing beside his bed, she crossed her arm and shook her head.

"Did you pour the drinks all over yourself? You smell like the inside of a vodka bottle," she scolded softly. Knowing how much his head was pounding, she tried to be considerate but the smell was just plain awful. "I'm going to wake the twins. When you're ready to relinquish your vampire status, do join us."

"No. Don't leave," he whined. Thinking he was just being ornery, she turned to leave when his hands suddenly grabbed her hips and pulled her over him. He rolled over until he was above her. His head up, he sent her a crooked smile and greeted her. "Good morning."

He looked incredibly handsome even when he smelled boozy—his hair tousled, his eyes lazy from sleep, his cheeks slightly flushed from the alcohol and sleep. *Why couldn't he look all disheveled and out of sorts like she does on the rare occasion she drinks?* Life was so unfair.

"Mr. Hallow—"

"Jason!" he corrected her sharply before burying his face against her neck. Startled, she tried to push him away but her arms were caught in between them. "If you continue to be stubborn, I'm going to punish you every time you call me 'Mr. Halloway'. I'll tell you your punishment later. We'll rest for now."

"Jason, I have to feed the twins. They're going to wake up any time soon," she told him gently. He shook his head childishly, still burrowed against her neck. Laughing quietly, she asked, "Are you still drunk, oh Mr. Vampire sir?"

"I like the sound of that. Come forth and pleasure me, servant girl," he said in a mock commanding tone. Her face flushed when she realized what he meant. Trying to escape again, all she accomplished was getting his attention back to her. Seeing her red face, his face took a decidedly lecherous bend. "Shy, are we? Well, there's only one way to remedy that."

Unable to grasp his meaning, she was caught off guard when he placed his lips on her. Not knowing how to respond, or whether she should, she just lay there until he grew more insistent. She tried to fight his repeated attempts to deepen the kisses, but she only felt herself melting into his kisses, giving in to his persistence. He let out a rumble of triumph as he managed to slip past her lips and invade her mouth.

She felt like she was drowning under his expertise and the pleasure they evoked. All she could focus on was his lips and his hands which were roaming about her body, managing to get under her sweatshirt and inching towards her bra.

A jarring sound penetrated the haze. She knew it was important, that noise. But Jason muddled her mind again. A second noise joined the first. *Oh, Tanner and Daphne are angry*, she thought absently. Then, like a thunderbolt striking her, she pushed him away and got off the bed before he even knew what was going on.

"We are not finished, April," he called breathlessly but she just shook her head, facing determinedly forward. Her face was redder than a tomato. Hadn't she decided to distance herself? This was definitely a setback. *But, with the way he was acting, surely he saw something more between them?*

No, April. Deluding yourself is not allowed here, she scolded herself, even as her fingers came up to trace her lips, wanting to retain any lasting impression of the kiss. She didn't know what to feel or how to interpret what just happened. She just hoped things wouldn't be awkward when they see each other again.

CHAPTER 12

Jason couldn't keep the smile off his face. All through taking a shower and getting dressed, the smile was ever present on his face. He didn't dare look in the mirror so as not to be confronted with the excessive happiness and smugness. Even the way he walked was different. He felt that there was a bounce in his steps. This was getting too cheery for him. He needed to stop.

But he couldn't help it. Who knew acting drunk could get him the hottest kiss in his entire life? Admittedly, he had still been in the fog of sleep when he'd pulled April into his bed, but he was wide awake and conscious when he decided to go in for the kill. And it was glorious. It felt like a part of him that he didn't know had been missing had just returned to him. The heat had instantly exploded and he was caught in the undercurrents of it so much that he didn't recognize his children's cries.

Now that sent a shard of guilt through his heart. The first time he was into a woman and all thoughts of them flew out of his mind. He felt like such a failure of a father. He didn't know how he could ever face them.

~

Pressing a kiss on Tanner's and Daphne's forehead with a murmur of apology when he entered the dining alcove, he greeted Harry and settled down for breakfast. His eyes followed April. Her sweatshirt was now riddled with blotches of porridge and she was currently trying to wheedle another bite down Tanner, who preferred to play with his toy.

"What are you waiting for? Get Jason his breakfast," Harry suddenly said coldly to April. April jumped slightly as she had been immersed with the twin. Or maybe she had just been studiously trying to ignore his cousin. She sent him an uncertain look but went to grab his daily dose of caffeine. Jason, on the other hand, was taken aback. He hadn't expected the barked order nor the coldness. Not wanting to create waves, because Harry will only be there for a few more hours, he let it slide but felt the beginnings of rage in his chest.

"Is that all?" Harry barked when she timidly placed a cup of coffee before Jason. Her face was stricken and her eyes were filled with discomfort and a tinge of fear. It was that fear that made him forget about letting it slide. He would not have April fearing anything or anyone when she's with him, especially not when he could help it.

"Stop it, Harry. Just because you're my cousin doesn't give you the right to order my employees around," he growled, placing his hand over the one she had over the cup handle. Her eyes darted from his to Harry's. She looked like a prey trapped between two predators. She only relaxed when he sent her a warm smile, going so much as to blush when the smile grew more heated. He hadn't known it was so fun to tease his lover. Or potential lover. He should do that more often. Letting her go, he turned back to Harry, his eyes growing decidedly colder.

Sensing that the argument was only going to become more heated, she decided to take the twins away. "It's time for bath," she said, her voice full of false cheer. They stopped what they were doing and squealed in excitement. Tanner absolutely loved bath time. Daphne, on the other hand, was indifferent. She only squealed because Tanner was doing so. This time, the smile on

April's face was genuine and so breathtakingly beautiful that Jason almost forgot about Harry. So much so that he was unprepared when April dropped Tanner in his arms. "Give your Daddy a kiss and off you go."

She let the twins loose on the floor after they'd given their daddy wet, sticky kisses. He almost asked her for a kiss, too, but she left like a bat on fire. Once she managed to herd them to their bathroom, and her beautiful behind was out of sight, he turned back to his cousin, continuing their staring contest.

He didn't know what to make of his attitude that morning. He would like to blame it on the alcohol but that wouldn't explain his general coldness and gloomy air. As he'd noticed before, this was not the boy he grew up with. And he didn't know how to talk with the man before him.

"I didn't know you were becoming soft," Harry said softly. Jason sent him a perplexed look. "Defending your employee? Why, if your parents saw this, they'd have your hide. I'm surprised. I believed you were the consummate businessman. Clearly, having children has changed things."

"Well, considering my parents are not here and that I have never cared about their twisted opinions, I can truly say I will sleep easy tonight and every night thereafter. What I can't understand is why you think defending my employee is making me soft. I hired April for a specific reason and what you saw just now was it. If I wanted a maid, I'd have gotten a maid. Her main focus is my kids and only my kids. And my main focus right now is providing the best for my children. If that makes me soft, I'll welcome that as long as my children are happy, safe, and secure," he finished.

He couldn't help the anger that burst forth when his cousin, one of his closest friends, brought his parents into their conversation. Harry knew that their relationship was strained at best. Their values and principles, in both work and personal lives, greatly differed from his. Something he had to thank his aunt for and, lately, his children and April.

"What happened to you, Harry? You've changed. Where's the guy who'd defend anyone from bullies? What happened to the guy who's quick to laugh but slow to anger? What happened to your morals?" he asked sadly. He remembered a snippet from last night and it worried him. "Do you know why I left so early last night? I saw how you were acting, all bursting with your self-importance and power, how the women were flocking around you and how much cold enjoyment you took from it. Then, I saw how you narrowed in on this one woman who was sitting alone. You invited her to dance and I knew she refused, but you pulled her to the dance floor anyway. When she tried to leave, you pulled her closer. I had to wonder if you'd have forced more of yourself on her if I hadn't decided to leave."

"I'm sorry you think so low of me," Harry said stiffly. Jason saw that his words had hurt him, but his cousin was too proud to explain himself. "I think I should leave. I know not to stay where I'm not wanted."

"What are you talking about? I want you here. I just want to know what made you change," he returned but it was unheeded. Harry left without another word, breakfast forgotten. Jason wondered if he would ever see his light-hearted cousin ever again.

~

April sat back and watched as her charges played around her room. Her heart was still beating fast from her nervousness. She had not been in that situation in a long time. Not since her mother and she left her dad. Hopefully, Mr. Halloway was alright.

The twins had learnt to use anything and everything around them to help them stand. It was cute, but she learned to keep away any fragile and expensive items off the furniture after the first few breakages. Luckily, Mr. Halloway was understanding and didn't deduct those items from her paycheck. Or she'd have to work for free for many, many months or years. When she'd found out how much one of it cost, her heart had literally stopped.

Lately, it seemed like Tanner was becoming stronger and more stable. He would try to stand on his own and succeed for a few seconds before the force of gravity and his tiny legs pulled him back down. Even so, it was a huge accomplishment for him. Taking him into her arms, she peppered his face with kisses and he shrieked with laughter even as he tried to escape. Daphne, not wanting to be outdone, demanded to be cuddled and kissed too.

It became a game after that. The twins would crawl around, trying to escape her, while she went on the prowl for cheeks to kiss. Once they were caught, she swung them around the room and kissed their entire face before letting them go again. They loved the game, scrambling away whenever they saw her and giggling when she looked visibly disappointed.

April was so focused on catching them, she was horribly surprised when male arms suddenly wrapped around her, pulling her back to a hard body. Catching the scent of his cologne, she relaxed into Mr. Halloway's chest. The twins were still crawling around, keeping an eye on her.

"How did it go?" she asked, not even trying to get out of his hold. She felt that he needed it.

"Bad," he replied as he rested his chin on her shoulder. "He's changed so much. The person I grew up with wouldn't say anything good about my parents. He hated them as much as I hated his." His words piqued April's curiosity. This was the first time she'd heard anything about his parents. She knew from some of what Mrs. Salvador said that Jason was not close to his parents. Even so, she knew it was not the time.

"He used to be so fun and fair. He was the one who preached about equality when I started to become too high; and respect, when Cameron became too promiscuous and callous with women. Now, it's the other way around. And I don't like it."

"Did you talk to him about it?" she asked, keeping the twins within sight. They'd lost interest in the game and returned to exploring her room. "Surely if he explained—"

"He left without another word. I may have been a bit too harsh—"

"A bit?" she teased. She felt, more than heard, his laugh.

"Yes, a bit, you minx. Now stop interrupting me," he scolded, his fingers dancing along her ribcage. Being the extremely ticklish person that she was, she jumped and yelped, almost banging her head on his nose. Luckily, he jumped back with a laugh. After he'd quietened and she allowed herself back in his arms, he continued. "Now, as I was saying, I was a bit harsh but I felt that it needed to be said. I thought we could talk it out, but he just left."

"I'm sure you'll have other opportunities to clear the air. You should take this time to reconcile yourself with your cousin's new personality and find a way to be comfortable with him again," she suggested softly. Looking to him, her eyes were caught in his soft verdant ones. Unable to look away, she didn't move away when he moved closer and even closed her eyes when his lips met hers. This kiss was softer, more for comfort and support. Unfortunately, before the kiss could become deeper and heated, his phone rang. With a harsh sigh, he pulled away and picked it up.

Using the distraction, she turned to the twins and immediately tried to push Jason out of her room, her face turning bright red. Busy, he moved a few steps before stopping, realizing what she was doing. Puzzled, his eyes questioned her but she refused to answer him. She didn't stop trying to push him out, but, seeing as he worked out and she didn't, it was an epic failure. With eyes filled with mischief once he found out the reason, he started to

71

tease her, but the warning in her eyes made him reconsider. Finished with his call, he bid the twins goodbye, kissing their cheeks, giving her lips a peck, and said, "I like the red one" and left before she could retort.

Cheeks burning, lips tingling, she turned to the twins and sighed exasperatedly, even as amusement bloomed. Why did she have to put her undergarments in the second last drawer?

CHAPTER 13

The week leading to Cameron's mother's party was fairly uneventful. The twins were quite well-behaved with some small fights that all siblings had. From what Jason had seen, it was mainly over toys. April had mentioned that sometimes they fought for her attention, but he had yet to witness that. Surprisingly, Daphne was the instigator and Tanner would sometimes give in, which was quite surprising because men in his family never gave in. Of course, there were those times when giving in was not an option. And those were when he had no clue on how to handle them.

April had to step in then. Most of the time, she'd squint at Tanner, which he'd return with an expression of utmost bewilderment. He'd see amusement lurking in her eyes but she'd keep her tough facade up. She'd then shake her head and split the twins up by pulling one from the other or calling their name sharply.

And that's another reason why he often called for her when they fought. They listened to her. With him, his calls for peace fell on deaf ears. And he knew they weren't hearing-impaired. They came at the call of food often enough to disprove that. He'd usually gift her with a deep, hard kiss as thanks and escape to his office. April would try to protest but would always fail. That was most probably because he did not give her enough time to do so.

He was currently in his office, trying to identify what was making him feel as if something was not right. The feeling had been nagging at him for the past few days and he wanted to make it go away. It felt very much like he was distrustful of April. Looking back, everything was the same.

The four of them ate dinner together, as usual, much to Mrs. Salvador's delight. She wasn't one to show her emotions but he knew when she did from all the years she'd worked with him. It was an admittedly messy affair with food flying about–courtesy of the twins–but April always managed to relate their day to him while he ate. Then he'd play with the twins while she grabbed a bite. After dinner, he'd go to his office to finish up some work while she prepared the twins for bed. Once the twins were out for the night, she'd remind him to go to bed early and leave before he could tempt her to go to bed with him. So their nightly routine was still happening but...

April had been acting differently. Now, every night, after putting the twins down, she would lock herself in her room. She didn't even come by his office. Maybe he was coming on too strong, he wondered. But that does not explain why her phone was always with her. Before this week, she'd always leave her personal phone in her room. Now, suddenly, she's carrying it around, along with the phone he provided, everywhere.

Maybe it was her family? he speculated. Truth be told, he knew close to nothing regarding that subject, which was a major oversight, especially since he intended to have a serious relationship with her. Even so... *No*, he decided, shaking his head. That wouldn't put that sweet, bashful smile on her face. His mind lingered on the smile. It was vaguely familiar. He had never seen it on her before so it couldn't be from her. But it was so familiar. As if he'd seen it on someone else before.

Where had he seen it before? Definitely on another woman. But surely not all women. He definitely had not seen it on his housekeeper. He'd recently seen it on the woman he took the elevator with. The woman he'd sent a friendly smile to. It could have been misconstrued as flirting but—

Wait. Flirting? When he put this in context to April, he sprang up in fury. Someone was flirting with *his* April? His mind didn't even shy away from his possessive pronouncement. He had resigned himself to the fact that April was his, enthusiastically even, and nothing was going to take her away from him. Not if he could help it.

He wanted to ask her about it, but he couldn't just do that. He needed proof. He had to take a look at her phone to confirm his suspicions. Hopefully she wouldn't be too offended by what he was going to do. Based from his knowledge of April's nightly routine, he had to wait until eleven—the time she'd check on the twins—to sneak into her room. Never had it occurred to him to just let it go. Or go through the conventional route to, maybe, ask her. That would reveal too much. Not that his numerous displays of affection or cuddling meant anything. *You do that to all the women you kiss after all*, a voice in the back of his head said sarcastically.

He ignored the annoying voice and looked for her phone which was conveniently located on her deliciously rumpled bed. Briefly distracted by how he and she could make it even messier, he brought himself back to the task at hand when her phone beeped.

Making his way to the bed, he recalled how the twins had ransacked her underwear drawer the last time he was there. He was sure she didn't want him to see that, but it made him realize he should take her shopping. Underwear shopping. Maybe even lingerie. He felt blood surging south as his mind wondered down a path that was both tantalizing and torturous. Luckily, another message came through and brought him back to reality.

His eyes narrowed when he saw who it was from. Connor. Wasn't he that guy who was hitting on her last week? Hadn't he prevented any further contact with *that man?* So how was he messaging her? He must have given him her numb—

All rational thoughts flew out of his head as he opened the message. Hah, she didn't even lock her phone. What if some evil character tried to steal it for information? He ignored his conscience that tried to point out that *he* was that character right now. He justified it by telling himself he was concerned for her safety. Even that tasted foul to him.

Shaking away the obvious lies, he read the messages and felt his rage worsen. They'd been messaging each other every day since the day they'd met. Even though her replies were innocuous, Connor's were definitely on the flirty side. *How could she not see he was flirting with her?* How could he let this happen right under his nose?

"Jason?"

He turned to the door, looking at how beautiful she was illuminated by the hallway light. All he could think of was making her irrevocably his.

CHAPTER 14

April eyed Jason warily as she closed the door behind her. He had this wild air about him, like he was some savage predator. She felt that one wrong move would kill her. Well, not exactly kill but somewhere along the line of something bad happening. Hearing her phone chirp, she searched her bed for it and found it in his hands.

"Why do you have my phone?" she asked in trepidation, hoping against hope that he hadn't notice who'd just texted her. It's not that she wanted to hide anything from him. It's just that she knew how he was going to react. And from the fire in his eyes, she was right in her assumption. "Please don't be mad."

"Mad? Why should I be mad? Is it because some man has been texting you? Or is it because he's been flirting with you?" he growled as he advanced towards her. She inched back even as her brows furrowed.

"He's flirting? Really? I thought he's just being nice," she confessed with a nervous giggle, hoping to calm him down. She swallowed back her next words when she saw he wasn't appeased. She started when she felt an immovable mass, most probably a wall, at her back. Having nowhere to go, she watched Jason approach with wary eyes.

"You are going to text this man right now and tell him you are not going to talk to him ever again. Right. Now," he growled as he pushed her phone in her hands. She noticed that he wasn't rough even in his anger. His movements were just jerky, as if he was trying his best to control his anger. His grip on her hand was not too tight and he hadn't tugged her arm violently, too. A part of her relaxed and trusted him, even as another part rebelled at his demand.

"But he's my friend," she mumbled obstinately. His hand tightened on her forearm, but she wasn't going to be intimidated.

"You are going to text this man right now!" he growled, bringing his face closer to her.

"Why?" she asked angrily. She refused to give in.

"Because you're mine!" he roared, making her jump. Then his words started to sink in and she was stunned. She didn't know what to say and what to think. She knew, from his actions, that their relationship was veering away from the typical employer-employee relationship, but she had no idea where they were heading. She'd hoped for a more intimate, exclusive relationship but knew that would never happen. The main reason being that they weren't equals. He's a billionaire. She barely had ten dollars to her name. He's in the upper echelon of Chicago society. She was barely scraping the bottom of the barrel of society in general, let alone Chicago society. She just couldn't see how they'd work.

Tanner's cry pierced through the silence that surrounded them. April managed to escape Jason's hold and went to attend to his son. She forced her mind to empty itself while she bounced Tanner in her arms, hoping to calm him and herself. Jason watched from the hallway, worry etched in his face.

"April, talk to me," he implored softly. She refused to look at him and instead watched Tanner's eyes flutter shut. He'd been awakened by his father's loud voice. Usually, she'd reprimand Jason for it but she didn't know how to treat him as she used to before his proclamation. She thought whether she should put some distance between them.

"What did you mean by... whatever you said just now?" she asked, unable to even voice it out. It was such a foreign idea. However, he didn't have any problem with it.

"You're mine, April. Meaning I won't allow any man to take you away from me. Or even be close to you," he said.

She could hear the bemusement in his voice but there was also acceptance. *He accepted his feelings? Wait, he acknowledged he had feelings? That's unusual for a man*, she thought, amused. *Mind, stop wandering*, she berated herself and brought her attention back to Jason.

"I don't know where this is coming from or why I feel this way, but I do know that I can't imagine life without you. I want to protect you. I want to give you everything that you can possibly need or want. I just want to make you happy."

"I-I don't know what to say," she croaked. Don't get her wrong. She's a woman and had always dreamed about a man sweeping her off her feet, and bringing her to his castle where they'd live happily ever after.

But it's the 21st century. Men no longer did the sweeping. And most definitely not a high-flying prince like Jason. Elation battled with disbelief and she didn't know which would win. "You can have any woman on earth—"

"And I choose you," he said firmly. Hearing the steel in his voice, she looked back at him. Seeing his vulnerability exposed with his stubbornness was jarring but all Jason. "Don't try to make sense of this. Just accept it. I have. And I most definitely want you."

April couldn't help but to acquiesce, looking into his beseeching eyes. A man like Jason did not ask and for him to do that, it boggled her mind. But it also helped her accept the depth of his proclamation. "I-I'll try," she offered wryly, shifting Tanner into a more comfortable position. "I mean, I will sometimes be inundated with insecurities. Especially when you're around women more beautiful than me. I just hope you will be patient when that happens and not become some crazed idiot when the situation is reversed." Even as she said that, she knew they still had ways to go before that would ever stop. Case in point, her phone was still in his possession. She just hoped nothing gets destroyed during their adjustment period.

Just then, her phone chirped.

CHAPTER 15

Jason suddenly looked mad and stormed to his office. Alarmed, April laid Tanner on his bed and chased after Jason. She was unwilling to call him back because she didn't want to wake the babies up. She hoped he wouldn't do anything drastic but from the noises in his office, it was only wishful thinking.

She stopped short at the entrance of his office. Jason was standing at his desk, with a satisfied smile, over pieces of plastic and metal that used to be her phone, his heaving chest almost distracting her. Almost. A substantial paper weight was clutched in his hand. And he looked like he wasn't quite done.

Unable to say anything, she walked in and closed the door behind her. Hearing the click, he looked up and sent her a savage grin.

"I've finally stopped any form of conversation between you and that man," he crowed hoarsely.

"B-But that was my mother," she managed to say, a slight wavering in her voice. Hearing her tone, his features changed. Paled. Became panicky. "She hasn't contacted me in weeks. She's always changing her number so it's difficult for me to get to her. Meaning she'd always initiated our communication. And now, my phone is gone. How's she going to contact me?"

She couldn't comprehend the amount of rage she was in. Admittedly, she and her mother weren't close—her mother was too independent to ever accept help—but they'd always kept in contact.

The fear of her father finding them kept their relationship alive. In hindsight, that was a very tenuous link but their relationship was still going strong. Seeing her phone in pieces, along with her sim card, her mind ached, trying to think of a way to contact her. *Who could she contact to get some clues?*

"I'm sorry," Jason said softly, wrapping his arms around her. Startled, April recovered enough to not acknowledge him. He had to learn he couldn't just apologize and they'd be hunky-dory. Not if they wanted their relationship to work. "I'll find a way to fix this."

"That's fine and all but why did you do this in the first place? Because of Connor?" she snapped softly. His arms tightened, giving her her answer. Turning in his arm, she told him, "Jason, he's nothing but a friend. Hell, seeing as we've only ever met once, he barely counts as an acquaintance. Even so, I'd like to see where this goes. Maybe make a friend?"

"We'll find you other friends. Friends who don't flirt with each other. Or have a working penis. Or a penis attracted to vaginas," he said through gritted teeth. Surprisingly, his use of words amused her but she smothered the smile that was trying to break through. He was adorable when he was acting all caveman-like. It helped that she knew he'd never hit her. "I'll introduce you to some people I know. You can be friends with them."

"No. I want to make my own friends. People with similar interests," she said adamantly. His face, which had relaxed when he thought that he had a solution, hardened again. "Jason, be reasonable. The people you know won't have any similar interests with me. What would we talk about? The weather? Good way to start a friendship."

"There are worse beginnings," he joked. She just sent him a dry look. "I don't like him and you won't have anything to do with him. Ever."

"So, is this how our relationship's going to be like? You dictating every move I make? I didn't know you wanted a puppet," she said through gritted teeth, moving forward in her anger. She'd had enough of his attitude. If they were ever to work as a couple, they had to be equals. It's difficult enough that she worked for him but they had to find a way if they'd ever have a chance to make this work.

"That's not what I mean and that's not what I want. This is just so new to me. Being in a relationship. Wanting to keep you away from other men—"

"Well, you'll just have to make it work," she decreed imperiously.

"We'll work on that," he said in the face of her decree. Realizing how close they were, April felt her face redden.

"It's late. We should get to bed," she said haltingly. Seeing the smile on his face, she rushed to clarify. "To our individual beds. Alone. To sleep. Good night."

He pulled her even closer when she tried to escape his arms. "No good night kiss?" he asked coyly.

"You're too old for that—"

His lips covered hers and she just melted into him. She had a momentary thought to move away but was swept by the heat they generated. What did she want to do again? It was getting difficult to think when he was pressing her into him and drowning her thoughts with one bone-melting kiss after the other. Finally, after an eternity, or maybe closer to five minutes, he let her up. Their breath mingled as they looked at each other. She noticed his eyes had darkened to a dark mossy color, sending shivers down her back. His eyes darkened further as he moved in for another kiss but her hand made him pause.

"Sleep please? The twins and I are going out tomorrow and I really need the rest," she implored. His eyes showed his

83

disappointment, but he respected her wishes. Placing his arm around her, they headed to their rooms.

"Good night, sweetheart," he said with a kiss on her forehead. They were giving each other nicknames already? She didn't have one for him yet! Her mind scrambled and blurted the first thing that entered her mind.

"Um, good night, hot stuff."

Of all things? "Hot stuff"? Am I going mad? I've never addressed anyone like that before—

"Yeah, I'm 'hot stuff' and I'm all yours," he said with a cocky grin. Rolling her eyes, she pushed him away and entered her room, closing her door before he could say anything else.

Trust her to find the cockiest guy on earth. But he's all hers. And he knows it.

~

The next day, April restlessly watched the twins. Her mind couldn't forget the call that had been rudely interrupted by Jason. As much as she was enamored by his show of possessiveness, worry dominated her mind when it came to *that* call.

Her mother—her proud, independent mother—had called her. That meant something. She didn't know what but there was a reason. And now, she couldn't know. *What if it was serious? What if her mother was bleeding on the floor—dying—because her phone was smashed into pieces?*

There was only thing to do. She had to see her.

~

Jason was rethinking his decision to allow April and the twins to visit her mother alone. It hadn't dawned on him that this side of town was rough and dangerous. Even so, he could have gotten his driver to accompany her. He didn't do much anyway, seeing as Jason preferred to drive.

He eyed the door to the apartment building if it can even be called that. He believed a hovel was a better description. It looked like it only needed one good punch and it'd collapse. Hoping there's still some sturdiness left in the structure, he entered and the scent of urine and other unpleasant smell he couldn't name assaulted his nose. To think that April had to suffer through this kind of accommodations growing up. Luckily, he'd found her or who knows where she'd be now. The cage elevator situated right across the entrance looked equally unstable and unlikely to withstand his weight. He decided to take the stairs right beside it instead.

His eyes darted from one stain to another, his mind supplying reasons behind the blotches even when he didn't need or want to know them. Stepping over an unconscious body, he finally reached the door of the apartment when he heard shouting. One voice, in particular, sounded very familiar and dear to him.

Provoked by her cry of pain, he kicked the door open and paused when he saw April latching herself onto a man's leg. Blood streamed down her face, but she still didn't let go. It spoke of her tenacity to keep the man from progressing toward her. He barely noticed the broken bottle on what could be called a dining table but was closer to a cat's scratching toy. His eyes were locked on the jagged-edged bottleneck in the man's free hand which was now rising, as if to deliver another blow.

Jason couldn't remember moving but the next thing he knew, he was across the room, throwing the man away from April. Away from the hall where he heard the twins.

"Jason?" he heard the tear-drenched voice from behind him. He just nodded, his eyes still fixed on the man who was now stumbling to his feet.

"Go to the twins, April. And call the cops. I'll hold him off. Now!" he shouted as he mirrored the man, pushing him back.

Despite his diminutive stature, being a foot shorter and less muscular than Jason, the man put up a fierce fight. Seeing the glaze in his eyes and the heavy stench of alcohol, Jason realized the man was drunk. Probably drugged out of his mind too.

Knowing he will be possessed with some unexpected strength due to the alcohol, Jason didn't let him pass. Even when April was shouting at the police on her phone. Even when he heard his children's cry. All he could think of was the fear he heard in her voice and the blood he saw on her face. The wound was still bleeding. More blood. More fear. All signs that he had failed his family.

All signs that kept his hold on the man so that he could finally protect them.

CHAPTER 16

"Hey. Where have you been? I've been looking for you," Jason said softly once he'd found April. She was in her room, looking unlike her usual open self, having cleaned up after the paramedics were done checking her and the twins. He still hadn't recovered from the scare and wanted to take her in his arm to assure himself that she was safe, that she'd never be in danger ever again. But she looked distant and withdrawn. He didn't know how to bridge the gap she'd made nor did he know the reason.

The aftermath had been crazy. The police had stormed in and pulled him off the man who was actually April's father. They were able to piece together what happened and took the man into custody. However, there had been a misunderstanding—or he hoped it was—because they almost took April as well.

"It is suspicious that your nanny knowingly brought your children into this part of town. We're just making sure that they're not working together and it's not a deal gone bad," they explained.

After Jason calmed down, and heroically refrained from punching the detective, he announced that April and her mother were off limits to everyone except the paramedics. He'd also offered to pay for any of their medical expenses. Of course, April's mother, Joan, didn't take kindly to what she considered charity, but April managed to convince her to accept it. The officers were harder to convince, but one call from him to their chief and they let it go albeit unwillingly. At least, they've dropped the issue. It only cost him a donation to their precinct but it was worth it.

They had to stay at the hovel for more than two hours. Jason was busy settling with the police while Joan helped April with the twins. Surprisingly, they were comfortable with her and she returned the favor. Daphne liked her the most and was often in her arms. Joan was gentle with them, encouraging their curiosity but knowing where to set the limit which was a load off April since she had a mild concussion from the blow to her head.

Once the police decided they had enough evidence and had taken all their statements, they returned to the penthouse. Joan went with them as April needed help with the twins and, of course, her apartment had been totally trashed. Surprisingly, she didn't kick up much of a fuss over him offering her a room. April had talked to her about it.

After making sure she was settled, Jason looked for April. And when he'd found her, he found it hard to keep his hands off her, but it looked like she still had some issues to resolve.

"I understand if you want to terminate my employment," she said softly, wrapping her arms around her body, retreating to herself. Jason was shocked. "I mean, the incident today pretty much showed how bad of a nanny I am. What kind of nanny brings her charges into a potentially dangerous situation?"

"April, I'm not going to fire you," he said gently. Initially, he'd thought she wanted to leave him and his mind and body rebelled. When he realized her confidence in caring for twins was shaken, he disregarded her distance and held her tightly against him. Her body was stiff, as if rejecting his comfort, but he was adamant. "I'm just sorry I didn't go with you. If anything, I think I should turn in my resignation as a dad and partner. I was so distracted with work that I didn't even think of providing bodyguards for the three of you.

"But I put them in danger." She suddenly sobbed. He pulled her closer, allowing her to cry into his shoulder. This was the root of her distance. "I could have killed them. They were lucky you came early or I don't know what would have happened."

"From your statement, I reckon that you didn't think your father would have found your mother. I'm sure you had no idea he'd barge in," he reasoned into her hair, but she shook her head.

"But I suspected. That's the only reason Mom would ever stop all contact," she said, looking up at him. The tears were killing him. He would do anything to stop her from ever crying. But he didn't know how to stop it or what to say to restore her confidence. A knock made him look to the door, his mind still in disarray.

"I'm sorry but these two want their nanny," Joan said, the twins at her feet, using her as a prop to stand. Their eyes lit up when they saw April and, plopping on fours, made a beeline for her. April tried to keep them away, but they surrounded her and flailed their arms up, a signal that they wanted to be picked up. She blocked them out, ignoring their pleas, but when Daphne started whimpering, she caved in and pulled them into her arms. Jason guided her to her bed so that she didn't strain herself carrying them.

They started babbling, as if telling April some exciting story, arms flailing about, shooting smiles up at her. She looked at them as if it was the last time she'd be seeing them and tears started to fall.

Tanner was the first to notice. He looked alarmed and started wiping them. Or his version of wiping them. It just looked like some ineffectual swiping. April smiled at his actions and tried to stop but her tears just kept falling. Tanner was starting to become distressed.

Daphne, noticing her twin's actions, looked fiercely up at April. She then planted her chubby hands on April's cheeks and said the most unexpected thing.

"Ma-ma, no!"

The adults were all shocked but Tanner liked it and mimicked his sister. Seeing the expression on their faces, Daphne decided it would be fun to do it again, and so followed suit.

"Say 'April'," April instructed them but they refused, calling her "Ma Ma" and giggling, sometimes kissing her cheek. April turned her shocked eyes up to Jason.

"Don't look at me. I didn't teach them that," he said defensively. He'd thought about it, but it seemed a bit underhanded. But the scene before him proved he need not do such thing. April did all the work and was now reaping the rewards. Satisfaction swirled inside him.

They kept saying 'Ma-ma' but when April told them to call Joan 'Ma-ma', they refused, patting her chest as if saying she was the only one they'd call that. Bewildered, she tried, softly, to make them stop but they refused. Instead, they became louder and rowdier.

"Well, there you go. Children know how to tell a bad person from good. If they'd accepted you as their mother, clearly you're doing something right," Joan said gruffly but she ran a comforting hand over her daughter's head. April sent her a small smile. "Don't let your father take this away from you, baby girl. They need you. You need them. And so does their father, judging from the panicky look he had when he thought he'd lose you. Heck, the four of you are starting to look like a family. Don't let that go just because you're scared. You'd never have made it this far if you let fear rule you. Let it go, sweetheart."

Seeing that it was going to be a teary embrace, Jason took the drowsy twins and left the mother and daughter alone. He was glad Joan had managed to convince her to stay. However, by the penetrating gaze she sent him, he knew he was going to endure some motherly concern. And he wasn't sure all his millions would be able to convince her he was worthy of her daughter.

~

Watching the twins sleep, April found it difficult to leave. It had been a week since the incident and she still woke up in cold sweat. Tonight had been an especially bad nightmare. She saw herself in a long corridor, running away from her father. Her clothes had been when she was a teenager—oversized everything with an abstract work of stains that she had received from some kind neighbors. Her father, who had been wielding a broken bottle, strode behind just as he had in their apartment. Nevertheless, he was slowly gaining on her. She knew it had only been a dream and that her father was in police custody, but it felt so real. The sick sour scent of drunkenness and neglect which she had always associated with him was breathing down her neck. Just when she had thought that it was the end, he was going to catch her. Then she heard a scream. It was a baby's scream. She knew that scream. It was Daphne.

Daphne? What was she doing here? She wasn't supposed to be here in this period of time when her father had reigned supreme. When her mother and she had been caught in the deadly web of his alcoholism and drug abuse. This time, when she heard the scream again, there was Tanner's shriek mixed in as well, and she had to turn around. In front of her eyes were the bloodied twins, their blood trickling from the wounds from their faces and bodies. Suddenly, they were in his arms, screaming and reaching out for her. She looked at his face, a face so similar to hers, but so different. With sunken cheeks and yellowed teeth, he smiled smugly at her, the gaps dividing his teeth into a more horrible form of greeting. As if to say that she was never going to get them back. He moved back, increasing the distance between them. Panicking, she chased after them. This time, she was faintly aware that her clothes

91

had changed to what she had on now. Clean clothes that was not as worn out and that actually fit her. But it provided no comfort as she raced for the safety of the twins. No matter how fast she ran, their distance only increased. Their cries, "Ma-ma, ma-ma", echoed down the hall, and the desperation within her grew. Until she suddenly woke up.

She needed to see them, the twins right away. Seeing them sleeping peacefully did a lot to calm her. Playing with their hands—putting her fingers and grabbing them out before the twins could grab them—she was surprised when a hand came between her shoulder blades. Looking up, she saw that it was Jason.

"What are you doing up?" he asked softly. Uncomfortable with sharing, she stayed silent and continued playing with their hands, smiling when Tanner shifted to his side. She snuggled into Jason when he slid his arm over her shoulders, and with the silence that ensued, she felt contented.

"Is it about your dad?" A moment or two of quiet enveloped them before April spoke.

"Yeah," she responded with a sigh. She quietly withdrew from the cribs, drawing him along as well, before telling him her dream. She thought it would be an uncomfortable sharing but, surprisingly, it was quite easy. It helped that Jason remained quiet throughout, his only action drawing her closer to him. When he swiped his fingers over her face, she was surprised when they came out wet.

"It's going to take a while for you to remember that he is gone from your life. For good. But no matter how long it takes, the twins and I will always be here for you. No matter how long it takes for you to forget, we will be here." Resting her head on his chest, she nodded and smiled when he dropped a kiss on her head. "Anyway, to take your mind off this, we have the party to look forward to."

"What party?" Looking up at him with a frown, she waited for him to explain.

"Cameron's mom's birthday party. It's going to be a wild one. Jen knows a lot of people and they are all coming down. You can mingle and talk to other people. Well, maybe not with the men but there's going to be other women as well."

As much as she was amused by his possessiveness, she had to refuse. "I don't think I'll be up for it—"

"Come on, I've already told Cam we'll be there. And Sharon is looking forward to meeting you." She was still uncertain but he convinced her with the next topic. "And with how many kids he has, there's bound to be a room for the twins. They'll like being around other kids, especially Daph, and you can spend some time with the adults."

"Fine."

~

April was glad that Jason managed to convince her to come to the party. The doctor had already declared that she had recovered from her concussion for the past three days. She tried to get her mother to come as well but she wanted to spend the day with Mrs. Salvador. Surprisingly, both of the older women had hit it off and were quickly becoming best friends. She tried to talk her way out, citing that she didn't have anything to wear and that she was still feeling unwell. Jason countered by revealing he'd bought a dress for her and threatened to call the doctor again to make sure she was truly fine. Touched by his gesture and unwilling to trouble the sweet doctor again, she gave in. And surprisingly, she was having a good time.

Sharon, Cameron's wife, was welcoming and had shown her around when they had first arrived. Jason had joined Cameron immediately, leaving April and the twins to Sharon. She managed to wrestle the twins away from April and refused to let her touch them. However, she did sneak away occasionally to take a look at them and they were amazingly well-behaved and were playing well with others. Seeing that, something in her chest loosened and she let herself enjoy the celebration.

Sharon was a darling and shared some pointers on raising children since she herself already has two boys, one baby girl, and another on the way. All of which were immensely helpful for future situations, especially with the twins becoming more active and mobile. April also marveled at the fact that she could move with so much energy and grace even though she's six months pregnant.

She also met Sharon's sister, Amelia, who was as kind as she was gorgeous. Her self-deprecating humor helped break the ice between them and they since had a rousing conversation, going from topic to topic. It surprised April how down-to-earth she was. She has her own share of children as well and her two sons were currently together somewhere with Sharon's elder sons, creating havoc wherever they went. April hadn't had the chance to see them yet.

She was currently standing alone, watching the party unfold before her eyes. It was a beautiful event, lavender and teal decors adorning the place, being the birthday girl's favorite colors. "Colors that won't clash with this hair of mine," Jennifer Ballard, the star of the day, had chimed in, pointing to her dark auburn hair, when Amelia and she were discussing the decor.

Jennifer was a wonderful woman. She was warm, approachable, and energetic. Before meeting her, April already had a positive impression of Jennifer and was predisposed to like her since she'd helped Jason with the twins when he first got them. And now, she loved her. Still, her energy was such that April got tired just looking at her flit from one group—accepting well wishes and having a good laugh with them—to another. And to think she was practically twice her age. *I hope I'd be as wonderful as her when I reach that age,* April thought wistfully.

"So, you are my son's nanny," a high nasal voice said, breaking the silence. "He could have done better."

Startled, April looked toward the speaker and saw an expensively made-up and dressed woman. Her features suggested that she was in the fiftyish range but her hands suggested an older age. She had a heart-shaped face and olive eyes that her son definitely inherited. However, instead of light blonde hair, hers was dark auburn, reminiscent of Jennifer's. So, Jason and Cameron were related through their mothers. Unlike Jennifer, however, this woman was cold with hints of malice in her eyes—eyes that clearly showed that April should be awed that such a personage was deigning to acknowledge her, a lowly maggot. April was stunned. This woman certainly could not be related to the warm woman she'd met earlier.

"Are you slow? Mute? It's just like Jason to pick someone who's clearly ill-mannered and unsuitable for the position," she murmured, as if April wasn't there. Rude, yes, but she was willing to let it go.

"Um, I'm sorry but I don't think we've met. I'm April, the twins' nanny," April said, introducing herself. The woman ignored her outstretched hand and April took it back, thinking it felt weird to leave it hanging. "You must be their grandmother. Jason has talked a lot about you."

And she could see why. This woman was cold personified. Clearly, she wouldn't be of much help with the twins. She'd likely leave the twins in some nanny's hands and forget about them. April wanted to be out of the woman's presence ASAP.

"Are you April?" a boy who looked a lot like Cameron suddenly stopped in front of her. He looked to be about five and was panting, as if he'd been running a lot. At her puzzled nod, he grabbed her hand and tried to pull her with him. It didn't work. "Hurry. The twins are crying like crazy and—"

He stopped when, at the mention of twins crying, April rushed past him and hurried to the nursery. She knew she shouldn't have left the twins alone. *Why didn't she listen to her guts?!*

CHAPTER 17

Their cries could be heard from the stairs. April's heart hurt just thinking about why they would be wailing like that. Running toward the room that was definitely *not* where she'd originally left them in, she could also hear a woman shouting, followed by the twins' louder cries, and Sharon's voice. *Who the hell was that and why isn't Sharon helping the twins?*

Bursting into the room, April was surprised to find a woman holding the twins in her arms, keeping them there despite their twisting around and crying. Sharon was carrying her baby daughter Cynthia and, along with Amelia, was trying to convince the woman to put her load down. It looked like an intense discussion so no one was aware of April's entrance at first.

The twins were the first to notice her and began twisting around even more violently, flailing their arms more vigorously, screaming, 'Ma Ma, Ma Ma.' The woman was so startled by their sudden action that her arms loosened and Tanner fell. Amelia, Sharon, and April tried to catch him but they weren't fast enough. He landed with a loud thud before screaming again. Only it was a pain-filled scream now.

April hurriedly picked him up and tried to snatch Daphne from that insane woman but she moved away. Tanner's arms were wrapped tightly around her neck and his cries had reduced to sobs while his body shook in her arms. April was glad he had stopped, but her eyes were still locked on Daphne. Her arms reached for

April, twisting her body and flailing her legs, but the woman kept moving away.

"Who the heck are you?" April asked through gritted teeth. The woman smiled smugly and flipped her hair prettily, despite carrying a squirming, crying baby in her arms.

"I'm their mother," the woman pronounced and shot a glare at April. *Their mother? Jason had mentioned her before. He said her name was Carrie Carter. This woman was her?* Looking at her, she was indeed beautiful but looked different from what she remembered. *Didn't she have black hair?* Of course, she only had vague memories of her. She'd never really followed fashion and the only reason this woman stuck with her was because of her controversial fight that turned so bad that she had been plastered in multiple news mediums. She couldn't escape her then. And now, neither could Daphne. "And you're fired, you skanky whore. Who do you think you are, trying to usurp my position in their lives?"

"From what I've heard, you've signed away your rights, bitch. So the twins are within their rights to look for another mother figure," Sharon said angrily, moving to stand beside April. April forgot about her; her entire being was focused on getting Daphne away from the crazy woman.

"I'm still their mother!" she screamed. For a beautiful model, she looked ugly when she's crazy. Or, more politically correct, angry. But who cares about that when there was a hysterical Daphne in the witch's arms? "I still have rights to them. I still can take them away with me if I want to."

During her raving, her arms had loosened around Daphne and April saw her chance. She grabbed Daphne and ran to the far end of the room with her bundles. She wanted to leave the room but the woman stood between her and the door. She didn't want to risk the twins in an attempt to leave. Plus, she was in a horrible shape while the woman looked like she had worked out her whole life. There's no need to guess who'd outrun who.

Carrie tried to follow but Amelia ran interference. Well, more like tried because the woman sidestepped her and went after April. Seeing nowhere else to run and no way to defend herself, April turned, keeping the twins shielded because she was under no impression that the woman wanted to have a civil conversation with her. Bracing herself for the impact, she was puzzled when it didn't come.

Turning around, she found herself shielded by Jason with his cousins not far away. Even Harry. Carrie had stopped short when she saw her protector and the manic look became sly and seductive. April didn't care about that. Knowing Jason would resolve this mess, she relaxed. Her attention was now directed to the twins.

They had stopped crying, but their bodies still shook with their infrequent sobs. Their arms were latched tightly around her neck and it looked like they won't be letting her go any time soon. Dropping to the floor—who wouldn't while carrying 2 ten-month-old babies?—she cradled them in her arms and rocked her body, smattering kisses on their heads. They relaxed further and stopped sobbing. Eyelids drooped and heads rested on her shoulders. The crying must have sapped all their energy. Their bodies slackened and soon they were in dreamland.

Her heart tightened and she internally cursed the woman. *What was she thinking, allowing them to carry on like that? Why was she even there?* April knew she'd signed her rights away; she'd seen the papers. So why did it look like she was trying to take the twins away?

~

Jason glared at the twins' surrogate. She still looked beautiful—she was one of the most beautiful women in the world,

99

after all—but his brief glimpse of her when she lunged for April revealed a side of her that he had already known but had only witnessed now. Her face contorting in fury and her eyes glinting with madness, she was the last person he wanted to see. It was a horrifying look. She reverted to her usual facade when she realized there were men in the room.

"Oh, I didn't see you there," she said and simpered, looking all sultry and coy. "I'm just here to visit my children. Surely you wouldn't keep them away from their mother. Who happens to be me!" At this, her eyes flashed to April, revealing her displeasure.

"You signed away your rights to them. You don't have any maternal rights. Anymore. The papers also state that you are not allowed to see them until they're eighteen. They can decide whether they want to have any relationship with you then but for now, you are not allowed any visitation rights or *any* other rights as a mother," Jason expounded, his brows creased.

He was puzzled. When he'd presented the papers to her lawyer and her, she'd been eager to get rid of them. Even when her lawyer had suggested they change some things that would allow her miniscule rights, she ignored his protests and signed it within five minutes of receiving it and left within ten minutes since entering the meeting room. So why had she returned, spewing bullshit left and right?

Her face had slowly turned red during his explanation but she tried to conceal it. "I'm still their mother. I took care of them for six months. Surely they remember me," she sneered.

"Oh, they definitely remember you," Sharon said, allowing Cameron to take Cynthia off her. Cynthia was surprisingly quiet, for which Jason was grateful. Two crying babies were his limit for now. "The minute you laid your hands on them, they crawled frantically away. They couldn't crawl fast enough to escape you, though, and once they were in your arms, they started crying and screaming, squirming to *get away* from you. True, they know who you are—you're someone they want nothing to do with."

"Lies," Carrie snarled. Sharon, unhappy with the accused, took a step toward her, scowling fiercely, when her husband put out a hand to stop her. Jason could hear Cameron murmuring to her, "Good god, woman. Think about the bun in your oven. She's not worth harming the bun." She sighed unhappily but took a step back, looking up to send him a scowl.

Fighting a grin, Jason turned back to Carrie and wondered how she got in. Surely she wasn't on the guest list. Sharon knew the kind of person she was and would definitely never invite her. When he asked, she just smiled coyly and didn't answer. Apparently, she'd decided to bury her anger and only show her social facade.

"Jason," he heard April hiss from behind him. Keeping his eyes on the viper in the room, he nodded to show he heard her. She understood so she continued, "Can you take Tanner and place him on the bed while I do the same for Daphne? My arms are kind of falling asleep."

"Let me do it," Harry said. Before April could do anything, he took Tanner and left her holding a squirming, crying baby. Harry almost dropped him when Jason took his son away from him. Tanner quieted, burrowing his head into the nook of his shoulders and immediately drifted off to sleep. "What happened? I just wanted to help. I didn't know they were so skittish around strangers."

"Normally, I'd say they're not but after being held hostage by Carrie, I say a bit of skittishness is warranted," April said wearily as she accepted Harry's help and pulled herself up. Jason forced down the possessiveness rearing in his head and reminded himself that this was his cousin. One of his closest. Despite the way he'd acted the last time they met, he redeemed himself when he rushed and helped April. This was his cousin.

101

Closest. Cousin.

Keeping an eye on Carrie, Jason followed April to the only bed in the room and laid Tanner down just as April was laying Daphne, too. They immediately started whimpering and squirming and only stopped when April placed her hand on their tummy. It was amusing to see the exasperation on her face when they all realized the twins wanted some contact with April. She was forced to keep her hand on them in order for them to keep quiet.

Everyone except Carrie was enjoying the tableau so they didn't see the other person entering the room.

"What is she doing to my grandchildren?" an imperious voice demanded loudly. So much so that the twins woke up and started crying again.

CHAPTER 18

April thought she couldn't believe their luck as she brought Tanner to her shoulder while Jason had grabbed Daphne. *Why was Jason's mother here?* Did they need another enemy in their midst?

Tanner calmed down after a while but wouldn't fall back to sleep. He was watching everyone with wary eyes and April felt her heart slightly crack. He's so young, but he has already learned that not everyone can be trusted. Babies shouldn't know such bitter truth before they could walk. They should be carefree and curious, exploring the world around them.

April took Daphne since she had been reaching for her. Similarly, Daphne didn't want to sleep. Instead, she surveyed the room with a small frown, shooting a glare at Carrie. April bounced Daphne in her arms to calm her down and she rested her head on April's shoulder.

All this took less than five minutes while the adults were busy looking at the newcomer. The woman just graced them with a haughty look and glared when her gaze passed April who could care less about her opinion of her. She was busy caring about the twins' well-being and a skinny harpy was very far from her radar.

"Mother, what are you doing here?" Jason asked, his voice and face as hard as a rock.

"I heard about the twins and wanted to know what was going on," she just said. "You have to vet your employees properly, Jason. Clearly, the woman you hired for the twins is incompetent.

Why, she was busy mingling with the guests when she should have been with your children. She doesn't know her place."

That stung and heaped more guilt on April. She herself had wanted to stay with the twins, but Sharon and Jason convinced her that they would be fine with the babysitter Sharon had hired for the night. And it was only after ascertaining they were happy playing with the other children that she went down. She'd checked on them ever so often but the fact remains that she'd missed Carrie and it weighed heavily on her.

"April does a wonderful job with my children. I couldn't have asked for a better person," Jason growled, stepping back to stand with April. He took Tanner as he was reaching for his father. April tried not to show her relief—the twins had definitely grown and now weighed a ton together—but must not have hidden it well enough. A smile graced Amelia's lips and she sent her a wink. Sending her a faint smile back, April returned to the situation at hand.

"Well, Mrs. Halloway, I've just been told that Ms. Carrie Carter here is your guest," Cameron said suddenly. Everyone's attention turned to him and April saw him returning his phone to his pocket. He had probably called the security stationed at the gate. "Surely you know that Ms. Carter is persona non grata to Jason. She's persona non grata to all of us. So may I know why you brought her along?"

"She's my grandchildren's mother. I can't ignore her or throw her to the side since she'd done her job," she said, glaring at Jason. As if saying he had not been doing that.

"Considering the fact that I had no idea about my children until three months ago and that she willingly signed her rights away when I knew, I don't think I've thrown her away," Jason growled. April placed her hand on his arm, restraining him from spewing more anger. More anger was not needed in this situation. She ignored the sharp look from his mother when she did. The opinion of one manipulative old biddy was not her concern.

Just then, Jennifer entered and stopped short when she felt the tension in the room. Her brows rose when she noticed Carrie. "It's time to cut my cake," she just said.

"Cake? You can think about cake at a time like this?" Mrs. Halloway sputtered angrily.

"It's my birthday celebration and I want it to be drama-free. But seeing as that's impossible right now, the next best thing would then be cake. So, unless you want me to reveal your true age, Hannah, you'd better put a cork on it," Jennifer warned. April bit her lips to stop the laughter that was trying to escape from her. Mrs. Halloway looked like she'd sucked on a lemon but kept her lips closed. "Ms. Carter, you are not welcome to any of my family's events. So, if I know of your presence in future, you'll be summarily escorted out regardless if there's paparazzi around or none. I know jobs are drying up for you. Surely you wouldn't want any bad press, would you?"

Carrie tried to protest but the warning look Jennifer sent her was enough to keep her silent.

"Well, did you say cake, Mom? I hope you kept the boys away if you still want a taste of it," Cameron said, slinging an arm around her and escorting her out.

Everyone moved to follow, except Jason and April. They had to settle the twins back at the nursery before returning to the festivities. She was glad this had been somewhat resolved but the glare that Carrie sent told her that this was far from over.

~

Jason swirled the whiskey in his glass in the living room, trying to forget about the evening. The celebration worsened after the cake cutting ceremony. His mother had been exceptionally shrill and nasty, complaining about the food, decorations, and guests and demanding changes to her food and drink. He commended Sharon for ignoring her increasingly vocal comments. Sharon was ever the gracious hostess and conceded to her ridiculous demands.

Carrie was also a problem. Sharon and Cameron decided not to throw her out, seeing as she'd been there long enough for people not to notice. Not wanting to fan the fires of the gossip mill, they allowed her to stay but asked the servers to keep an eye on their uninvited guest. Carrie took advantage of them, however, and tried to create some sob story about April mistreating the twins and how she'd somehow manipulated them to see her as their mother.

Of course, she was not blatant about it and a word in the right pair of ears created the desired ripple effect. It reached Jason when he was preparing to return home and tried to rectify the story. Even so, he knew the damage had been done. His protective instincts went to action; he only hoped April would agree to the measures he'd thought of to protect the twins and her.

"Hey, what are you thinking about?" April asked softly, dropping onto the sofa beside him. She'd left him to his own devices and, along with her mother's help, settled the twins down for the night. He surmised she had a harder time that night seeing as she took half an hour longer than usual. Probably due to their scare in the evening.

Realizing the distance between them, he pulled her to his side and cuddled her close. He slung his arm over her shoulder and laid his cheek on to the top of her head. She tensed slightly at first but relaxed beside him a few moments later. Silence ensued for several moments—the kind that was quiet, and soothing; each one of them knowing that the other needed to unwind before they could talk. The soft lighting in the room helped them relax further into each other.

"How are the twins?" he asked as he put down his brandy and entwined his free hand with hers. He smiled at her discomfort.

He knew he was unfairly increasing the pace of their relationship but he didn't care. He *did* care about her thoughts and feelings about it. He was just impatient and wanted her to be as comfortable with him as he already was with her.

"They're fine. They required a bit more attention and fussing but fell asleep quite fast considering the evening they've had. I'm glad Mom is here to help," she told him, settling into a more comfortable position.

"How's she settling in? Any more mentions of finding her own place?" He felt, more than heard, her scoff.

"Every hour of every day. And she won't stop. Even though she's broker than a homeless person, she's too independent and proud that she would have left if I hadn't told her I needed help with the twins," she grumbled. Jason found her worry for her mother endearing which reminded him of his own facsimile of a mother.

"I wish mine acted remotely as warm as yours," he said softly. She squeezed his hand and pressed a kiss onto it. He didn't know if it was the soft light creating an intimate atmosphere, her presence or everything combined that encouraged him to speak. "Clearly, my mother is a cold human being. She has an agenda for everything. Nothing comes free with her. And she's a stuck up bitch, which is weird since she came from a middle-income family before managing to capture my father.

"Despite that, they were two peas in a pod. Every move made and every word spoken is with the intention to further their agenda. Whatever that may be. They're like a team but not one founded on love and loyalty. Their teamwork was so cold and calculated I'm surprised they haven't turned to ice."

"Then why are you different?" April asked lightly, smiling up at him.

"I was sent to Aunt Jen when I was seven. My parents had a hard time keeping nannies. They said I was too noisy and wouldn't listen to instructions."

"Now I see where the twins got their aversion to nannies," she said, laughing. Jason joined but explained once she stopped.

"I didn't see it like that. To me, it was a bid to get my parents' attention. In my mind, I thought, '*Dad would like me now*' or '*surely Mom won't scream at me again if I show her this*'. Sadly, I was mistaken and was shipped to Wisconsin before I knew it."

Throughout his rant, April ran a soothing hand along his arm and rubbed her cheek against his shoulder. He didn't know why, but it helped to ease the hurt and sense of abandonment from his seven-year-old self. He knew those memories won't hurt him anymore.

It also helped ease the slight sting of hurt and betrayal that his mother's presence issued that night. He didn't know why it surprised him to find that she'd invited Carrie and allowed her near his children; he thought she'd cared about her grandchildren and wouldn't want that viper anywhere near them. Now *that* hurt and destroyed his hopes of ever repairing their relationship.

They lapsed into silence after, similar to their earlier silence. However, he was now more aware of her breast pressing into his arm and her soft curves fitting perfectly against his hard body. The jasmine and apple scent of her body wash tantalized his nose. He was not used to the women he's with being covered with the cloying scent of perfume, no matter how expensive or nice it first seemed. All these factors caused a stir in his chest. Trying to hide his growing excitement, he shifted in his seat which made April look up.

Her face lightly flushed, making him believe he was showing his lust and attraction. Her eyes darkened, her tongue peeked out to wet her lips. He couldn't help but take that as an invitation and swooped down for what he'd been craving for the entire day.

CHAPTER 19

April let herself be swept away by the kiss. Her arms locked over his shoulders, her legs came up and tangled themselves with his as she was lowered onto her back on the couch. The kiss started off soft and slow, letting her be comfortable with the contact and kissing in general. His hand stayed at her waist the entire time.

Then, slowly, it became deeper and more heated, his hand starting to creep under her shirt and crawl up her body. Deeply under the influence of the kiss, she didn't notice his progress until she felt his hand cup her breasts. Startled, she tried to push him away and he retreated a bit. But he would repeat his actions again once she's back under his spell. His hand under her bra and his intoxicating kisses both made her forget about her inhibitions.

Suddenly, the sound of a throat clearing penetrated their sexual bubble. April managed to get a few inches of separation and tried to find the source. It wasn't hard to find.

There, at the entrance of the hall, was her mother with Daphne in her arms. Feeling like a teenager caught with her pants off, she pushed Jason away and scrambled to her feet, straightening her clothes and hair. It was disconcerting to be caught making out by your mother. Even if you're twenty-six years old. She was slightly annoyed that Jason didn't have the same reaction. He just sat up and sent her a charming, crooked, annoying smile.

Daphne, having seen her, demanded to be in her arms. April went to get her but Joan stepped back.

"Are you sure you want those dirty hands on her?" she asked, passing a look of reprimand over April then Jason.

"Mom! We didn't do anything like that," she hissed, mortified. Maybe there was some justification for her mother to get her own place like not humiliate her in front of her employer/boyfriend. Once she'd determined that was true, she allowed April to take Daphne. Daphne laid her head on April's shoulder, eyes drooping. "Why are you up, baby girl? Couldn't sleep?"

"Weeeeell, if the both of you hadn't been so busy exchanging spit, you'd have heard her cry out," Joan scolded. "Is this what you've been doing before I was here? Making out and ignoring the babies?"

"Mom, no. It's only tonight. The stress and everything," April said exasperatedly. She looked to Jason for help and was not amused when he just shrugged. At her glare, he immediately straightened himself and moved to support her.

"Yeah, Mrs. Saunders. We were just talking and one thing led to the other. I'm so sorry if the little girl woke you up," he said, looking appropriately contrite and ashamed. Her mother looked satisfied with his explanation, her face softening slightly. April just rolled her eyes. He's such a charmer.

"Well, make sure it doesn't happen again," she said sternly before leaving. April heaved a sigh of relief. Having her mother around was both a nightmare and dream. She just hadn't realized which side outweighed which. On the one hand, she was a great help with the twins. However, her presence was getting into her time with Jason. Pouting, April began to relax into Jason again when Joan realized April wasn't following her. Like a Valkyrie descending with vengeance, she came back and dragged her out. The last April saw of Jason was a wink and a blown kiss.

~

"I don't want you to get hurt, April," Joan said for the millionth time that morning. April stopped banging her head against the wall as she was holding Daphne's upraised hands, supporting her attempts to walk. Her mother was doing the same thing with Tanner. She knew this was a discussion waiting to happen, but she wondered why it had to take her mother three days to bring it up. She must be using up all her patience. And her store of it was low on a good day.

"Mom, as I've said before, Jason and I are together. I know the risks and accept them. I've tried to ignore this thing between us but Jason is like a force of nature; you can't ignore him especially his possessive side," she said with a grin, occasionally cooing at Daphne when she was able to take five steps by only holding her fingers. Daphne giggled and jumped, gripping her fingers tightly.

"But still—"

"Oh, stop it, Joan," Mrs. Salvador cut in as she bustled into the living room with a tray of refreshments. The twins demanded to be let go and made a beeline for the table. Mrs. Salvador and Joan helped supervise the distributions of food while April took a break. As expected, the twins were clingier these days, unwilling to let her leave the room. So, it was much appreciated that her mother and Mrs. Salvador didn't need any prompting to take charge of them whenever she needed a breather.

Speaking of Mrs. Salvador, that's one of the things that changed with the advent of her mother's stay. Usually, the housekeeper would keep to herself, playing with the twins when April was busy with other things. But with Joan being there, she would join the conversation. April had ceased being surprised whenever she spoke her mind.

"I've been with that boy for close to fifteen years and I have never seen him act with any woman like he does with your daughter. It's almost sweet, if not sickening."

And that's another change. She was more forthcoming with information. Her voice could finally be heard frequently. Even if her opinions were unwelcome. Like now.

"But you have to heed your mother too, dearie. That man just had his life changed so this could be a temporary phase," she warned. Blunt with a dash of sweetness. Who wouldn't want a housekeeper like that?

~

"What is this woman trying to do?" Jason roared when he finally realized the papers he'd been handed. His lawyers took a step back in the face of his anger, hunching their shoulders. Jason was blind to that. He was seething, his thoughts darting all around his mind, trying to understand the implications and possible solutions.

But he couldn't stop thinking about April. He'd spent the entire morning trying to contain the news about her father and her brief trip to the less popular side of town with the twins. He'd told the guards at the condo to keep away any reporters and any publications from her. He'd barely retained her. He didn't want anything that would cause her to go away.

He knew who had spread the news but knowing it and stopping it were two entirely different things. He'd shelved the woman to a later point in time when his lawyers suddenly showed up with a summons to court. Carrie Carter was fighting for the custody of his children.

"Have you seen the alleged medical report?" he growled.

"We have but we have yet to determine if it's legitimate. It'll take a few days—"

"I want it on my table by tomorrow. It doesn't matter how much it takes or who you have to bribe. Tomorrow," he reiterated harshly, emphasizing each syllable. They nodded and hurried out. Exhaling a sharp breath, he slumped in his seat and massaged his temple. *What was he going to do?* Carrie was claiming that she hadn't been sound of mind when she signed the documents, rendering it void. With news showing April in bad light, his case was less than impeccable.

His phone rang. "Halloway," he barked into the phone.

"Hey, Jase," he heard April say. He smiled slightly. She'd finally grown comfortable enough to use a shortened version of his name. He didn't count 'hot stuff' since she won't use it anymore so this was a step forward in their relationship. However, he heard a hint of apprehension in her voice and the smile went away.

"Hey, babe," he replied, racking his mind for any reason for her uneasiness. "How's your day?"

"Well, my mom warned me about you with Mrs. Salvador backing her up. It was a nightmare." He chuckled, relaxing into his chair. She was the only person who could make him laugh even if his mood was dark as hell. She and his children.

"Thanks. I needed that," he told her softly. He could sense her interest but knew she wouldn't press until he gave the green light. Instead he asked, "So why did you call? Not that I don't welcome a call from you but this is different." He sensed her hesitation so he prompted her. "April."

"I just had a chance to turn on the television and the news is full of Carrie claiming that you took her when she was at a low point in her life. Something about depression and that nonsense. Then she went on to say that she's fighting to get back her, and I quote, 'lovely bundles of joy'. What's going on?"

He had grown steadily angrier as she related the news. Damn that woman. She wasn't even going to keep a low profile. The whole world was going to hound his family for answers and he felt helpless to stop it. Buckling under so much pressure and stress, he lashed out.

"Why aren't you taking care of the twins? Is that what you do all day? Watching television? Maybe that's why you want your mother to stay with us so that you can shirk your duties and have more time to use my money," he snarled.

"If that is what you believe of me, I'll wish you a good day, Mr. Halloway," she said softly and hung up.

Hearing the dial tone, the feeling of panic rose to overwhelm him. He couldn't believe what he'd just said. He didn't truly believe whatever he'd just blurted out. It was just the situation and his fear that he'd lose the twins. He tried to call again but only reached her voice mail. He might not only lose the twins; he might just also lose the only woman who meant the world to him.

CHAPTER 20

April knew she was being childish. Her mother was vocal enough when they were putting the twins to sleep. Mrs. Salvador's squinty eyes brought about that point well enough, too. But, she just couldn't help it. Jason's outburst had hurt.

She tried to tell herself that he didn't mean it, that he was just stressed about the twins' mother suddenly claiming mental instability which would mean losing his children. But it didn't create a dent on the bubble of hurt surrounding her heart.

"Oh, don't be so stupid," she groused to herself softly while checking on the twins. She smoothed her hand over Tanner's head, enjoying the softness, and grew concerned when she touched the bump on his head. He'd been whimpering in his sleep and it wasn't a good whimper. It was like he was having a nightmare.

She's worried about the consequences if he or Daphne were ever in that woman's hands again—their safety and their future if Carrie became a permanent fixture in their lives. Something in her chest knotted painfully when she thought of what they'd have to endure.

This was the third time she'd been trying to convince herself not to take Jason's words to heart. It was still not working. "His work is already stressful, April. With this new development, he's in even more pressure. Your stupid phone call didn't help, either—"

"Your call wasn't stupid," Jason suddenly said from the doorway. Startled, she whipped her head around and was struck dumb. She didn't know what it was—the lighting or the sweat glistening all over his arms and shoulders—but all she knew was that she felt light-headed and her mouth went drier than the Sahara.

Jason had just obviously come back from the gym; he was in his tank top and basketball shorts. And he looked delicious enough to eat. *Maybe with whipped cream or chocolate. Wait, definitely chocolate. But he's ticklish. She would have to tie him up.* Her body heated up just thinking about it.

"If you are done mentally stripping me, can we talk?" she heard Jason ask wryly. When his words finally penetrated the fog of sexual heat around her, her face went red but she nodded. He moved into the room, keeping her in sight, as if afraid that she was going to run away. Silence engulfed them for a few moments.

"First off, I'd like to apologize for my behavior this evening. It was, and is, embarrassingly extremely juvenile of me," she said in a rush. His eyes widened in shock but he nodded.

"Apology accepted. But can I ask why?" Discomfort assailed her. She didn't want him to know the whole, pathetic truth of her past because their relationship was still young. But it's best to let it all out now when she had a more vested interest in it rather than later.

"It's mainly due to two reasons. As we both know, I'm not the most attractive person. Ever. No let me finish," she told him when he was about to interrupt. His lips compressed, showing his disagreement, but he didn't cut in. Relief filled her. She really only wanted to say this once. "Because of that, I've not been in many relationships. Actually, I've only been in three relationships. And they were not what one would call a healthy relationship. Worse, I knew it wasn't healthy but I still stayed.

"Which leads me to the next reason: my whole life, I've been told that I'm worthless, not smart, not pretty. My whole life. Mom isn't like that but she's often out working so much that her love and support on the days she was there couldn't get through the hurtful words that was an everyday occurrence to me. My opinion of myself had always been low and it is only now—with you, the twins, Mom and even Mrs. Salvador—that it's slowly changing. But, today, I-I just reverted to my old self. I didn't want to give you more reason to get angry with me. That was my mentality. So, I created the distance between us. By acting like a servant," she finished quietly. She felt drained. It had been so difficult, airing it all to him. And now, waiting for his reaction was nerve-wracking.

His arms suddenly appeared around her, pulling her to his chest. Startled, she stiffened before relaxing into him. Surely, he wouldn't be hugging her if he was revolted?

"I'm sorry for lashing out on you," he finally said. She didn't expect that. She wanted to turn and dispute that but his arms became bands of steel. With his index finger against her lips, he silenced her. "It's my turn now."

"Fine," she murmured.

"As I was saying, I'm sorry. It's difficult for me to admit this, but I knew I shouldn't have said all that I'd said to you earlier. I know you don't use me for my money. I know you didn't have any ulterior motive for wanting your mother to stay with us. I'd like to say that it won't happen again but, knowing me, we both know that's unlikely." She smiled at that. Jason was extremely hot-tempered, especially when he's under pressure. "As long as you won't repeat what you did tonight, I think I can survive anything."

Surprised by the vulnerability in his voice, she looked up at him and saw how weary he looked. She hadn't expected that her withdrawal would affect him so much but now, remorse filled her.

Wanting to comfort him, she nodded, turning to hug him. Suddenly, he buried his face in her shoulder and held her tight.

And, in his embrace, she finally had the strength to ignore the taunts that still lived in her head.

~

Jason sat back in his office chair after his lawyers left. He couldn't believe what they'd just told him and what they'd just found. By some miracle, Carrie's claims were true. Apparently, she was under some emotional stress when she'd signed away her rights. She claimed that she didn't want to let the twins go but he, Jason, had forced the contract on her. Having felt horrible for giving into him, she immediately went to seek legal advice and spoke to a psychiatrist.

This was an utter lie. He didn't believe it even in the slightest but decided on getting a private investigator to delve further into it. Right now, he went over several scenarios with his lawyers to keep her grubby hands off his children.

His phone rang and from the ringtone, he knew it was April. A smile briefly landed on his lips but, recalling that he had to break the bad news to her, it left as soon as it arrived. Taking a deep breath, he answered.

"Hey, sweetheart. How has your day been?" he asked.

"It has been fine. Mom and Mrs. Salvador are out buying grocery. I'm preparing the twins so that we can go to their first-year checkup," she replied in a rush. She must've been having a bad time because he could faintly hear her calling the twins under her breath. He heard her put down the phone, probably to chase after his mischievous children. Allowing the normalcy of it wash over him, he decided to shelve the bad news for the moment. He wished he was with them. Even if he wasn't going to be of any help, their presence was like a balm to his soul. Her voice came over the line again. "Hi. Sorry for that."

"No worries. It gave me time to unwind," he told her.

"That bad?"

"Yeah. The doctor seems to corroborate the evaluation. But I don't trust it. It looks too good to be true," he told her. She *hmmmed* in response but he knew she was listening. She only did that when she's thinking things over. "I'll have to get an investigator to look deeper into this. Hopefully it'll clear this mess. In the meantime, I have to fight Carrie for custody. It's going to be difficult, though."

"I wish I could help but my influence only goes so far. Meaning not far at all," she responded worriedly. He smiled. Her support meant the world to him and it eased the burden, knowing she was with him.

"My driver is on the way to send you to the appointment along with some guards for safety. Don't argue," he told her fiercely when he heard her preparing to do just that. "The press is lapping all this up. Carrie has been putting on a show, accusing me of abusing my kids and you of neglecting them while in pursuit of me. They will target you to get a reaction and I don't want you to be in a situation where you're mobbed by them."

"When did she do that?" she asked curiously while–he assumed–putting the twins into their strollers.

"Just this morning." He heard her sigh, and the knot in his chest, when he realized she could be in danger, loosened. He knew she'd capitulate to his precautions. "Have fun at the doctor's."

"Haha," she deadpanned. He had to hide a snigger, knowing the twins would be having their shots as well. "We'll be going to the park after. Do you want to join us?"

"It's not safe—"

"It'll take their minds off the shot," she countered fiercely.

He had to agree to that. The twins loved being at the park, especially when they got to play with the sand. Knowing that and their impending trip to Shot City, he couldn't begrudge them this. Even so, he couldn't shake a sense of unease.

"And didn't you hire bodyguards? We'll be fine."

Famous last words.

CHAPTER 21

April laughed as she watched Tanner shower himself with sand again. He loved to do that. And having learned the lesson that getting sand in his eyes was not fun, he'd be careful and close his eyes while he did so. Daphne laughed as well, briefly distracted from her bucket of sand. Tanner, looking mischievous, threw sand at April, stopping her laughter. She reached out and tickled him and knowing he expected retribution, he squealed and tried to crawl away, totally forgetting about the traumatic trip to the pediatrician. Something April herself, couldn't forget.

Reporters had swarmed them like ants on sweet. She hadn't heeded Jason's concerns and thought they would respectfully keep their distance because of the twins. Boy, had she been wrong. She'd barely taken a step out with the twins in her arms when they suddenly swarmed on her like mosquitoes in summer.

The twins, shocked, had clung tighter to her, burying their faces into her neck. She'd tried to take a step back but some of the reporters had moved to the empty space behind her, blocking her escape. Trying to muscle her way forward didn't work either since they wouldn't move and she was hampered with the twins. They screamed questions at her, scaring the twins. Daphne started crying.

Luckily, the bodyguards Jason told her about came and created a barrier that allowed her to get to their car, although the bodyguard riding with them loved to lecture. She hadn't strapped

Daphne into her car seat since she was still hysterical. But apparently that had been a no-go for Professor Bodyguard; he'd refused to let the car move until she complied with car safety. Usually she'd be more reasonable and explain. However, he wasn't being helpful with the situation. His stern tone incited Daphne further, even extracting a whimper from Tanner. Seeing the situation's grim future and pumped with adrenaline, she snapped, told him to shut up, and ordered the driver he'd better move or she'd call Jason. The threat of calling Jason was enough for him to step on the gas, despite Professor Bodyguard's protests.

Alas, the checkup hadn't been any better. They had been fine when the height and weight were taken. However, the twins didn't like being away from her so one of them would play beside her chair while the other was being examined which raised questions from the pediatrician. She had to explain the situation leading to their visit to the clinic. Apparently, it was not convincing. It wasn't until they left that the doctor saw the severity of it.

The twins didn't like anyone touching them. April assumed their aversion to touch was because they felt they were being mobbed. It was understandable but it had made the examination more difficult. Daphne had even pushed away the pediatrician's hand when he wanted to check her lungs. April had to use baby biscuits to distract them. It had worked up until their shots. Luckily, the pediatrician had left that 'till all the other stuff was over. So, she didn't have to leave Tanner alone for long while Daphne was getting her shot.

Waiting until they'd calmed down, April heard Tanner say a new word. While in the reception, he pointed at the pediatrician's closed door and said tearfully, 'Ma Ma, bad'. Startled, she burst into laughter, the receptionist grinning as well, and corrected him but he resolutely refused to listen, continuing to say, 'bad'. Good thing Daphne had exhausted herself into slumber by then so she wasn't influenced. April wouldn't know what she'd do if both of them started throwing a tantrum.

Pulled back to the present, she brought a crying Tanner into her arms, having fallen from an attempt to stand on sand. Daphne crawled over to her, using her shoulders to stand, then laughed, taunting her brother. Tanner frowned at his sister but smiled immediately after. Puzzled, April was then alarmed when she didn't feel Daphne's weight beside her. Whirling around, she saw a dress shoe behind her and jumped up, with Tanner in her arms, throwing herself into Jason's arms.

Being enveloped in his scent, she felt her tension and stress just melt away. Something about being with him made her feel like everything was going to be fine.

~

"I take it it has been a bad day?" Jason asked as he and April pushed the twins in the swing. Her grimace said it all. He didn't need for her to tell him. His driver and bodyguard had told him what happened. He'd been angry that she hadn't listen to him; she was so resistant to the idea that everyone will now be interested in her. She didn't even want to entertain the thought. So, he wasn't surprised that she hadn't realized the enormity and severity of Carrie's attack.

"I was so shocked when they came at me. And I was carrying the twins since they didn't want to stay in their stroller so they could practice walking. If I'd known they were going to be so vicious and relentless, I would have brought the stroller as well," she told him softly, smiling when Tanner shrieked with delight at going so high. Daphne, jealous, swung her legs furiously and sent a demanding frown at her daddy. Chuckling at her antics, Jason pushed her as high as her brother and smiled at her laugh.

He faced April again and sighed. He didn't know how to impress on her Carrie's deviousness and how she could present

April in a bad light without making it look like he, himself, thought of her that way.

"You have to be warier now, sweetheart. Carrie isn't just some obscure member of the public and I, the guy you are dating, have quite the presence in the media. With Carrie forcing herself into the spotlight, people are now interested in you. You can't hide from it, no matter how much you want to," he told her, being as honest as he could, painful it may be. She didn't say anything but just took Tanner to the slide. Hoping he hadn't driven her away, he followed her with Daphne.

"Well, I have to know. Are we dating? Because sure, we're living like a married couple but we haven't even had s-e-x, much less been on a date," she said after a while.

She was right. And looking at their relationship objectively, it surprised him. He'd treated his hookups better than this—with this person, he wanted to make his wife.

Before he could rectify it, she continued. "And I just don't understand why they are so interested in me. I'm very boring. My life revolves around you, the twins, and my mother. That's it. So why would they be running over each other, trying to get a picture of me and hear what I have to say?"

"Because you're with me and, by association, you become newsworthy," he told her. But he was still struck by her statement before. He hadn't realized how small her circle was. Along with how shabbily he'd treated her, he felt that he wasn't a great partner after all.

Watching her laugh with Tanner helped ease the pressure, but he knew he'd have to improve the way he treated her. True to his resolve, he'd take her out on a romantic date, no holds barred. It wasn't out of guilt that he wanted to do this, but he wanted— needed—to treat her better than those women he did not truly care about. Because how else would she know of his affection for her?

When he saw the horde of reporters closing in, he knew their little escape was over. They were attracting the attention of other park users who were turning their heads, wondering who the reporters were there for. Luckily, April brought the twins there often enough without him, that they didn't think they were important enough to garner their attention. That's the only reason he'd allowed her to come to this park. That and there was a lesser known route to the parking lot right beside the playground.

"We have to leave," he told her, collecting Daphne and the bag she brought. Seeing what he was seeing, she nodded and picked Tanner up. The twins were surprisingly cooperative. Maybe they sensed a disquiet between the adults.

Jason led them to the car, relieved that the reporters hadn't found that route. Yet. He pressed a kiss on Daphne's head when she released a whine, probably uncomfortable with the speed they were moving in the darkness under the tree-lined path. He kept his eyes peeled for anything out of the ordinary. Feeling April's hand slide into his free hand, he turned to her with a smile. Only to feel it leave his face when he saw how pale she was, her eyes darting to every sound they heard.

Wanting to comfort her but knowing how limited their time was, he gave her a quick soft kiss, hoping to reassure her that he was there for her. The smile she sent him told him she was fine.

As long as he was with her.

CHAPTER 22

"I just want you to be prepared for the malicious reports tomorrow." Jason's words echoed in April's head as she read headline after headline of her. With the twins. With Jason. By herself. How she wished she wasn't bothered but his words didn't prepare her at the least.

Some of it were rather flattering but most were horrendous and spiteful. There were baseless accusations about her care of the twins, snide comments about her weight, her choice of outfits, and comparisons of her to Jason's previous lovers. It was all too much.

"Stop looking at those papers," Joan scolded her, taking away said papers. "They're all lies anyway."

"It's just so real now. Before, it was just an abstract concept. Something that only happened to people who wanted it or those who have achieved something good or bad. Now that they're hounding me, it's a nightmare. And I'm questioning if I'm worthy to be with Jason now. I'm not beautiful or well dressed. Why is he even with me?" she asked herself softly.

"He's with you because you have something those other female dogs don't. And he is smart enough to see and grab it before some other man steals you away," Mrs. Salvador said firmly, her eyes daring April to argue. Usually she wouldn't but she couldn't let the matter drop.

"But all these women, they look so beautiful. Actresses. Models. I feel so dowdy in comparison," she grumbled glumly, sending a shadow of a smile to Tanner when he glanced at her. He returned her smile and went back to playing his game.

Before she was able to fall further into the abyss of insecurity, the bell rang. The doorman told them they had some visitors. Recognizing who they were, April gave him the all clear.

Opening the door, she froze when arms suddenly reached for her, pulling her into a tight hug. Only the huge baby bump kept her lower body from being crushed. She hesitantly wrapped her arms around Sharon, and all her tension faded away.

"I hope you don't mind us crashing," Amelia said as she maneuvered around Sharon's bulk. April sent her a smile in response as Sharon had still not let her go. Amelia's sons, along with Sharon's, followed her along with two women, one of who was carrying a sleeping Cynthia. "Sharon, let the poor woman go."

"No. She must be horrified by what those monkeys wrote. And obviously needs comfort," Sharon said tearfully, stubbornly clinging to April. Amelia just shook her head and mouthed, 'hormones' behind her back.

"Sharon, I'm fine. Not happy but—"

"Don't say you're fine. We saw what was published. It's all full of lies and exaggerations," Sharon countered fiercely. It touched April to know she had such a strong support system. Of course, she knew Jason would be there for her, but she didn't want to take his focus away from fighting Carrie.

Also, she'd been alone for most of her life. Having to move often and Joan constantly being away for work, she'd not been able to maintain any friends especially female friends. Realizing that she had a bond forming with Jason's cousin-in-law and her sister, it filled a void in her she hadn't known was there.

"Thanks. It means a lot to me," she told Sharon and Amelia, finally able to release Sharon's hold on her. Joan and Mrs.

Salvador retreated to the kitchen, leaving April to entertain her guests.

"I have never seen anyone vilified so badly as you. *I* have never been attacked like that before when the world, along with *their* mother, found out I dated Cam," Sharon said as she seated herself at the dining table, picking Cynthia up when she crawled to her. The penthouse was becoming quite loud with Amelia's and Sharon's sons running around in the rooms with the twins watching them in fascination. Good thing April had already stored the fragile and pricey items, so they were free to do as they please.

"It must have been Carrie fanning the flames," Amelia said decisively.

"And how do you know that?"

"It's so obvious. Why else would they be so nasty with her? Usually, the press would release an announcement and her background whenever Jason is seen with a woman. But the way they wrote it, someone must be supplying information—false ones—to make her look bad."

"Is that true?"

"Well, the one about my dad is right," April confessed, bracing herself for the withdrawal of their support. What she wasn't ready for was the hug from Amelia. It was doubly surprising because Amelia didn't look like a "huggy" sort of person.

"You poor thing. Our mom was bad but not to the point of threatening to kill us," she cried. April awkwardly patted her back and smiled when Sharon mouthed, 'period.'

"Well, luckily, Jason came along just in time," April said stiltedly, trying to get out of Amelia's hold. After successfully pushing her away, she rubbed her neck. "Thanks for coming guys. It really means a lot."

"April, do your guests want refreshment?" Joan asked pointedly.

"Oh, where are my manners?" April said, flushing. "Do you guys want anything? And before I forget, this is my mother, Joan Saunders. She's living with us since her house got trashed."

"Water is fine but some snacks for the kids would be great too," Amelia said with a smile. Sharon just nodded, busy playing with Cynthia. Joan nodded and went to get the requested items.

"Stay and entertain them, sweetie," Joan told April when she made a move to follow her.

Right. Entertain. This should be easy. Of course, she'd had no experience but how hard could it be?

"Oh, I know that look," Sharon said once she had set her daughter down. "That look says you're about to do something you don't want to."

"Are we that bad?" Amelia chimed teasingly.

"No! No," she said. "I just have not entertained before. I don't know what to do."

"How about we go out?" Amelia suggested, surprising April. She didn't even ask why. But it was a huge relief.

"Sure. Let me get the twins ready—"

"No. Just *us*. It'll be good to get away once in a while." April wasn't comfortable with that. And it was so last minute. Surely Jason wouldn't allow it. "Don't worry. I'll talk to Jason."

"But—"

"Well, it's decided then. We're having a girls' day out," Sharon announced.

~

Jason wasn't having a good time at work. His lawyers have yet to find a way to prevent the judge from granting Carrie temporary partial custody. Her tearjerker interview was gaining supporters, and petitions had been signed to release his twins to her. To appease the press and public, the judge—a people-pleaser in Jason's opinion—had caved in, fanning the flames further.

He was not pleased.

Furthermore, more articles were published regarding April that were just plain nonsense, most of them blatant lies. He's working with his public relations office and lawyers about the possible actions in a bid to clear her name. That had been a nightmare.

His lawyers told him to sue but his PR office told him to wait; let the fires die before attacking them and instead, proposed releasing a statement regarding the publications to which his lawyers had countered saying that if he didn't strike when the iron was hot, it wouldn't be as effective. His headache worsened. He finally snapped, forcing them to come up with a solution by the next day, then left and focused on his company.

Unfortunately, the part of his life that usually worked like a well-oiled engine had a wrench thrown into it, dissolving it into chaos. Janice, in a desperate attempt to get his attention, stripped to her underwear when he called her into the office. Seeing this attempt a step too far, Jason instantly terminated her employment, offered her severance pay, and when she resisted, had security escort her out.

He had to share his new vice president's assistant. However, she was not able to handle the load and had a breakdown in his office. He released her to her former duties and had to use a junior clerk who, while desperate to please, didn't have the firmness to be of much help.

Finally, hoping to calm down and not snap at his new assistant, he called April.

"Hey, Jase," April said cheerfully into the phone. He felt his mouth curve up. He didn't know why, but her voice drained the stress out of him. Relaxing into his seat, he greeted her. "Are you OK? You sound stressed out." He didn't know why but everything that had happened up 'till that point, poured out of him—his anger, frustration, and helplessness.

"Oh, boy. That sounds bad. Why don't you just take the day off then? Nothing seems to be going your way," April suggested.

"I can't. I have to make sure your name is cleared. I won't let Carrie win," he said hotly.

"Well, that would take a while. But I see that you need something to take your mind off the problem."

"You are not a problem—"

"I know. I was referring to Carrie," she returned drily. He felt his cheeks suffuse with red. Luckily, she wasn't there to see. "Look. I'm currently out with Sharon and Amelia. I barely got away from Sharon so I could answer your call. Why don't you get Mom to come in? She'd be the perfect person for this. Even though she doesn't have any secretarial experience, she's firm and knows her way around the computer. I'm sure she can help— I have to go. Sharon's found— Sharon, let me go! I was just about to finish the call!"

There were sounds of a struggle and Sharon's voice, saying, "Let it go. You can have this once we reach your house—" More struggles and shouting.

He hoped they were treating April well. She'd called earlier to inform him of the change in plans. Seeing as she'd not asked for time off for the two months she'd taken care of the twins, he couldn't begrudge her this opportunity. Plus, he trusted Amelia to leash them if need be. Especially when Sharon's hormones got the best of her.

The line went dead after that, leaving him smiling. April could definitely make him smile. He considered her input and decided to try it out. *How bad could Joan be anyway?*

CHAPTER 23

"You didn't have to pull my hair," April grumbled as she rubbed her scalp. Sharon just ignored her and kept choosing clothes for her. She didn't know why but she felt like someone's pulling strings on her. "Please know that the only reason you won is because I abhor hurting people weaker than me. And, with you expecting, I consider you weaker."

Sharon gasped, her emerald eyes sparkling with outrage, taking a step in her direction before Amelia stopped her.

"Good god, you guys are like teenage boys always trying to get a rise out of each other. Can you stop?" she said, exasperated. Then she saw what Sharon had picked and her mouth went wide open in disbelief. April knew she'd be in disbelief if she saw it either. "What are you doing? Why did you pick that?"

"It's nice," Sharon said defensively, snatching away the neon pink polka dot batwing blouse.

"On a clown. Seriously, after all those years being groomed by Elliot, that designer you model for, I'd have thought you'd already pick up some styling tips," Amelia muttered, grabbing everything Sharon had picked and dropping them into some poor store assistant's arms. April laughed and glanced outside, seeing her bodyguards preventing anyone who looked like a reporter or paparazzi in. Sighing, she wished she was old news.

They were currently at one of the stores in the Michigan Mile. Most shoppers didn't care who April was, seeing as they were newsworthy themselves, so she was able to walk uninterrupted. Amelia and Sharon were unfazed by the snapping cameras and questions when they'd left the condominium, allowing April to show a strong front as well. In the car, Sharon surprisingly threw her arms around her. Even so, April had drawn comfort from her embrace.

Once they'd arrived, Sharon then dragged them into the closest store and proceeded to take everything off the shelves. Unfortunately, her choices were, in April's inexperienced eyes, less than spectacular. But who was she to say? She didn't know what to pick either.

Like ducklings, Sharon and she followed Amelia, trying to absorb whatever nuggets of information she was willing to dispense. Well, April was. She didn't know what Sharon was doing, apart from sulking. It felt like following her older sister shopping while lugging around their reluctant pregnant younger sister which was really funny considering Sharon was six years her senior.

She couldn't help but dub her the younger sister since that was the vibe she was currently exuding. Even so, seeing as she had never had a sister, the experience was heartwarming.

"Can we stop? My feet are killing me," Sharon complained for the fiftieth time, after their visit to the sixth shop. Amelia and April shared a look but agreed to her request. They stopped at a café, requesting a table indoors. April wished they could dine al fresco—it was such a nice day out—but seeing the crowd growing, it seemed prudent to keep away from the public eye as much as possible. Her bodyguards sat a few tables away, far enough to afford privacy but close enough to protect her if the need arises. Her eyes widened when she saw what Sharon ordered. It was enough for her husband's entire team! April remembered that Cameron had once been the quarterback for the Giants and she could just imagine their appetite, which probably wasn't impressive now that she's seen Sharon's plate. Sharon then turned to them, asking for *their* order. She looked at her in shock but Amelia took it in stride and ordered a club sandwich. Shaking off her shock at both the sisters' appetites, April ordered a grilled chicken sandwich.

The café was nice, the interiors very open and airy. It felt like sitting at the patio but with air conditioning. The patrons glanced up from their plates but once they saw who it was, they returned to their meals. Well, all except for a group of young— probably in their mid-twenties—well-dressed, pretty and fancy women, seated near the front. They were and are still glaring at her. April's companions didn't see them so she didn't want to make a fuss. Hopefully, ignoring them would work.

"That was a fruitful trip," Amelia said, satisfied. April nodded, forcing those women out of her thoughts. She dared not disagree. Amelia was a tough taskmaster when it came to fashion. She couldn't believe the countless times she had to model outfit after outfit, shoes after shoes. Her calves contracted just thinking about it. And whenever she'd gathered the courage to argue, Amelia would just fix her army sergeant eyes on her and the fight fizzled out of her.

Of course, Sharon had been exempted. But she didn't just sit quietly in the chair provided. Commenting on every outfit, it had made for an even more trying afternoon. Even so, she wasn't so strict and stringent about combinations and color contrasts as April. Basically, she was less sophisticated and approachable than Amelia. April found it easier to joke with her and even argue on her assessments. Often, they'd dissolve into giggles, with Amelia looking on, less than amused.

"Well, we have manicures and pedicures next," Sharon said around her appetizer, a stuffed jalapeño. April wrinkled her nose at her to which she responded by popping another jalapeño and chewing with her mouth open.

"Gross," April cried with a laugh. Amelia scowled at her sister and hit her hand with the back of a spoon. Sharon furrowed her brows at her but closed her mouth. "Anyway, I don't know about the mani-pedi. I've never been away from the twins this long before. Rain check please?"

"I felt that way when I first had Derrick. But as they grow, you also grow to treasure the time away from them," Sharon finished with a cackle. The other two looked at her askance which she took offense. "Don't lie, Ams. I know you sometimes take work trips to get some alone time. Away from Scott and the boys."

"Yes, yes, baby sister," Amelia hastened to agree, looking around to see if someone else heard Sharon. "But we're wondering about your cackle. Since when did you cackle? Are you somehow transitioning to a witch? I knew all those suspicious herbal drinks were bound to transform you—"

"Um, excuse me," one of the women from the glaring table interjected which startled April, Amelia and Sharon. April had been so caught up with the argument that she hadn't noticed her.

"Yes?" Amelia prompted politely when the woman didn't continue. April found it weird that the woman kept her eyes on Amelia and Sharon only. It was like April was invisible.

"What are you doing with that woman? Both of you are so classy that we can't tell why you're with such a trashy bitch. I mean, look at her. That shirt. Those shoes. The only reason we can think of is she forced herself on you. If that's the case, you're welcome to join my friends and me," the woman said. They were dumbfounded. They all knew who she was talking about: April.

April bowed her head. It hurt to have such hateful words flung at her. Something about saying it to her face made the wound inflicted by this woman even deeper. She thought she had become immune to negative opinions. Clearly, she was wrong.

"Who the hell are you talking about?" Amelia asked coolly. Her face was frozen and her eyes were like ice chips while Sharon's face was red and her hands clenched around her fork. Worried about her health, April wrapped her hand around her fist, giving her a small smile when she turned her fiery eyes to her.

"That trash masquerading as a woman," the woman sneered, finally deigning to look at April. April looked impassively up at her, tightening her hold on Sharon.

"I suggest you walk away, little girl, and do your homework. Or, better yet, mind your own business," Sharon said through gritted teeth. The woman took offense.

"Sorry if I was just trying to help."

"Well, I'm sorry but we don't need your help," Amelia countered.

Finally realizing they were serious, the woman turned away, flipping her hair. "Well, it's like what they always say. Birds of the same feather flock together. So naturally, trashy people will join other trashy people."

Apparently, that was too much for Sharon. She sprang up, leaned across the table, and despite her pregnant belly, grabbed the woman's hair. The woman shrieked, flailing her arms, trying to regain her balance. April and Amelia tried to release her hold. The woman's friends rushed to her aid and tried pulling Sharon.

"Let go, Sharon. Think about your baby," April cried when she realized where the other women were pulling. Their hands were directly on her stomach, probably jeopardizing the baby. Once Sharon was aware of the danger, she released her hold and pushed the other women away, cradling her tummy.

The woman turned to them, eyes ablaze and shouted, "My daddy will hear about this!"

"Just shut up," April snarled, moving to see if Sharon was alright. Suddenly the manager came to their table. She didn't pay attention as she thought the manager was going to throw the other women out. Or, at least, do some damage control. So, she was shocked by what she heard next.

"I'm sorry but I have to ask you ladies to leave," she said. Thinking she was talking to the interlopers, April didn't think much of it until Amelia said, "What? Why?"

"You are causing too much of disruption in this establishment. We've overlooked those reporters out there but this is too much," she said firmly, looking pointedly at the pack of women huddling around their injured member.

"But she started it," Sharon cried. April rolled her eyes. Way to be helpful.

"I'm sorry but from what I've seen, it was you, ma'am, who assaulted her." Under Amelia's hard gaze, the manager fidgeted.

"Well, ladies, I didn't want to come here anyway," Sharon said, picking up her bag. Amelia and April were startled by her sudden decision but supported her by getting their bags as well. "But don't think I won't let my husband know about this and you, little person."

"My husband, too," Amelia said.

"And my... boyfriend," April said after the not-so-subtle nudge from Sharon. The manager looked stricken but they left, heads held high before she could say anything else.

Their bodyguards surrounded them, forging a path through the suddenly crazy crowd. Once in the car, they all slumped into their seats.

"God, Share, couldn't you have controlled yourself better?" April sighed. To which Sharon responded by bursting into tears.

~

"Jason, your cousin is here to see you," Joan told him over the intercom. He debated correcting her usage of his personal name but decided against it, not wanting to give her any ammunition.

138

This was his future mother-in-law and she had already warned April of him. Letting her know to let him in, he set his work back on the desk and awaited Cameron's entrance.

"Did you know there's a horde of reporters outside your building?" was the first thing out of Cameron's mouth when he entered with Scott, Amelia's husband. Jason just nodded wearily. "Man, I don't want to be in your shoes. They're like piranhas. Avaricious for blood."

"Avaricious? Did Sharon force you to read another book?" Jason asked, amused, chuckling when Cameron's cheeks turned a burnished red. Scott shared his amusement.

"So what?" Cameron said defensively. "At least my wife cares about my vocabulary."

"You cursed in front of the boys again, didn't you?" Scott asked wryly. He and Jason laughed when Cameron admitted defeat and nodded.

They all knew how much he hated reading. He avoided it like a running back avoided being tackled, destroying any book he had to read. He barely graduated high school because of that. So, as a punishment, Sharon had chosen one that would burden him the most.

Of course, she hadn't settled on that instantly. At first, she'd done the usual and enforced a cuss jar. A dollar for every cuss word anyone uttered in the house. That hadn't worked so well since Cameron had always been willing to shell out some cash. So, she changed it, trying from increasing the fine to keeping the boys from him.

It wasn't until she'd found a book and wanted to share it with Cameron that she'd found his weakness. And the funny thing was, Cameron didn't try to negotiate with her. When she handed him a book, he found a quiet spot and read it.

After they'd stopped laughing and Cameron stopped grumbling, Jason asked what they were doing in his office. "Scott wanted to talk business with you," Cameron told him as he made himself comfortable on the sofa. Or tried to. "Can't you find a more uncomfortable couch?" Ignoring him, Jason and Scott continued their discussion.

However, less than half an hour later, his door burst open and Sharon rushed in. Or waddled at a fast pace. Amelia was not far behind, holding out a hand to hopefully catch her sister if, God forbid, she falls. Cameron went to his wife and barely caught himself when she threw herself at him, burying her face in his chest.

"Baby, what's going on? Why are you crying?" Cameron asked worriedly. Amelia, seeing as her sister was in good hands, went to sit in her husband's lap. She didn't look that happy either. "What? I can't understand you. Mean? Who's mean? Did anyone offend you?"

"What's going on?" Jason asked Amelia, the only rational woman in the room. "And where's April?"

"She's outside with Joan. And Sharon's just high-strung," she answered wearily. At that, Sharon lifted her head off Cameron's chest and glared at her.

"I'm not high-strung. I'm *never* high-strung," she spat angrily.

"Well, I'm sorry if I'm mistaken," Amelia retorted, rolling her eyes.

"Alright, what's going on? Why are you crying?" Cameron cut in before the sisters could devolve further.

"April and Amelia are meanies. And I want you to destroy that café," Sharon finished.

"'Destroy' is a bit too much. Maybe ruin them?" Amelia added. The men looked at them, lost.

"What did they do to you?" Scott asked warily.

"They kicked us out," Sharon cried, outraged. "And to think that I was going to go back for their food. Such a waste of good food." Scott and Cameron looked between the sisters, knowing there was more to the story. Finally, Amelia told them.

Jason didn't hear much of it. Seeing his friend and cousin with their partners made him yearn for his. Quietly making his way out, the rest too engrossed with the story, he went to fetch April. His arms felt surprisingly empty without her.

But when he saw her, anger coursed through his entire body. What the hell happened at that café?

CHAPTER 24

"You have to click there to save it," April told her mother. Joan brought the mouse carefully to said button and electronically saved Jason's appointment for the first time. Her brows furrowed as she went to the calendar. Once she saw the information was there, her brows unknit, and jumping up, she hugged her daughter.

"Oh, thank you, sweetie. I've had experience being a secretary in the old days and such but all these lights and buttons confuse me too much. Being as poor as we were, I've had no training in this. Nor were there any companies willing to hire me once my skills went obsolete," Joan gushed. April just laughed and returned her hug. It was especially comforting after the day she had.

"Thanks, Mom. For getting me out of there," she said in answer to the questioning look Joan gave her. Her face softened and she moved to place a kiss on April's forehead. But, before she could enjoy this quiet time together, Jason Halloway, suddenly swiped her daughter out of her arms like a force of nature.

"What happened? Why are you crying? Don't lie to me, April. I know those are tears on your cheeks. Did Joan say anything mean to you? Because if she did, I'll have her out in a heartbeat—"

"Jason, stop. My mom didn't do anything. In fact, I'm glad she's here," April said, placing a finger on Jason's lips.

"Are you sure?" he asked suspiciously around her finger, turning skeptical eyes on Joan.

"Yes," his girlfriend said exasperatedly. She appreciated his care but sometimes, he just went overboard with it.

"Then why are there tear tracks? Don't tell me it's water. I know tears when I see it," he peered worriedly into her eyes.

"I was upset and overwhelmed. The articles first thing in the morning. We even made it to the first page! Then a woman approached us at the restaurant, spouting lies the media has fed her and trying to get Amelia and Sharon to join their table because they didn't want me with them in the first place but were too polite to say no when I joined. Of course, we set her in her place but, somehow, she offended Sharon so badly that she—the crazy pregnant woman—actually lunged across that table and grabbed her hair. Then the manager kicked us out. It was so unfair. The woman approached us first and said so many hurtful and offensive things. It's just not fair," she cried out.

During her rant, she'd broken free of Jason's grip and paced about the room. She felt so out of sorts, unlike her usual self. Normally, she was able to put things into perspective, even when panicking but today, everything was just coming at her all at once and she couldn't take a step back. She felt so lost and alone. And she felt that, since Jason was so used to the limelight, he didn't understand her. She didn't have any friends growing up, so she became an intensely private person. To suddenly have the entire world become interested in every little aspect of her life was mind-boggling and uncomfortable.

"April, you know I'll be there for you. Even under the close scrutiny of the media," Jason finally said, gently placing his arms around her, stopping her frantic movement. She tried to put some distance between them but the unrelenting pressure on her shoulder blades forced her to rest against his chest. Even so, she kept as much distance between them as possible. Ordinarily, she felt comfort being in his arms but today, anger grew instead—a flaming, fiery rage that came from nowhere. She just couldn't understand the animosity she was suddenly feeling but knew she had to explain it.

"I know that. At least my mind does but something in me wants to place all these stuff on you. The cameras. The reporters. My sudden lack of freedom. *The twins'* lack of freedom. I don't like it and it's all your fault," she grumbled, pushing him away and storming off. Feeling the room closing in around her, she had to get away. To breathe. To think.

And to get away from him—the root of it all—even as her heart cried out for him.

~

Jason was stunned. He hadn't expected April to react in that manner. He'd told her countless times that he would always be there for her to protect her, to support her. No matter what anyone else said. So, he didn't understand her outburst. And, for once in his life, it hurt.

"Don't let this come between you two," Joan said, sliding her arm into his. So focused on April, he'd forgotten of her presence and jumped.

"How can I not let it? Didn't you hear her? She blames me for everything. Even when I told her I'll always be with her. What else does she want from me?" he growled, masking his pain with anger.

"Understanding," Joan said sharply. He turned his bewildered eyes on her. "Look, you have to understand. She didn't have any—let me stress that—*any* friends growing up. Some of it was due to her father but most of it was due to her personality. She doesn't like to show her inner thoughts and emotions. It makes her feel too vulnerable so she bottles it up. Of course, some people may take her silence as weakness but she'd always been able to put it in perspective. 'Only one more year,' she always says. And that helps to siphon off her negative emotions, problems.

"Now, with the papers and media jumping at her, she can't find the space or time to take a step back. To look at the bigger picture. So, it all pours out of her in one big explosion. In fact, you should take this in a positive note. It shows a level of trust I have never seen her give to anyone before," Joan told him, keeping a firm hold on him but looking anywhere but at him.

Jason felt his heart soften. She was clearly uncomfortable with the frank talk but would do it for her daughter. If that wasn't a testament of her love for her child, he didn't know what was. And he could see the similarities between the mother and daughter.

They're both reticent but were willing to break that shell for their loved ones as what Joan was doing for April now, and as April always did for the twins and him. He couldn't forget how she took charge when he was sick. Butting heads with Janice and his idiot of an ex vice-president. He had believed he was starting to fall for her then. Maybe even before. But that's when he had been aware he had feelings for her.

So, it wasn't much of a surprise when he felt his anger abate. His arms came around Joan. And, just like her daughter, she involuntarily flinched from the initial contact but relaxed into him a few moments later.

"I understand what you're saying but how do I make this better? Because I don't think my usual methods will work this time," he muttered.

"Usual method? You mean showering her with money?" Joan asked, her voice ringing with a note of derision. Jostling her slightly, he nodded nonetheless. "You can do that but, let me tell you, that method rings of insincerity. And you're still not addressing the underlying issue. She doesn't think you understand her side. All she sees is you going to work and not doing anything to keep those reporters away."

"That's not true. I am on her side. I'll always be on her side. Why would she ever think that—"

"Do not kill the messenger," Joan grumbled, making him stop.

"I just don't understand it. I assumed that, since she's being so calm with it, she didn't mind those sharks shoving their cameras and microphones into her face."

"She did when she thought they were only interested in you. But when they turned their beady eyes on her, it all became too close for comfort. Anyway, you know what they say about assuming. It'll make an ass of you and me," she said hardly. Then she relaxed and continued, "If you'd looked out for it, April showed some signs of her anxiety."

"I didn't know that. How am I supposed to know what to look for? This is the first time I've been in a relationship. A serious, committed relationship," he admitted reluctantly. Then looking at her, utterly clueless, he asked the most important question. "How do I make this work, Joan? I'm as lost as April right now. I want to make this better but I don't know how."

"Why don't you ask your friends in there? I'm sure you'll think of something."

CHAPTER 25

April felt horrible. She hadn't meant to hurt Jason like that. And she didn't know where all those sentiments and words came from. But she did, and she had hurt the only man she'd ever truly trusted and cared about. She'd seen it when she'd left. The shard of pain his eyes expressed in an otherwise impassive face. It had startled her but she hadn't expected his hurt would induce her own pain.

She sighed as she dropped onto a seat by an open room. Having wandered around the offices and endured the curious and often snide gazes of the people working there, she finally found an empty hallway, just off the copy room. It gave off an eerie feel, but she needed the space to think.

Growing up, she wasn't the most confrontational person. She just didn't like the spotlight. Her throat would thicken, unable to get the words out, and tears would fill her eyes when she got angry. So, often, she wasn't able to express her anger. Instead, she became a hot mess and got picked on more.

As she went from elementary school to middle school and finally high school, she decided that being angry was a waste of energy and eventually became the woman she was today. Especially since she could never get the words out. Or so she'd thought.

The way she tore into Jason surprised her. She had been angry, for whatever subconscious reason, but her eloquence shocked her. The words weren't stuck in her chest, unable to get through her suddenly thick throat. Her eyes hadn't watered. Her face wasn't wet from angry tears. She marveled over this surprising change. But she wished, for once in her life, that she hadn't been able to put her anger into words.

Searching her mind, trying to figure out where the words had come from, she realized she wasn't actually angry with Jason. She understood and accepted that the reporters and cameras were a part of his life. Maybe she'd wished he'd explained the exact magnitude of it but it was like an on-the- job training. Once she went through these hellish few weeks, she could get through anything.

Instead, she found a simmering pot of anger for Carrie. It'd started when she first met the twins and had steadily grown with every reminder of her. Be it from the twins' clinginess to this recent debacle. And April blamed her for her sudden restrains whether it was right or wrong.

Because, with or without Carrie, she knew once their relationship was made public, it'd have the same result. Microphones would be shoved into her face and cameras would flash left and right. So, essentially, Carrie only sped up the timeline.

"Son of a bitch," a male voice suddenly rang out angrily, echoing slightly in the empty hallway. April sat up straight, her eyes searching the doorways, trying to find the source. But most of the doors were open, making it difficult to pinpoint. And she didn't want to poke her head into any room because the anger intimidated her.

Not wanting to wait for the angry person to get out of the room, she quietly got up and retraced her steps. After rounding the corner, the male continued. She paused, deciding it was harmless to listen in.

"I can't get too close to her and the computer security is tight. My attempt to get into the server has already raised a flag," he said, frustrated. He must have been on the phone because she didn't hear any reply. "Yes, I've erased any traces of me being here but I can't help you. Of course, I love you but I'm not willing to put my neck out while you stay safe in front of the cameras."

Who was this man talking to? Why did his voice sound familiar? She didn't exactly know a lot of people and her circle of male acquaintances was so small it could be constituted as a dot. *And what about the computer he mentioned?* Seeing as his voice was coming from one of the rooms, the computer must be one of Jason's. That made it very suspicious. From what he's saying, she presumed he didn't have clearance.

"Well, fuck you, bitch. I've done everything you've asked of me. If that's not enough, then we shouldn't be together. This is very dangerous. I don't want this to bite me in my ass later in the future. And I'll have other opportunities. If they catch me now, it'd be difficult to find another chance."

Hearing footsteps from the room, April decided her presence was no longer necessary and skedaddled out of there. The last she heard of him was, "I love you too, baby. Let's get together later."

She couldn't wait to let Jason know about this.

~

"What happened? Where's April?" Sharon asked once Jason stepped back into his office. Sighing, Jason prepared himself for a deluge of relentless questioning. Sharon applied her job as an agent for athletes to all parts of her life. She'd always try another angle, both to get answers and the best offers for her clients. She was relentless but her methods were effective.

"What happened? I heard her raise her voice which is very unlike her," Sharon repeated. This was one area of his life in which he didn't want to be proven right. She tried to get up from

Cameron's lap but his arms stopped her. Turning to glare at him, she demanded, "Let me go. I have to make sure April is okay."

"At least let the poor man explain himself," her husband offered, smiling at her futile attempts. Huffing, she folded her arms and turned accusing eyes on him.

Taking a deep breath, Jason gathered his thoughts and began to do one of the most important things he had ever done in his life. And probably the hardest.

"I need your help. April is angry at me and I don't know how to make it better," he said in a rush. Everyone was stunned except for Sharon.

"Well, of course, she's angry with you. You have not publicly shown her any support nor did you ease her into this life. She was practically shoved into shark-infested waters with no ability to swim nor provision of any flotation devices aside from you standing on the platform, saying, 'The sharks are dangerous and they will bite but I'll be here. Supporting you.' All the while she's being eaten by those sharks. Alive—"

"Sharon," Cameron said, trying to cut in but she just talked over him.

"And since she's being understanding and all that—what with your work and fighting Carrie—there is the issue of the world not knowing about your relationship. All the world knows is that SHE only accepted the job so as to get close to you and not because she genuinely wants to help you with the twins—"

"Babe," Cameron tried again but the bulldozer kept going.

"So now every woman who has a soft spot for children will judge her all the harsher and her sense of worth as a mother will be seriously compromised—"

"Sharon, will you just shut up?" Amelia cried. That did the job but it brought her sister's ire on her.

"Well, that was uncalled for," Sharon huffed but closed her mouth when her sister shot her a glare.

"Did you not listen to him? He's asking for help. *Jason Halloway is asking for help*. And you're not helping," Amelia hissed.

"Well, why didn't you say so earlier?" she mumbled but kept quiet when Cameron jostled her slightly.

"You're protective and that's what I love about you," he told her and moved to kiss her when Amelia spoke again.

"Alright. So, April is angry with you. Do you know why?" she asked Jason.

"Yeah. From what Joan and Sharon kept saying, I'm not very demonstrative. And I need to show my support. Show it openly and in a manner that would be difficult to misconstrue," he said, slightly distracted. He was still processing all Sharon had thrown at him.

He hadn't known April had it so bad. The press had never hit him as badly as they were apparently doing to April. And there were the abuse rumors floating about. He knew his children were in good hands but the rest of the world don't. Usually, he wouldn't care what others thought about him but his children were now involved. And April. He had to do something. Fast. Mentally reminding himself to contact his public relations office and lawyers, he tuned in to the discussion at hand.

"So, we've agreed. You have to frequently take them out, show your affection openly to both April and the twins. And we'll be seeing you in Los Angeles next week," Sharon said decisively.

Los Angeles?

"We're going to Los Angeles?" a voice said from the door. Turning around to see who it was, he threw his arms around April, bringing her close to him. He didn't know why she came back but her presence brought relief to a side of him that always worried when she was out of his sight. He was startled, though, when he felt her arms come around him, and she buried her face into his chest.

"I'm sorry for exploding on you," she murmured. He smiled.

"And I'm sorry for not being so demonstrative," he returned. That surprised her. She looked up at him. "I believe that's why your subconscious is so angry with me."

"Is it? Hmm. I haven't thought of that—"

"Alright. Enough with the lovey-dovey stuff. We still have an evening gown to buy," Sharon said and pulled April out of his hold.

"Evening gown? What are you talking about? Is this about Los Angeles? Hey, isn't that where Harry is?" April asked, her hands desperately holding onto his arm. Not knowing why but wanting to show his support anyway, he grabbed her away from Sharon who shot exasperated looks at them.

"Yes. And he's having an auction. He's selling off female employees for a night like the pimp he is. Normally I wouldn't put up with this but the both of you need the publicity. So, we're going there," she explained and latched on to April again. "Now we have to go. We only have a little time to get a gown before Amelia and I leave in a few days. Let's go."

Jason was stunned as he watched April being dragged out against her will. And April, too slow to call for help, was gone before Amelia shut the door.

What just happened?

"Alright. We'll return late so you guys will have to look after the kids at Jason's house. Knowing the boys, your house will have been trashed by now. Send the invoice for any repairs and replacements to us, alright?" Amelia mumbled as she pressed a kiss on Scott's cheek and hugged the remaining men. "Don't worry. I'll take care of her."

"What just happened?" Jason said into the room at large.

"My wife and a cause," Cameron answered glumly. "May the Lord have mercy on us."

CHAPTER 26

"Is she gone?" April hissed from the bathroom in Jason's room. She'd made a beeline for it once Sharon had deemed them "prepared for the battle ahead". Or something along that line. All April cared was getting out of that madwoman's clutches.

"Yes, she is," Jason said, amusement lacing his voice. Heaving a sigh of relief, she smacked his arm when she came out. How could he be enjoying her misery at a time like this? "Hey!"

"This is not funny," she whined as she threw herself, arms akimbo, on his bed. Thinking of all the shops she'd been dragged into, she wished Amelia had taken charge. Instead, the traitor had allowed Sharon to lead, trying on gowns after dresses after outfits. She wasn't even allowed to choose her own undergarments. Sharon said in order to portray sexy, she had to feel sexy. And sexy undergarments were supposed to help.

'Supposed to' being the key word. These types of undergarments have always baffled her. They looked unnecessarily intricate and too uncomfortable to wear. How was that supposed to help her feel sexy?

After helping her get her shoes off, Jason went to check her shopping bags. Of course, being male, he immediately zeroed in on the Victoria's Secret bags.

"Sweetheart, what is this?" he asked, dangling one of the bags from one of his fingertips. Rolling her eyes, she brought her knees up and lay on her side.

"What else do you think is it?" she grumbled. He cast her a rakish grin and started taking out some pieces. Too exhausted to care, she just relaxed into the bed.

"Mind modelling it for me?"

"If I wanted my boobs to touch my chin and ass to look floppy and unsupported, yeah sure," she replied sarcastically.

"Come on. It'll be fun," he cajoled and slightly pouted. She turned away, trying to escape his beguiling pout but he just pulled her back. "Also, seeing as Sharon would force you into them, with or without your consent, this will be a great time to get used in it."

"Ugh, logic," she cried angrily. And what did the imbecile do in the face of her anger? He smiled and cajoled some more. She could have resisted him if he'd only used logic. But once he tried to tickle her, she had to do something to stop him. "Alright, alright. I'll do it tomorrow."

"Great. I'll be back by the time you put the twins in bed," he said with the most excitement she'd ever heard in his voice. Her response was to roll her eyes again and turned back to her side. However, her agreement was not sufficient for him. He just had to share his excitement.

Yelping in surprise, she suddenly found herself on her back, her bewildered eyes locking with Jason's burning verdant eyes. Before she could recover her balance, her lips were caught in a heated kiss that lasted for five seconds but was enough to disperse some of the fog in her mind.

"What was that about?" she asked, dazed. He just smiled and gave her a peck on her nose.

"I'm going to have so much fun reminding you about this tomorrow," he chuckled before getting off her and tucking a blanket over her. She didn't know what he was talking about but the warmth and softness of the bed almost lulled her into oblivion. The last she heard finally allowed her to slip into dreamland.

"I'll look into the twins later. Just get some rest."

~

"Do you know why Jason is so excited today?" Joan asked as she helped April and Mrs. Salvador prepare dinner. April sent her a puzzled look.

"Jason? Excited? I've never heard those words used together," Mrs. Salvador said with a smile. She did that a lot now especially when their relationship went public. It was nice to have someone, other than family, show a positive response.

"I don't know if it could be classified as excited but he alternated between telling the driver to hurry up and looking at his watch. He barely stayed in his chair as the time moved closer to five. All appointments had to be either moved to before five or rescheduled. So, if it's not excited, then I'd at least term it as anxious." They all shared a perplexed look. "Oh, why don't you ask him, April?"

"Me? Why do you guys think he'll tell me—Hey, wait! Stop pushing me. Alright, alright. I'll go, I'll go. Sheesh," she groused. Trying to protest didn't work because their combined strength was much greater than any roots she might grow on her feet. So, mustering up all her confidence and affection, she headed to the living room.

She paused by the door, and the domestic scene before her brought warmth to her heart. Jason was still in his office shirt and pants but had kicked off his shoes, and his tie was lying in some obscure corner of the room. But he looked as handsome as always. He had Daphne's hands in his and was supporting her as she practiced her walking while Tanner played with some toy cars and trucks.

Daphne still needed support, even after close to three months of practice while Tanner was strong enough to walk on his own. Their difference in progress was largely due to Daphne's stubbornness. She had refused to stand on her own, demanding help every time April had encouraged them to exercise. It was only when Tanner had shown significant progress that she became more independent. April could see this trait will be a cause of friction in future and raised it up to Jason, but they agreed to cross the bridge when it happened.

As always, Tanner saw her first and got to his feet, wobbling the ten steps to her. Cheering, April took him into her arms and gave him a tight hug. Jason smiled at that and he brought Daphne to them. Giving April a kiss, he inquired of her presence.

"Mom wants to know why you're so excited," she told him, setting Tanner down. Jason gave her a look of chagrin and did the same to Daphne. "What?"

"You forgot your promise, didn't you?" he asked, although from his tone, it was more of a statement. Releasing a sigh, full of barely concealed disappointment, he said, "Never mind. It was of no importance."

Confused, she continued to look at him until a snippet of last night's conversation came into her mind which didn't clear her confusion at all. Instead, her confusion transformed into disbelief.

"You're excited because I'm going to wear some lingerie later?" she asked. Instantly, his downcast face brightened.

"But-but it's just me. With most of my flabby body on display and only two small pieces to cover the important parts. I don't see how that can ever induce excitement."

"It's because it's *you* that's why I'm looking forward to it," he told her earnestly.

"I'm sure you've seen fitter, more beautiful women strutting their stuff before. *That* I'd get excited about but me? I'm just going to wear it, show it to you, go back to the bathroom, and take it off. That's not exciting."

He had an unexplainable look of outrage but before he could explain it, they were called to dinner. Promising to talk about it later, they brought the twins to the table.

April still could not understand what was so exciting about her wearing lingerie.

~

Jason had never felt this level of excitement before—the kind where he couldn't stay still. The closest he could think of was when he made his first million. And it had been a momentary blip in his radar before he had to get back to his work.

He was situated in a chair in his room furthest from the bathroom because he had a plan. And he couldn't wait to put it into play.

Finally, April came out. And his sweatpants immediately sported a tent. She was magnificent in a simple navy silk set that was nearly the same color as her eyes; it was a startling contrast with her creamy skin. Apparently, she'd bought a size too small because her breasts were spilling over the top and side, making it difficult for him to peel his eyes from them. God, his eyes traveled down her body.

His mouth became drier as his eyes roamed her body. He had never been this aroused. Ever. And never at such speed. His fingers itched to traverse her body, explore every nook and cranny, every sensitive spot that would drive her crazy. His mouth wanted to lick every expanse of her skin, gathering the taste that was purely April. His dick just wanted to be inside her.

However, his brain knew he still had a plan to see through.

"Jason, what are you doing all the way over there?" she asked curiously.

"Nothing," he replied guilelessly. Her brows furrowed and she moved to reenter the bathroom. "Why don't you come closer?

It'll help you get comfortable in it. And so I can see you much better."

"Said the wolf to little red riding hood. Do you think I don't know what you're doing?" she demanded crossly. He just shrugged, and she stomped her feet. "You just want to watch me model it for you. Like how those Victoria's Secret models do."

"Would that be so bad?" he heard himself ask and wanted to snatch back the words as soon as it escaped him. When did he become so soft and vulnerable? He, who callously dumped any woman when they start to ask for more in a relationship? He, who told a woman straight up where they were lacking? But looking into her eyes and downturned lips, he realized a show of vulnerability would help her gather the courage to cross the room to him.

"Please, sweetheart? I promise I won't laugh. Hell, just by looking at my groin, you know that I want you. Just you. The only thing in my mind is you," he entreated. She appeared to be chewing on her lips. She thought his idea over but he was hard-pressed to stay in his seat. He needed her soft weight in his arms. Stat.

Just when he decided to bound over to her, one of her legs moved hesitantly away from the bathroom door toward his direction. With her eyes trained to the floor, she released her death grip on the doorknob and slowly but surely, came closer to him.

His heart pounded; he felt like he'd won a race. He felt elated with adrenaline coursing through him. Trust. This showed she trusted him. And what a sweet revelation that was innocent even. It mixed with the lewd thoughts running through his head—of how he could easily bend her over, push aside her panties and enter her as she passed the dressing table he had never used; of how he could tie her arms at the bedposts, rise over her in his soft mattress, and tease her with the head of his shaft.

He must've made a sound because she paused and looked up into his eyes. He knew he should look away to hide the fire running through his veins but his head refused to move. Knowing she was going to run back to the bathroom soon, he didn't waste any time and feasted on her displayed body.

Just as he was preparing to look away, her legs started moving in the wrong direction. She was placing one leg in front of the other like she was coming to him. Shooting his eyes to her face, he became more inflamed when he saw how flushed she was, her moist lips slightly parted. And her eyes. Her eyes were pure desire.

And then, she was there. Right in front of him. He wanted to touch her but knew the first move must be hers. Fingers digging into the arms of the armchair, he tried to predict where she would place her hands first. *His arms? Chest? Face?*

But when a finger trailed along the erect length of his shaft—the last place he'd ever thought of—his brain turned off, and he reacted.

Her sweet moans forever etched into his mind.

~

Pulling the comforter over both their bodies, Jason brought April right next to him. Despite spending the past few hours getting to know each other better, he still couldn't get enough of her. Never enough.

"There goes my plan to return that set," April yawned, laying her head on his chest.

"Never return them. In fact, I believe I'll have to increase the limit of your card just so you can buy more sets," he said into her hair. Feeling her body shake with a laugh, his lips curved into a contented smile.

"Well, if you insist, we do have to test every set the same way we did this," she teased, making him release a bark of laughter. "Against the wall, in the armchair—"

"That table finally has a purpose," he added. Just thinking about the past hour was getting his juices running again.

"The shower, the closet—Wait, you just came ten minutes ago. You can't be ready again—"

Pushing her onto her back and rising over her, he pressed his lips over hers. When he finally felt her respond by arching into his body, he let up.

"I'm always ready when I'm with you."

CHAPTER 27

The next day, their world crashed on them.

Seated beside Jason by his desk, April looked up at him in shock and then shifted her eyes to his lawyers, who were looking decidedly uncomfortable, then back at Jason, whose jaw was clenched so tight that it looked like it was carved from granite.

"Jase, tell me they're wrong. That-that she can't have them," she demanded softly. He refused to look at her. Fear grew and with it anger as well. "Jason! Tell me they're wrong."

"The court has ruled on it. Barring any further evidence, a parent is granted visitation rights if they're not the custodial parent. And they've decided alternate weekends for Ms. Carter," one of the lawyers offered. She nodded but still looked at Jason, demanding he tell her he has failed.

"I'm sorry," he finally murmured which was the impetus for her explosion.

"We can't bring them with us when we go for the auction and now this? You told me she won't get her hands on them. You told me you'd protect them. That they won't ever have to relive their fears—"

"Look, I tried and I'll keep trying. But they blindsided me with the speed of the decision. There's no compelling reason why they should withhold her rights although I know there should be," he said, ignoring her snort. "Even so, I'm still compiling evidence against her but she's working with someone. Her tracks are being wiped away so clean that my investigators can't get anything to hold on her."

Biting her lips, April looked away, tears brimming in her eyes. She knew she had to let the anger go. He's already working so hard both for the twins and his company. She tried to help but the only way she could was to keep out of his way while he worked. And it made her feel so useless and helpless.

Suddenly, she was lifted and placed on Jason's lap. Startled, her eyes went to where the lawyers had been and only found empty space. She turned to her boyfriend, bewildered.

"Alright. Tell me what's really going on," he demanded softly, green eyes boring into dark blue. Unable to answer him, she began biting her lips again. "Baby, I know this isn't like you—"

"How do you know this isn't me? Maybe I'm just hiding a part of me who is angry and nasty," she cut in belligerently, ignoring his raised brows. "And why do you think this has anything to do with me? I'm angry because some psycho woman is going to take our babies away from us."

"You can never be nasty unless it's warranted and only if you can ever bring yourself to do it. I know a portion of your anger is because of the custody battle. But your explosion is about something else. Something you've been keeping inside for quite some time," he stated confidently. His fingers moved to tickle her chin but she turned her face away, avoiding him and the issue. "Sweetheart, how am I supposed to help you if you don't tell me what you're worked up about?"

"You're doing everything for the twins," she blurted out. "And I'm doing nothing. Ergo I'm useless."

"W-what?" he sputtered, moving her to face him. His fingers didn't give in. Even so, her eyes were trained on his chin. "Where did this come from?" She truly didn't want to expound but some part of her refused to let her keep it in.

"It's true," she cried, jumping off his lap. "I stay at home and take care of the twins. That's all. I don't clean or cook since Mrs. Salvador is there. I can't exactly let you pay me since we're together. My sense of self is being eroded just by my inactivity. And-and I really want to work."

"Alright," Jason began, uncertain in the face of her tirade. "I'm sure I can find you a position in the company—"

"No. I don't want to work for you. Sharon and Amelia have their own jobs and identities away from their family. I want that." Somehow, that made her feel like a child and she moved to explain herself further. "It's not that I don't love you and I want to spend most of my time away from you but our relationship is not balanced. You're giving me everything I've ever wanted but I'm not contributing anything. I don't even have any money to buy gifts for you. I can't exactly buy you a present using *your own* money."

"You give plenty into this relationship," he countered. "You're my light whenever I'm bogged down by my work or fighting off Carrie. You always make me smile. The twins have grown wonderfully under your care; they're more independent now. My home is much homier than it was before. Something neither I nor the twins ever had before. Before you, it was just a place for me to rest. Now, it's a home. *Our* home. And I feel that's more important than anything I can ever give you."

"That's great and I don't want to sound ungrateful but that's not enough for me. I've always had to work and now that I don't, I feel lost. Right now, with us adjusting to each other and Carrie, I'm pretty preoccupied but what about later? When the twins are in school and you're busy with work, what am I supposed to do? I can never be a woman of leisure," she cried as she dropped into her chair.

Her eyes trained on the floor, upset. She didn't look up when Jason's polished office shoes appeared in front of her. Her emotions were a jumbled mess, with one emotion always overpowering the other. But, right now, after pouring it all out, shame was the dominant one.

What did she exactly have to complain about? Most women would kill to be in her position. And she was telling him it wasn't enough? When she'd spent most of her life fighting and scraping to get to where she was now—happy, contented and in love? Who'd do that?

But there was still a nugget of discontent still buried in her heart of hearts that won't relinquish its hold. And no matter how much she told herself she was blessed to have Jason and the twins, that little ball would never go away.

"Hey," Jason said as he crouched down to meet her eyes. Bottom lip sticking out, she moved her head to the side, avoiding his gaze. She folded her arms when he moved to take them into his hands. Jason resorted to placing his hands on her thighs, squeezing them gently.

"Look, I know we happened unexpectedly and a bit fast. And so much has happened during this time that should have just been about us. I know you have some reservations about me, your feelings, and your future, but just because I've been the obvious provider now doesn't mean it will always be that way. And it doesn't invalidate your feelings of dissatisfaction.

"I know how your mind works. You feel that because I've done so much for you, but you don't deserve feeling as you do right now. Don't look so surprised," he said with a laugh at her shocked expression when she finally deigned to look at him. "I've been doing a bit of thinking since that day you exploded. And with your mom being here, she provided a bit more insight."

"Big mouth," she muttered crossly, making him smile. Even so, she felt much better as she realized further explanation was not needed, seeing as her ability to put her emotions into words was a work in progress.

"Well, I appreciate her candidness and hope we'll continue to work on our issues with her help. But you don't need to rush into a decision right away. You still have years before the twins would ever be independent enough to not need you around. How about you take this time to figure out what you really want to do? Explore the options available. Make some bad decisions. Don't worry, you won't make me bankrupt anytime soon."

With tears streaming down her cheeks, her lips curved into a delighted smile and she slipped her hands into his. She didn't realize how having someone who knows her well could bring so much comfort and peace. The edges of discontent were smoothed down by his words, and they weren't poking at her heart anymore. But…

"I don't want to use your money," she said through her tears. Seeing him smile, she growled, making him chuckle. She shook his arm and implored. "Jason."

"Okay, how about we make it a loan?" he offered and before she could refuse, his intercom interrupted them.

"Jason, there's a group of antsy lawyers in front of me. I don't like antsy lawyers. Now stop coddling my daughter and deal with them. Dang, I think one of them jumped." Joan giggled.

Sharing a look, they laughed and Jason went to answer her mother. But not before she pressed a kiss onto his lips. And what was supposed to be a short thank you kiss became a long heated one. So much so that Joan had to interrupt them again.

~

Pushing Tanner on the swing, Jason felt his heart become heavier with every squeal of excitement his baby boy let out. His family was currently in their favorite park, spending the last few minutes filled with laughter. But he wasn't enjoying it. Instead, dread and guilt filled his entire body.

Despite the agreement he managed to finagle from April yesterday, their mood immediately plummeted once his lawyers entered. He hadn't been able to postpone Carrie's weekend. Even after his lawyers left his office that day, his investigators were still unable to find any dirt on his ex-lover. Not even a dust bunny. It made him mad enough to consider firing them all. And the psychiatrist who had made the diagnosis on Carrie had disappeared. No one knows where he was. Not even his wife.

Even April wasn't taking it so well herself. He watched her play with Daphne on the slides and her eyes were almost black with sadness and anger. She didn't say it, but he knew she blamed him. Hell, he blamed himself too. What's the use of having so much money and power if he wasn't able to keep the ones nearest and dearest to him safe?

And his children were not safe with Carrie. He didn't even know if she'll give them the minimum level of care which was why he was so grateful that the judge agreed to his stipulation: Carrie was only allowed to exercise her visitation rights if there was a competent, experienced nanny in her employ. Hopefully, that would be enough to keep them safe. And if it wasn't, at least he had another card up his sleeve.

Suddenly there was a surge of people moving toward the playground. Worried about their safety, Jason took a squirming Tanner out of his seat and joined April who already had Daphne in her arms. They let the twins down in front of them and watched the group of people warily.

Knowing who was responsible for the cameras and microphones in the area, his anger grew. *Why did everything have to be on camera with that woman?* Even a simple handover wasn't going to be easy. Jason wrapped an arm over April's shoulders and brought her close to his side as the viper approached them in five-inch heels, sinking every few steps into the sand.

As a model, a smile was ever present on her face but her eyes were shooting fire at him. She was accompanied by a young woman in an expensive revealing outfit who was sending alluring smiles in his direction. He wasn't interested, but April brought her arm around his waist in a proprietary manner, resting her head on his chest. He didn't know why exactly, but unexpected comfort filled him.

"Ah, my sweetums. Are you ready to spend your time with mommy dearest?" Carrie cooed loudly when she neared. The twins, merrily playing in the sand with each other, looked up, immediately crawled to April and practically climbed up her legs. April brought them into her arms and they clung fiercely to her. Unhappy with the twins' reaction, Carrie placed the blame on their appointed savior. "You poisoned them against me," she spat.

"What? No," April denied as she tried to calm the children down. Bouncing them in her arms, singing softly to them. They wouldn't let up. Instead, the more Carrie talked, the tighter their hold on her became. "Maybe they just don't like you."

"Maybe," Carrie drawled, surprising them. He hadn't thought she'd accept anyone not liking her gracefully. "But the court has ruled and you can't keep them. Not for the next two days. So, give them over. Chantal will take care of them."

With a snap of her fingers, the woman with her stepped forward and basically pried the kicking and screaming twins away. She placed Tanner into the arms of a man who they hadn't noticed was there (probably a bodyguard) while she took Daphne into her arms. April moved forward to try and take them back—they were screaming for her, arms outstretched in her direction—but Carrie got between them.

"Don't even think about it, bitch. And don't get too comfortable. I'll be in your place soon enough. First my babies and then Jason," she hissed.

"I don't think so," April shot back angrily, her hands fisted at her side.

Jason stepped slightly in front of April. "I believe I have a say on both issues. And, trust me, your hold on the twins will be gone as soon as I find something on you," he growled.

"Hmmm. And how well is that going for you?" she smirked before starting to head off, picture-perfect smile ready for the cameras.

"Wait. At least let us accompany you to your car," April requested, her eyes fixed on her bawling children, not caring that she was giving more ammunition to her opponent. Jason fell more in love with her then. Slipping his hand into hers, for both comfort and support, he waited for Carrie's answer. But her fiery eyes were arrowed on their joined hands.

"No," was her reply before she smirked triumphantly at them. "Let's face it. The chicks have to leave the nest soon enough. And I'll take such good care of them that they won't want you anymore." Wrapping his arms around a distraught April, he watched his children leave, screaming his name, and not being able to do anything about it.

Even so, they trailed after Carrie. Neither of them spoke nor did they take any heed of the cameras and Carrie's unobserved glares. April hid her face into his chest after the SUV left the car park, the twins' cries and screams still ringing in their ears.

"What are we going to do?" she sobbed.

~

Ignoring the cries, Carrie looked impassively as the hired nanny, Chantal, tried to soothe them. Everyone in the car knew that this was just an act, though. They were all acting out the role

169

appointed to them. Roles that weren't assigned by the great Carrie Carter. Try as she might, she didn't like the setup but even she herself had someone else to answer to.

Once the car had left the park and slid smoothly into traffic, she told the driver to drop her at the airport. Her rage grew when she saw his lips lifting into a smirk in the rearview mirror. Swearing to herself that she would teach him a lesson once this job was over, she glared at the two devils that had made her lose her figure and job for more than a year. If it hadn't been for them, she wouldn't have to do what she was doing now.

Accepting this job that heaped humiliation upon humiliation on her. She needed the money and she had no other choice left. If it were not so, she would never see the little pipsqueaks again. Fate was cruel and seeing them now, squirming in that fake nanny's arms and annoying the hell out of them, she wondered why she went through all the trouble of getting rid of them before, leaving Jason to take care of them. She realized they've become a hindrance in getting booked.

And now, she had to take care of them while their bloody father was enjoying himself. *Urgh! Well, if I couldn't get rid of them, I might as well let others join in on the misery then,* she thought.

The more, the merrier.

CHAPTER 28

The drive to the auction was silent. In fact, the entire trip had been silent. In the jet, all the way from Chicago to LA, they hadn't spoken a word. Jason had been absorbed in his work while April only sat in one corner, moping. In between that, she imagined all that could go wrong with Carrie. She just couldn't let go of the fact that she had just left her babies with that woman.

It wasn't during hair and makeup that she'd realized how distant and quiet Jason was which wouldn't have worried her on a normal day but, on top of the twins, it only concerned her even more.

April looked over at him. Sitting on the other end of the seat, the distance between them felt insurmountable. He was still hush as death. Ever since they'd left the park and handed their babies over to a monster over a day ago.

His eyes were shuttered, his emotions kept close only to himself. She didn't know how to reach him. She hadn't even been able to get a smile out of him. And he said she was the light of his world. Worry for both the twins and Jason were clouding her mind. She couldn't do anything for the twins but Jason, she could work on.

Gathering her courage, she slipped her hand into his, cuddling into his side, twining their arms together and laying her head on his shoulder. She nuzzled his shoulder, and started the ball rolling.

"Jason, what's wrong? You've been silent for so long that it's worrying me."

"Nothing," he said briskly. Trying hard not to let his detachment hurt her, she gave him a warm squeeze and carried on.

"Is this about work? The twins?"

"April, nothing's wrong," he snapped, intensifying her pain but also igniting her anger.

"Come on. You can tell me. I may not be able to help but they say a listening ear could ease the greatest of burdens," she chirped brightly. This was her final attempt to broach the distance. Not that she was giving up, but the fury in her chest just wouldn't allow her to be slapped down like that again.

"Nothing's wrong," Jason barked, pulling his arm out of her grasp. And that did it.

"Well, sorry for caring. I was only genuinely worried for you, what with our babies gone. I thought maybe you'd be more affected than I'd be seeing as you know the kind of damage that woman can inflict on them. But maybe I'm just misreading you. Maybe the bedrock of our relationship revolves around the twins. And with them absent, we don't have much of a bond anymore," she said, moving jerkily to the other end of the limo. She wasn't exactly aware of what she was spewing. All she knew was that she was furious.

"Baby, no. That's not it," Jason beseeched, remorse thick in his voice. But she wouldn't relent. He always forced her to be open about her feelings but now, he was acting aloof and closed off. Their relationship was already rocky. Communication must be the one area where they were equals. "Pull over," he called out and April felt the limo slowing to a stop. Looking out the window, she saw that they were parked in a near-empty parking lot just by a library. Once they were not moving, Jason tried to lift her onto his lap but her flailing arms discouraged him. Exasperation and a tinge of fear filled his eyes as he looked at her. In her ire, she refused to look at him, only stealing glances through her peripheral. Silence engulfed them for a few moments. Then, in a broken voice Jason said, "Don't tell me I've lost you too."

Shocked by both the desolation in his voice and his words, she turned to him. And another wave of shock crashed onto her when his ravaged face and teary eyes greeted her. Her anger left her in a heartbeat. Moving closer and taking his hand, she reassured him gently. "Of course not, baby. You'll always have me. But you're acting distant and I don't like it. It scares me."

"I'm sorry," he whispered as his hand curled into hers. Sensing that he needed a more affectionate contact, she wrapped her arms around him tightly. He responded by pulling her even closer to him so much so that she was half on and half off his lap. She stroked his shoulder and waited for him to continue.

"I'm sorry for being a bad boyfriend and a horrible father. I can't protect my babies. All the money in the world can't help keep them from harm. Why work so hard for it if I can't keep them safe? And now, I'm hurting you. I don't blame you if you hate me and want to leave me."

"I don't blame you," she finally said. It took a while to process his words but she found his uncertainty, perversely, all the more appealing. Maybe it was because he'd always been the strong, capable one. Or maybe she was just a sadist. Hoping to reassure him, she continued. "As what you've said, there's no proof of her unsuitability as a parent but I'm sure you'll find something, some way, somehow. You're stubborn and tenacious. That's how you got to where you are now."

"Y-you don't blame me?" he asked, hope shining in his eyes. Shaking her head, she laughed softly when he pressed a kiss onto her forehead.

"Of course not. We both know what a slippery eel that woman is. We just have to dig deeper and harder to get our babies out of their clutches," she stated, determination ringing in her voice. "How about we put this off for now and enjoy a night out with your cousins? We don't have to forget about them but we don't have to bang our heads against a brick wall either. Who knows? Maybe we'll find another avenue to explore during the auction."

Wiping away the lone tear that escaped, April remained in that position for the rest of the ride. They still didn't have a plan and they couldn't see the light at the end to the tunnel. But she felt they'd passed a hurdle in their relationship. A huge one.

~

Jason looked around the crowded room, anxiously looking for his girlfriend. He smiled when he spotted her laughing with Sharon. He felt slightly embarrassed for breaking down in front of her, but he knew it had strengthened their bond. There was an air about her that told him she had more confidence in him. In them. And that brought an inner peace in him about her, and his children—everything in his life. It made him feel everything was going to be alright.

"Hey, how are you?" Cameron said as he stepped beside him. Everyone in the family knew he hadn't been able to prevent Carrie from exercising her right and it hurt his pride so much. He'd always been the one who had his life together and for it to fall apart in the public eye, it felt like he failed.

But his family had been nothing but supportive, so he was able to let his discomfort and anger go. Grimacing, he just shook his head and drained the wine. Cameron clapped his back in support and changed the topic.

"Have you seen any of the people being auctioned later on?"

Sending him a raised eyebrow, Jason's eyes moved from his cousin to his girlfriend and back. "Do I really want anyone participating in this when I already have April? Everybody else pales in comparison," he espoused passionately, making Cameron laugh. Realizing how pompous he sounded, he joined his cousin. "I'm sorry. Just the thought of looking feels like cheating. And our relationship's still too new to survive that accusation."

"I don't know. You guys have gone through more than what Sharon and I went through in the same period. If push comes to shove, I think you guys can survive through anything," Cameron said. Feeling bashful in the face of such confidence, Jason masked it by shoving his cousin's shoulder playfully.

"You're waxing poetics and your grammar is the most proper I've heard in a while. Maybe there *is* some benefit to your punishment," he teased. His cousin shushed him while looking around.

"Don't say that. That'll only encourage Sharon to give more difficult and lengthier books," he whined.

"Don't you want that?" Jason egged on then excused himself when a close friend from across the room suddenly signaled for his attention. Curiosity piqued when his friend entered a deserted hallway and then an alcove. He made sure no one was paying attention to him before subtly entering behind his friend.

"Don't tell anyone I told you this," his friend began softly the moment they knew no one was following. Still clueless, he nodded nonetheless. "I've been hearing some whispers that you're planning to buy over the tech company."

Jason didn't have to clarify. There's only one company he was interested in at this point of time and the plan was still in the preliminary stages. Only the executives were privy to the information. The said company didn't even know he was interested in them. *How did anyone get wind of it?*

Nodding in the face of his stupefaction, his friend slipped out. Jason barely noticed him disappearing. This was an indication of a serious breach. He could barely wrap his head around it. *How was he going to do any work if he couldn't trust anyone in his company?* He had to find the mole. Fast. Because if he trusted the wrong person, it would be a costly mistake. Very costly.

CHAPTER 29

April was enjoying her time with Sharon at the event. It was surprising because the last time they'd spent time together, April barely fought the urge to strangle the woman. But, as she found out, without any plans or agenda, Sharon reverted to how she was when they'd first met. It was refreshing. Amelia wasn't able to join them then because she'd promised to help Harry with the wardrobe, makeup, and hair of those being auctioned.

April found her first event more bearable than she'd expected. The food was delicious, despite being in bite-sized pieces. She had to refrain from chasing after every server she saw. It was that good. The music being played was a mix of classic and indie, and the eclectic mix was surprisingly enjoyable to the ears.

However, she could have done without everything else. Every time Sharon brought her around the room and introduced her to people, some who could possibly be beneficial contacts to Jason. April was met with cold stares and a flurry of whispered conversations once she left. It was infuriating and disgusting.

These were the people who were in charge of the Fortune 500 companies—people who were in charge of innovation and creativity that would power their country and future. Preposterous. Surely not. Who would've thought they'd give so much credence to hearsay? And blatantly false ones at that.

Even so, there was a silver lining—she didn't care about their opinions. It gave her a sense of peace to realize that. She wasn't fretting over making a great impression. A good impression was all she could muster, and, surprisingly, she was fine with that. She was still representing Jason, so she didn't allow it to get to her head. And she was having a good time. A fun time in fact.

It was just as Jason had ordered in the car. That and "forget about all the cameras." She believed they went past the cameras in record time. He'd barely paused to greet Cameron and Sharon. Just a bro hug between him and Cameron while she scarcely had the opportunity to get her arm around Sharon. It felt good to give the press a proverbial middle finger by barely acknowledging them.

Sighing contentedly, she took a sip of her wine, scanned the room and almost spat it out when she spied an elegantly-clad figure that looked like someone who shouldn't be there. Blinking rapidly, hoping it wasn't true and that her mind was just conjuring *her*, her heart almost escaped her chest when her eyes confirmed what her heart wanted to deny.

What was she doing in Los Angeles? And, most importantly, who was taking care of her babies? Surely not her poor excuse of a nanny. April had suspicions on that woman's credentials. And while she may not be the person to spit on inexperience, the way that girl handled her babies proved her lack of interest in her job.

Her eyes followed Carrie as she greeted people warmly and the greeting returned with the same degree of welcome, some of whom had been especially cold to April. Apparently, the viper wasn't just feeding the press falsities. Her spread of influence was wider than she'd expected.

She placed her glass down on the tray of one of the roving servers and moved to follow her, stopping short when her target entered an alcove. Using a plant and pillar as cover, she waited for her next move.

"What are you doing?"

Jumping slightly, April turned to the man and scowled, shushing him at the same time. Harry's brows furrowed over his light blue eyes and he repeated his question softly this time.

Deciding he wouldn't be leaving her alone anytime soon, her eyes moved to Carrie and back. She did it three more times, fairly giving herself a headache, but he was still clueless. Only his brows moved. It furrowed deeper. Sighing, she pulled his face to where Carrie was. Finally, he understood.

"What the heck is she doing here?" he exclaimed, only quieting down when she smacked his arm. Even while doing so, she was faintly surprised at how comfortable she was being around Harry. Their first meeting had been horrible but the ice between them had thawed during their second interaction. Turning worried eyes on her, he moved to assure her he hadn't invited that vulture, but she just shook her head. She trusted him.

"That's what I want to know too," she said as the both of them watched her like a hawk. Their prey was having a great time conversing with an influential fashion mogul. Resentment mixed with her worry. Why did she get to have a wonderful time with those people who had done their best to make April almost regret their trip to LA? Did she have an ulterior motive for being here? Like further blacken April's name? More importantly, who was taking care of her babies?

It was getting boring watching her talk and flit around different groups. And April's back was hurting from stooping over. Finally, deciding not to waste any more of her time on that witch, she resolved to tell Harry to let it go when their target received an unwanted phone call. Carrie stomped out with a thunderous scowl on her face.

Without discussing, they discreetly followed her. And by "discreet" they acted as if they were talking or Harry was pointing out notable guests to her. Once they reached a deserted hallway,

179

they dropped all pretense and openly followed her but still at a safe distance so as to make sure Carrie remained unaware of their presence.

Again, it looked like a dead end. The viper was just traversing hall after hall with no apparent end in sight. Hoping they would garner some leverage from snooping, April persevered. Harry had to come along for her safety. He protested often but she always shushed him.

"What the hell are you doing here?" a male voice suddenly said when their enemy stopped in front of an open door. From the sound of it, the door most probably led outside.

"I don't know what you're talking about. I'm just here to network. You know how important that is for me to get a job," Carrie replied insolently, looking at her nails. She grimaced when she noticed a chip. "And why did I have to meet you here? My manicure is now ruined."

"Are you sure it's just to network? Or is it to keep an eye on your baby daddy?" he mocked. April frowned. That voice sounded very familiar. She'd already placed him in the office along the empty hallway when she'd gone to think. But he really did remind her of someone. She just couldn't put a finger on it.

"What does it matter if I do? I don't want to sit at the penthouse, listening to his brats cry while he's having fun with that troll."

Brats? Did she even want her babies? And they were crying? That bitch wasn't doing anything to comfort them? How dare she! Anger flaring up, April almost came out of their hiding spot to confront her but Harry held her back with one hand around her shoulder and a phone in the other. *Wait, why was his phone out?*

He was recording the entire exchange! Delight replacing anger, she berated herself for not thinking about that. What kind of 21st century woman was she?

"That was not part of the plan," the man said, fury thrumming through his voice. April shifted, trying to get a glimpse of the man but all she saw was an alleyway with some lights shining in it. Frustration mounted in him as he snapped, "You're supposed to show what a loving mother you are. And you can't do that miles away from those brats. If someone takes a photo of you here during your first weekend with them, no judge will ever believe you ever again."

"Alright, alright. I'll leave. And no, no photo was taken. Harry enforced a strict no-photograph policy during his events. So, we're safe," she sneered at the still hidden man, stepping out of the door. Putting her nose up, she sashayed past the man, moving under a light.

"What did I even see in that bitch?" the man sighed as he followed her. And, although they couldn't see his face, at least they now knew he had blond hair.

~

"Hey, where've you been?" Jason asked as April slipped into the seat beside him. She pressed a kiss on his lips and sent him a bubbly smile. Startled by her unexpected exuberance, but welcoming it with a warm smile, he laced their hands together. "That's unexpected."

"Well, I may or may not have found something against Carrie," she whispered with a giggle. Still not understanding, he sent a puzzled smile her way. April could barely able to contain her excitement. She squeezed his hand and was about to answer when the emcee announced the auction was about to start. "I'll tell you later."

"You guys have so done it," Sharon suddenly stated from across the table. They both just looked at her. Jason understood what she meant but this topic wasn't usually brought up at such functions. So, he was slightly lost on how to respond. "I mean, you guys are so touchy-feely. And April initiated the kiss. You must've crossed some boundary that has made her more comfortable around you."

"And why are you talking about this now?" April asked with furrowed brows, her eyes darting around. Clearly, she was as uncomfortable with the topic at hand as he.

"Because you kissed." At April's disbelieving stare, she huffed. "It just came out, alright? I was in in a state of shock. Humor me."

"Fine," April sighed, rolling her eyes. Jason was, again, glad that April had found some female companions. He knew she lacked friends, and taking care of the twins wasn't exactly helpful in the friend-making department. So, he saw Sharon and Amelia as a start. Hopefully, she will widen her circle of friends soon. So long as it's not with those who have working penises.

"So, what did him in? Was it the lingerie?" Sharon teased, attempting to be circumspect. Attempting being the key word.

"Babe," Cameron reprimanded with a laugh. Her response was a slight shrug.

"Maybe. We should definitely go lingerie shopping again," April said with a cheeky smile and laughed when Jason called her name in a scandalous manner. She had clearly been influenced by his cousin-in-law. "What? Don't tell me you don't want me to."

"Wh-yes but I thought you don't like to talk about this *in public*," he whispered, flabbergasted. With a soft smile, she just pressed a kiss on his cheek. Jason was distracted by the kiss that he was unprepared for her next words.

"I don't but teasing you is so much more fun. Plus, I'm wearing the red one right now," she whispered softly. Soft enough that only he would hear. His little guy down south immediately stood to attention.

"I'm not going to survive this night," he groaned, pulling her closer to his side. Laughing at his misery, she rested her head on his chest.

"Sorry. I was held up at the back of the stage. One of the people being auctioned off threw herself at me," Harry said as he sat down, along with Amelia and Scott.

"Yeah. It was so funny," Amelia said with a snort followed by a laugh. To Sharon, who was looking all curious, she said, "I'll tell you later."

"And I'll tell you what *I* found out later," Sharon returned excitedly and became silent when Harry shushed them.

Jason studied his cousin curiously. He looked quite nervous. His eyes continually darted to the stage then looked away when someone was introduced. Jason hadn't studied any of those being auctioned because he wasn't going to bid on anyone. But, from his cousin's actions, he may have to make an exception.

Finally, the last girl to be auctioned came up. She was blonde, petite, and slim. He was too far away to determine her eye color but Jason believed it was a shade of green. Clad in a soft pink sleeveless gown, she looked quite presentable—pretty even—and very reluctant to be there. Her hands came together before her and her head was slightly bowed; her body practically thrummed with tension. She barely made any eye contact, but when she did, the only eye contact she made caused her to blush redder than a tomato.

The recipient of the eye contact was no other than Harry.

Jason found it intriguing that Harry was intensely focused on this one individual. He hardly paid attention, much less close attention, to the previous women. But when it came to this woman, however, he appeared to be anxious, scanning the room as if waiting for something.

There was a moment of silence after the introduction was done. The emcee was waiting for someone to offer a bid. Jason saw her share a look with the closed-off auctioned person and concluded they were friends. He suspected that she had been probably roped into doing this by her friend, the emcee.

From his peripheral vision, Jason saw Harry's hands curl on his lap. His dark eyes were trained on the poor woman on stage. People were starting to talk—some women even snickered—at the lack of response. April was shooting glares at them, most likely wanting to reprimand them for their tactlessness.

Suddenly it hit Jason. Harry couldn't or even start a bid. He's her employer and it wouldn't be appropriate. Jason raised his hand.

"Ten thousand."

His voice seemed to travel everywhere in the silent room. Then, it appeared like everyone turned to look at him. But he wasn't affected. He only cared about the woman in his arms and her opinion. And from her smile, he knew she approved.

"T-ten thousand from Mr. Halloway," the emcee said, recovering well from her shock. The now-sold girl sent him a faint smile, full of gratefulness. He just returned her smile and kissed the back of April's hand that was being laced with his. "Any other bidders? Ten thousand going once, going twice. Going thrice. And Mr. Halloway gets Elena Hamilton for a full twenty-four hours. Now, Missy will now join your table, Mr. Halloway. We'll be starting on the men now. So, ladies, get ready your checkbooks." With the speed in which the emcee closed that bid, Jason surmised that she wanted her friend to be out of the limelight as soon as possible.

As Missy made her way to their table, Jason glanced over at his cousin and knew he'd made the right choice.

~

After the auction, while everyone was in a hurry to leave—probably to go to another party or event—Jason and Harry were able to find a quiet spot to take a breather. Enjoying the silence but ever watchful of April, Jason was unprepared for Harry's question.

"So, what's your plan for Elena?" Harry asked oh-so-casually.

"Oh, we talked about having a threesome when you were making your speech. Maybe include Cam and Sharon, once she's given birth. It'd be fun," Jason answered with a barely suppressed smile at Harry's thunderous look. He enjoyed pulling his leg.

"This wasn't part of the deal!" he fairly shouted, garnering some attention from the remaining people.

"Well, she consents to our plan. So, I don't see how it's wrong," Jason further egged him on. Seeing his face turning red, almost to the point of explosion, Jason burst into laughter, leaning onto the wall for support. Harry then realized he was just being teased. He grumbled and shoved Jason's shoulder, almost toppling him. "You should've seen your face."

"Hahaha, very funny."

"To answer your question, April and I suggested that she could come and babysit for us one of these days. After everything is settled," Jason revealed between laughter. "Anyway, I made that bid for you."

"Me? What are you talking about?" Harry looked guileless but his suddenly crossed arms told a different story.

"Oh yeah, her blush. *Your* tension. It's clear you guys are attracted to each other. *This* will give you guys time to get to know each other. Maybe find out if she wants you for your money—"

"She doesn't know who I am. She's pretty much a homebody and doesn't read magazines. We met at the changing room and it just knocked me over...how much I want her," Harry hesitantly revealed. His hands were busy, moving from his blazer pockets to his trouser pockets then his belt loop, before he folded his arms again. Jason had known him for years and this was a clear sign of nerves and uncertainty. Harry? Uncertain of a woman's response to him? That was a first.

Jason raised his brow. Such instantaneous attraction was rare, and Harry had never looked so vulnerable before. Not for the past decade or so. If this woman was able to evoke such a reaction, then Jason didn't feel so bad for meddling.

"This will be an excellent time then. April and I have to go. Our plane is leaving tonight so we can get enough rest to deal with our babies tomorrow." With a man hug, he moved to leave and collect April but Harry latched on to his arm.

"Where's Elena then? Is she going with you?"

"I sent her to your room. Have fun getting to know each other." He bade and tore his arms out of his grasp. With a jaunty wave and smile, he left his cousin staring after him, dumbfounded while Jason had a new disturbing realization.

Having a hand in other people's lives was fun.

CHAPTER 30

April tried to slap whoever was trying to shake her awake.

"Five more minutes," she mumbled as she turned over. Or tried to. Consciousness slowly returning to her, her neck started to shoot shards of pain as her body was inclined in an uncomfortable angle. Brows drawing together, she slowly opened her eyes and slapped away the hand that was shaking her.

She found herself looking at Jason, and she remembered where they were. And, stupidly, only one thought filled her mind. Be it commercial or private, airplane seats were forever uncomfortable especially for someone of her height. Shaking her head, both to clear the cobwebs of sleep and drive that irrelevant thought away, she stretched her arms up and looked sleepily up at Jason.

"Hey, are we almost there?" she asked around a yawn. He smiled and shook his head, making her frown. "Then why did you wake me up?"

"Because you look so cramped and in pain. Why don't you sleep in the bedroom?" he asked as he pulled her up. Her muscles still not fully awake, she let him direct her to the said room and instantly awoke.

The room was big. And spacious. And big. Did she mention 'big'? It was so big that it could fit five of the king-sized bed that was currently occupying the center of the room. It had bare essentials: just a drawer, a door that probably leads to the bathroom and a dresser. Still, her eyes were focused on the bed. The big, soft, bouncy bed.

"I'll let you go back to sleep then," Jason said with a chuckle, turning to leave. But April grabbed his hand. She could see his laptop still open and a stack of papers and files occupying the table. She also saw the dark circles forming under his eyes and his complexion looking paler than usual. Signs of exhaustion for him.

"How much longer is the flight?" she asked as she tugged him to the bed. It was a confirmation of his tiredness that he allowed her to do so.

"Another two and a half to three hours," he replied. When she tried to get him on the bed, however, he resisted.

"Baby, I can't rest just yet. I still have to find whoever is leaking information and the babies. I've sent the video to some lawyers and I'm waiting to hear back from them."

"And they can still contact you later. You'd be no good to us if you become sick again; you're well on your way there now. I don't think the twins can cope with you being sick now especially after being with Carrie for the weekend. They'll need you to be at your best, to play with them, to still add a sense of normalcy in their lives." Jason looked away and thought about it, struggling to choose between what he wanted and what he needed to do.

"Please. Rest," she pleaded, staring deeply into his eyes, relating her worry. Finally, he sighed.

"Fine. Let me just keep everything in the safe first," he said, relenting. Barely able to stop celebrating, she just smiled and allowed him to leave.

"Ten minutes," she called as she made herself more comfortable. Cursing herself for deciding to wear jeans on the flight, she struggled to get the apparel off of her unresponsive legs. Sighing in frustration, she waddled to a nearby chair and finally managed to get the offensive piece of clothing off.

"What are you wearing?" Jason said, his voice caught in his throat, from the doorway. Jumping slightly, April tried to cover her legs with her jeans. She'd thought he'd take longer but maybe she's the one who did.

"Um, why don't you go to the bed and I'll join you—"

"Are you wearing the purple set?" he cut in, shutting the door. She thought he might have locked it but her eyes were trained on his tense face. His eyes, a bright green, were fairly burning as they raked over her body. "My favorite one?"

"D-don't you like the red one?" she asked from her suddenly dry throat. He flashed her a rakish grin.

"Babe, you in lingerie is my favorite one," he whispered, stopping in front of her. April tried to keep her eyes on his face but the part of him straining his pants kept calling her. Her hands itched to wrap around it.

Suddenly, Jason tugged her out of her seat, making her lose her balance, stumble, and fall onto his laps. Still surprised, April had the presence of mind to place her arms onto his shoulders.

"Tell the truth. You wore that to join the mile high club," he teased. She felt her face flush but sent him a coy smile.

"Maybe."

"Why, miss? Are you out to seduce innocent, old me?" She had to laugh at that.

"Innocent? You? Puh-lease. I saw the way that air stewardess was looking at you. You're a veteran of the club, mister," she mock-scolded. He furrowed his brows.

"I'm sorry but I seem to have lost my memories. One look into your gorgeous eyes and every other woman fled from my mind," he said in an English accent. It was a fairly good one too.

"That's so cheesy," she said, giggling.

"Too much cheese or not, I don't think I can last much longer without seeing you in nothing but that purple creation."

"You won't last much longer than three seconds before getting it off me," she snorted but willingly took off her shirt.

And she was right. He only lasted two.

~

"What do you mean you won't let me leave with them unless Jason is here? The court has agreed to let me fetch them on his behalf," April growled. She was reaching the end of her patience with this woman. Having accommodated every ridiculous change made by that viper just so April could get her babies back, this was the last straw.

Ignoring her sneer, April pulled out her phone and called Jason. She had been reluctant to call him, knowing he was busy finding the leak and chasing his lawyers and judge to repeal Carrie's visitation rights. But this was just getting out of hand. Hoping he was able to answer, April kept the woman in her sights.

"I can't talk right now," Jason barked the moment he picked up her call.

"I know but this is important," April appealed and suddenly there was a change in his demeanor.

"Oh, sorry, sweetheart. I'll always have time for you. Just let me clear the room," he said apologetically. Smiling slightly when she heard him dismiss his lawyers, April studied the apartment.

It was big but not as big as Jason's. The design was modern, minimalist—empty tables; hard, uncomfortable pieces of furniture; and abstract paintings. It made April feel like a bull in a china shop. She feared messing it up. And it was definitely not an appropriate place for the twins.

"Alright. So, what's up? The twins giving you hell?" he asked jokingly.

"No. I haven't seen the twins. Carrie has changed the time and location. I'm now at her apartment and she's refusing to let me collect them without you," April complained, upset. Carrie remained in her seat, lounging in it as if she had no care in the world, a slight smirk plastered on her face.

"What? Why?"

"I don't know. I don't care. I just want to get the twins and get out. So, get your ass here pronto," she ordered fiercely. From his laugh, she knew he found it amusing but also knew she could count on him. He'd be here soon and this whole nightmare would be over.

Hanging up, April scowled at Carrie. She wished she could just ignore her and grab her children but she didn't want that witch to have another thing to whisper to the public and complain to the judge. So, in order to protect herself as well as to have someone corroborate her, she brought two of her bodyguards along to act as witnesses on top of their assigned jobs in case the witch becomes deranged.

"Don't be disappointed, honey. Jason will never put off work for anybody, let alone a woman," Carrie said in a fake sympathetic voice. Furrowing her brows, April just looked at her, lost. She knew Jason cared about his work but he wouldn't leave her hanging with this whore. Especially since she's holding their children captive. Carrie continued, unaware of her confusion, "We can have some bonding time while we wait. I'm sure he'll be here in an hour or two."

"What are you talking about? He'll be here in twenty minutes. Maybe less if he speeds and ignores the lights." At that, Carrie's face changed. It became harder and her eyes lit up with a rage that made April take a step back. Not wanting to be in her company any longer than she had to, April decided to look for her babies. "I'll just—babies—yeah."

Taking her silence as consent, April went to search for her twins. It didn't take long because, despite its size, the apartment didn't have a lot of room. She paused at the doorway of the room

191

where her babies were. The room looked as stark as the rest of the apartment. Despite the various paraphernalia that were needed to take care of them, the room itself was lifeless. The walls were bare of color and decorations. She didn't expect Carrie to decorate the room herself but some indication that she was trying would help corroborate her sudden interest in the twins. It was the least thing she could do to show interest in the twins. It's not that April wanted her to have a stronger hold on them but it was like she didn't even want them. And, from what she'd heard last night, April had a strong inkling that she really didn't like them.

After taking some pictures of the lifeless room—in case it was needed to show her absolute disinterest and charade—April excitedly approached the cot and smiled when she finally set eyes on her babies after fifty hours without them. Both were asleep in the same cot, arms and legs tangled together. In the back of her mind, she was surprised by this because, usually, they demanded their own space. But her heart was just happy to see them.

"Hey, babies," she whispered as she ran her hand down their body, face, hair—basically anywhere she could touch. Smoothing Daphne's hair away from her face—the long hair that was starting to irritate the little baby—April found a slight discoloration on the skin just before her hairline. There was a slight bump too.

Frowning, April untangled them and turned Daphne to her back. She barely made a sound. If April hadn't seen her chest move, she'd be worried, but then an injury on her baby's head caught her eye and alarmed her. She lifted up Daphne's shirt and was horrified to see bruises littered all over her torso, like she had been pinched. Turning her to her front, April's heart broke, and tears welled in her eyes, when her suspicion was confirmed and she saw more bruises. *Who would do such a thing?*

She inspected Tanner as well and tears began streaming down her face when she saw the same thing on him. *How had this happened? Why?* They had only been in the witch's hands for barely more than two days. How could she have let this happen? That witch had them for more than six months and there had been no show of abuse. This was rather alarming. Maybe it's her nanny? Even so, surely she wouldn't have allowed it to continue. The bruises were a mixture of old and newer ones, probably done a few hours ago.

When she heard someone pounding on the door, April dried her tears and started packing all their stuff that she'd sent to that monster as a sign of goodwill. Now she wished she'd fought harder to keep them from her grasp. Hearing Jason shouting, April hurried out and was barely surprised when she saw Carrie, in just her underwear set, clinging to Jason.

"Jase, we have to go," were her only words. Jason, seeing how distraught she was, managed to tear himself away and followed her. When he tried to talk to her, she just said, "We'll talk in the car."

Sending her a worried look, he shouldered the bag and took Tanner. He shot a warning glare to Carrie, before they left that house of horrors. And, if April had a say, they were never coming back.

Once they were all strapped in the car and their bodyguards in their own, Jason started for home but stopped when April told him woodenly, "Bring us to the nearest clinic."

CHAPTER 31

Jason was shocked and horrified. *Why would anyone hurt his children like this? Why?* He'd been surprised when April demanded they go to a doctor but agreed to it, thinking she needed to assure herself that the twins were alright. Now, he was glad she'd done that. They were hammering another nail into Carrie's coffin.

But that was the businessman in him talking. The father in him was shocked and angry. Rage flamed in him and he wanted to knock down the bitch's door and do the same thing she'd done to his children. Her gender will not save her from his fury.

They were currently waiting for the doctor as he carried out his examinations. They were able to see him, even though he was about to close the clinic, only because April had shown the bruises. His children had barely made a sound, just some whimpers, while he prodded their bruises. And it was starting to worry him and April. Her hand was squeezing his hard. After a few more minutes, the doctor talked to them at his desk. They decided to let the twins rest on the bed of the doctor's office. It was less disruptive that way.

"So? What do you make of the bruises?" April asked worriedly.

"From the redness and blackness of some of it, I'd say they happened one to two days ago. And from the quantity, I have some suspicions that it's abuse. I hope the both of you know I'll have to report this to Child Protective Services," the doctor, a jolly-looking middle-aged man, told them, looking at them with suspicious eyes.

"We just took them from their mother. She and I are not together so only she has visitation rights. It's been barely an hour since we left her house," Jason explained through gritted teeth. *Abuse?* He hadn't expected Carrie to stoop that far. She'd had them for six months prior. Why would she start abusing them now? Did she think they won't notice?

The doctor frowned. "I still have to report this. They'll investigate your claims and work from there." April nodded her understanding. She looked so broken. Jason wrapped his arm around her and pulled her closer. Thinking that was all, they were surprised by the doctor's next query. "May I know if your children are heavy sleepers? Just out of curiosity."

Jason had a bad feeling.

"Not really. I can barely put them down for a nap for half an hour, never mind an hour. They'll just play in their cot when they think I'm not there," she related with a teary smile. "May I know why you're asking?"

"I don't want to alarm you just yet but I'm asking permission to take a blood sample from them," the doctor said. His vagueness was fanning Jason's anger. The doctor, realizing how volatile Jason was, rushed to reassure them in a lame attempt of explaining the matter. "I truly don't want to conclude anything. Maybe they're just extremely tired. Or don't want to wake up—"

"Just tell me, damn it!" Jason roared, slamming his fist on the table. The doctor jumped in his seat while April wrapped an arm around him, hoping to calm him down. What alarmed him, and also April, was the fact the twins didn't react. They were still asleep, oblivious to the world.

"I'm sorry, Mr. Halloway. But I can't tell you of my speculations right now. It'll only raise unnecessary anxiety."

"Can you please just tell us?" April pleaded, tears running down her cheek. Jason didn't look up. His shoulders were slumped, his head bowed. What could be worse than what they'd already found out? "Please? It's killing us."

"I suspect they've ingested alcohol."

~

Jason was still shell shocked. After the doctor's pronouncement, he and April didn't waste any time. Jason had called in a favor from an acquaintance to expedite the blood test. Then, because they wanted to be safe rather than sorry, they headed to the nearest hospital in case any treatment was needed.

Along the way, his contact had confirmed the doctor's suspicions. There was enough alcohol in them that could possibly kill them. Jason told him to send his results to the hospital they were going. Luckily, the hospital was one where he was a benefactor of. They were quick to take their babies in and immediately started on the necessary treatments. One of which was to pump their stomach of any alcohol left.

It was heartbreaking to see a plastic tube being inserted into their mouth and down their throat. They were still so small and fragile to undergo such a harsh procedure. He struggled to think how they were going to heal after this.

Having been kicked out of the room after he had caused a fuss about the tube, Jason and April sat in the hard, uncomfortable chairs and waited for the doctor. For their babies.

"I blame myself," April suddenly said from where her head rested on his shoulder. "I should have fought harder."

"Hey, I'm supposed to say that," he croaked, his throat dry. He was so devastated and exhausted that he had no moisture left in his body. "And it's not your fault, baby. It's mine. I should have never left them alone with her. I should've fought harder. Be sneakier. Hell, I should've asked for another judge. Anything to keep them safe. But it's too late now."

"I suppose we're both at fault for underestimating her. I would never have thought she'd hurt them. Maybe neglect them but this? This is worse," she said with a sob. Pulling her onto his lap, Jason let her cry. For both of them. He couldn't allow this release now. He needed the drive, the anger to sustain him or else he'd become a complete mess.

"Jason! April! Oh my god, we got here as soon as we could," Joan said as she and Mrs. Salvador came to a stop beside them. "I've cancelled and shifted all of your appointments and meetings for the next week or so. And I've also notified the others. They'll come as soon as they can. How are they?"

"They're still in there, having their stomachs pumped," April said, still sobbing into his shoulder. He wrapped his arms around her, head pressed on her shoulder, letting her presence soothe him slightly.

Feeling a hand on his other shoulder, Jason looked up. His eyes, heavy with tears, connected with the eyes of the second maternal figure in his life. Her eyes reflected his worry but also showed concern for him.

"You can't control everyone, Jason. There's only so much you could have done. Just learn from this and not make the same mistake," Mrs. Salvador advised softly, rubbing his shoulder in a comforting manner. He wanted to take her advice but his children were in there because of him. How could any parent ever forgive themselves?

~

They were all currently in the twins' room. They had to stay in the hospital for the next day or two for observation. And they've yet to wake up. Needless to say, everyone was in a somber mood.

Cameron and Sharon arrived soon after, with Cameron informing him of the reporters outside. Apparently, someone—most probably a hospital staff—had let it slip that the twins were brought in under suspicions of abuse. Jason told his team to release a statement that would hopefully keep the wolves at bay while they sorted things out. He had already received a call from the Child Protective Services despite the late hour. He'd answered truthfully. For once, he thanked the media because they had documented his every step from the moment he'd passed the twins to Carrie to his return from LA. His alibi was tight and so was April's.

They were just waiting for his children to wake up. The doctors had told him they'd pumped all of the remaining alcohol from their bodies and were going to observe them for further compilations. The alcohol that had already been metabolized would dissipate and they'd wake up soon within the next twelve hours. Which was a shit time frame, in Jason's opinion.

"Go and get some food, the both of you," Joan ordered. Cameron and Sharon had left for their hotel. They couldn't stay long as Sharon was not feeling well. He didn't begrudge them. Sharon's pregnancy should be their priority and not his family problem. A problem he had brought on upon himself.

"I'm not hungry, Mom," April said, her eyes never leaving the cots the twins were in. Jason didn't have any appetite either but was aware that they hadn't eaten since lunch. If they wanted to take care of the twins, they had to take care of themselves first.

"Come on, baby. We have to eat something. We need to keep our strength up in order to take care of them," he said softly, slipping his hand into hers.

She rejected his hold. Turning to him, fury bright in her eyes, her fisted hands slammed into his chest. "I don't want to do anything but wait. Why would you think I can do anything else when my babies are lying there so pale and sick? I can't and I

198

won't," she said through gritted teeth before turning back to the cots.

Jason wasn't surprised by her outburst. She'd slowly retreated to herself as time ticked by, refusing to do anything other than look at them. It broke another part of him, a part in which April had a hold of. Seeing his loved ones suffer made him wish he could do anything to change it, but he was only human. Waiting was his only option too.

But he couldn't let her waste away when he could do something about it.

"You have to eat. You won't be of much help to them if you're too weak to hold them," he told her, a hint of steel in his voice that cut through her hurt and anger. He didn't want to hurt her anymore, but some things just needed to be done. "Look, I'm not saying we go out and eat. I'll just order in and we'll eat here. You can still look after them but get some sustenance as well."

Her eyes glazed with tears, she nodded and tentatively slid her hand into his. He recognized an apology when he saw one and drew her into his arms.

"I'm not angry, sweetheart. This has been an arduous night for all of us. I just don't want you to keep everything to yourself," he said into her hair.

"I'm sorry for being a bitch," she said, her voice muffled into his shoulder. He laughed, his mouth slightly wet with tears of his own. Letting her go, he took out his phone to place the order when a text message caught his eye. It was from his head of IT. They had traced the leak. And he couldn't believe who it was.

Joan was the leak?

CHAPTER 32

He could not believe his eyes. Jason read the text again. It couldn't be. Joan was a huge help around the office. She was similar to Mrs. Salvador, except she exercised her competence around the office. Things had become more efficient and work satisfaction had increased which was mind-boggling to him. She'd done so much. *Why would she release sensitive corporate information?*

Wanting to get to the bottom of this but not wanting to worry April, Jason waited outside for Joan. She was surprised to see him, having just returned from a smoke break. He couldn't detect any nervousness, like she was hiding something. All he could see was worry and anxiety for those she'd considered as her own grandchildren.

"Have they woken up?" she asked, eyes bright with hope. Jason wanted to reassure her but he needed to get this done and over with.

"Why did you release company information?" he asked bluntly. He saw no other way to bring it up. It could be that his exhaustion was clouding his diplomatic skills. Joan looked taken aback and anger replaced her hope.

"What are you talking about? You think just because I'm poor I'll do something so shady and deplorable? Let me tell you, Mr. Billionaire, I still have my dignity and I will never do something like that," she said heatedly. Jason sighed, wanting to massage the headache that was forming.

"I know. I'm sorry but with everything that's been going on, I'm just not thinking clearly. I know you won't do it. I know that. But the IT department found that the information had been sent to a competitor email and it came from your computer," he told her, hoping his honesty would appease her.

How wrong he was.

"And you immediately accuse me? What kind of person are you? Don't you know it's 'innocent until proven guilty'? Or something along that line? To think I live with you and my daughter's dating you," she mumbled angrily. Jason didn't know what else to do. He didn't want to anger her further, but he needed to resolve this issue.

"Mom, what's going on? Why are you so angry?" April asked from the doorway. Jason's heart sank. He was going to get it now.

"Can you believe this man is accusing me of being the leak? Can you? After all that's happened, you'd think he'd know me better," she told April. April just sent him a look and he told her everything.

"Mom, did you change the password?" April asked once he was done. Password? His mind was too tired to grasp her meaning. "The Windows password. I know everything had been a rush and you have yet to get your own ID but you aren't using the same password under Janice's ID, right?"

"You can change the password?" Joan asked in a small voice. Jason just sighed. He couldn't believe he didn't think of that. They both knew that they'd erred: Jason with his lack of tact and Joan with her internal angst. Now to mend their bond.

"I should've told you about it. It's an unforgivable oversight," April said with a grimace.

"No. It's not your fault. It's mine for letting my exhaustion get the better of me. I hope you'll accept my apology," Jason said to Joan with a tired smile. Her small smile indicated her acceptance.

"And I'm sorry for just attacking you with my insecurity. It's still a shift from working in diners to helping you run a corporation. And I guess the whispers from those stupid bitches got to me," Joan revealed. He wanted to pursue that revelation but April interrupted.

"So, did you notice anything strange in the office? Aside from the hyenas just waiting to see you fumble."

Joan's brows furrowed in concentration. Jason hoped she'd recall something because he didn't want to be back at square one again. There was no camera right outside his office.

"Well, I do remember this guard—a cute one—making a lot of rounds in the office. I didn't even make anything about it. I only thought his girlfriend was probably working on that floor. But, there was one time when I was walking back after making some copies that I saw him leave my office. I was worried he was trying to access the computer but everything was fine since my computer was still locked. And everything was right where they were. So, I just thought maybe he only wanted a tissue or something," Joan related before scowling. "I should have said something, right?"

"Yeah, and so should I," April seconded, sending him an apologetic look. Jason braced himself for more bad news. "I'm so sorry, baby. I know I should've told you this before, but it slipped my mind. I guess I'm not any better than Mom."

"What is it?" he asked, dread pooling in his stomach. He didn't think he'd receive more bad news.

"Remember that day when I had my first outburst?" He nodded slowly. "I actually came back to the office because I just overheard a very interesting conversation." And she told him all about it. His eyes widened. "I know. I'm such a lousy girlfriend for forgetting something that is so important."

"You're not lousy, forgetful maybe, but not lousy," he corrected, kissing her forehead before hugging her tightly. A squeak of surprise escaped her.

Relief coursed through him. He could finally find the mole. He knew he was looking for a male, maybe two, and that both or one of them was a security guard. He had cameras everywhere else in the office that could pinpoint the person. Finally, he could find some answers.

Pulling an unsuspecting Joan into the embrace, he hugged them a moment longer before releasing them.

"Now, let me order some food."

~

A cry woke April up.

Make that two.

Blearily sitting up, April absently gathered the twins into her arms, wondering why her back was so painful. It was quite a stretch since she had been resting between their cots but now that they were awake, they readily climbed into her lap and clung to her tightly. Smiling down at them, she frowned, suppressing a yawn. *Why were they crying? To the extent that their faces were turning red?*

Wait.

Willing the fog to clear, she suddenly wrapped her arms tightly around them. They reciprocated, latching on to her neck with unexpected strength. Tears poured out of her and streamed down her cheeks.

They were awake! They were awake!

Thanking the higher power for this blessing, April kept kissing them, wherever she could reach within their tight embrace. She was unable to suppress the sob that escaped her as she bounced them in a bid to comfort them. Burying her face into their body—first Tanner's and then Daphne's—she relished their warmth and breathed in their familiar scents.

She vowed never to let them out of her sight ever again. Especially not with Carrie.

~

A few hours later, after updating everyone and the doctor's visit, April settled down with the twins in Daphne's cot. They didn't want to remain apart and were also adamant that she not leave their sight. So, with the help of a nurse, Tanner's drip was transferred so that the needle wouldn't be accidentally pulled out of him.

She wished she could get the needles out, but they still needed the drips; it was still too early to get them off the glucose. Currently, they were rolling about in the cot, drinking milk to help the abrasions left from the tube that had been shoved down their throats. And they demanded that she hold their bottles for them. Something they'd usually didn't allow. It was another indication of their trauma. She toyed with the thought of undergoing therapy but decided to discuss it with Jason first.

On the television, which she'd turned on so as to catch the statement Jason released regarding their stay in the hospital, Carrie was currently swarmed by reporters and paparazzi. And she didn't look too happy about it. Satisfaction filled her as she watched Carrie's poorly concealed rage which further encouraged the swarm to be more aggressive. She tried to show an impassive front but grew a bit too violent when one of the reporters asked about the alcohol.

April frowned. She didn't know how the press knew about it. Jason had only said that they were being cautious as the twins had run a fever when they returned from Carrie's. That's all. There had been no hint of censor towards Carrie in his tone or expression. But that had been enough for the media to mount a hunt for that bitch.

As much as she wanted to enjoy her suffering, she also wanted to know how the media received knowledge of their ingestion of alcohol because only four parties knew—the clinic, Jason's contact, the hospital, and them. So, seeing as the hospital had the loosest ends, April talked with one of the hospital officials. She realized just a mention of Jason was enough for anyone to do her bidding. Which was to search for the snitch. That done, she returned to the twins.

They were still sleepy which was most likely an aftereffect of the alcohol still left in their bodies. Drowsily playing with each other, they soon drifted off to sleep but not before fiercely gripping her finger. One for each of them.

April contented herself with just looking at them. She felt so grateful that they hadn't been more seriously harmed from the alcohol. She'd had the time to look into the matter while waiting for them to wake up and it scared her how grave the effects of alcohol were on toddlers; it could have been fatal. If the doctor hadn't suspected it, she wouldn't have known they were well on their way to danger. She was also grateful for their resilience. If the twins had been any weaker, they'd be arranging their funeral this day.

Her thoughts turned to Jason then. He was having a hard day. The press release must have brought in another deluge of frenzied media reporting. His voice mail didn't have enough space for another message as it was. Then he had to deal with the search for the rogue security guard. Or guards. His security and IT were working on it and had narrowed the time frames for both incidences. It was just a matter of time before they found him.

Finally, he had to deal with the judge. His lawyers had presented the numerous evidences against Carrie to the man. They were all damning. Even if Carrie's lawyers argued she didn't inflict

205

them, it was proof of negligence which should be enough to suspend her rights until a thorough investigation was carried out.

Surely the judge would be on their side. Right?

CHAPTER 33

Storming through the building and making his way to the man who'd inadvertently traumatized his children, Jason absently marveled at the anger coursing through him. He'd never felt such atomic levels in his emotions before. It made it difficult to think. To plan. He was at his most primitive at that moment. He wanted very much to beat the man into a pulp. But he knew he couldn't and it rankled because, as much as he wanted to, he knew he couldn't be thrown into jail. Who'd protect his family then?

"Are you sure this is a good idea?" Cameron asked as he easily kept up with Jason's strides. He had been with Jason when his lawyers delivered the bad news. He'd been too dumbfounded that he wasn't fast enough to stop Jason. He only hoped his cousin wasn't going to do something rash—like getting thrown in jail. "I mean, you don't exactly have an appointment. I don't think they'll let you pass."

"Who says I'm going to ask for permission?" Jason countered, elation filling him as they rounded the final corner. The man was just past that door. Ignoring the frantic cries of the assistant, he slammed open the door.

His prey was behind his desk, looking innocuously up from his work. Jason didn't trust that man, much less that look. Barely suppressing the urge to wrap his hands around his beautifully vulnerable throat, Jason walked with measured steps to the desk.

"May I know why you refuse to protect my children?" Jason growled. He moved to place his hands on the desk but, in a fit of anger, his hands slammed into it with a force that made the coffee cup jump and spill some of its contents. The judge was unperturbed.

"I believe you do not have an appointment, Mr. Halloway," Judge Walter said coolly. Ice blue eyes met fiery verdant eyes, both unwilling to look away. From his peripheral, Jason smirked when Cameron backed away from the tension surrounding the table.

"And I cannot believe that, having young grandchildren of your own, you'd subject my defenseless children to that woman. Would you leave your granddaughter alone with her?" Jason demanded and was not surprised when Judge Walter's eyes slid away from him, some strong emotion shimmering behind it. From all accounts, the judge was a family man. Everyone in his family loved him and vice versa especially his grandchildren. So, it boggled Jason's mind that he was willing to let that viper have power over Jason's babies. There must be something he was not seeing.

"Of course not, Mr. Halloway. But the evidence does not show that Ms. Carter herself inflicted them on your children. And the video is not conclusive evidence. How do I know you didn't create that video just to incriminate Ms. Carter? In this day and age, that is something I have to take into account. It's just not enough to deprive a parent of their child. Or children in Ms. Carter's case," he said frostily. However, he refused to lock eyes with Jason. Instead, he shuffled some papers around his desk.

"Even so, surely you can suspend her rights while Protective Services investigate," Cameron spoke for the first time since they'd entered. And Jason was grateful at him for bringing it up. He couldn't trust himself. If he spoke to that man again, he was liable to get kicked out of the office.

"I can't do that just because another parent has something against the other. It's not fair to the parent being investigated. Now, enough of this issue. I have made my decision and will abide by it. If you have nothing else to say, I suggest you leave. And next time, make an appointment—"

"She has something on you."

Jason felt so stupid. Why didn't he see this before? That would explain why a family man would suddenly support the inveterate party girl. And Carrie was definitely a party girl. She drank, she smoked, and she partied hard. And as much as she was trying to portray a loving mother to the media, she could never outrun her past especially since that past was barely a month ago.

"What are you talking about? Ms. Carter is just a model. What could she possibly have on me?" Judge Walter said in a tone that tried to convey disbelief and amusement. But his eyes—well, they were truly windows to the soul—showed discomfort and fear. Fear? Well then. There must've been some truth to his statement.

"If not Carrie, then the person helping her then. Someone powerful enough to rope you in too," Cameron deduced while Jason smirked at the judge. Finally, a breakthrough.

"Thank you, Judge Harris. You have been a great help. Wonderful, in fact. Please forgive my intrusion. It won't happen again," Jason said with a facsimile of a pleasant smile. He couldn't help but savor the judge's discomfort and suspicion. Who wouldn't?

~

Jason returned to his office, and he was grateful that Joan had managed to clear his schedule. His company was in good hands, his new vice president having proven himself to him. Even so, he was still keeping an eye in case of any glitches. Joan, on the other hand, was at the hospital with April.

209

Cameron ignored the glare Jason shot him. Instead, he took a seat across from him, his face serious. Seeing him making himself comfortable, Jason resigned himself to his presence and decided to use him as a sounding board.

"Do you think I'm making too much out of it? Seeing something out of nothing?" he asked nervously. As much as he wanted to be right, he didn't want to hit another dead end. His children's well-being was at hand and it was imperative he release Carrie's hold on them.

"I don't know. It seems plausible. He's always been a huge advocate of children first. Especially for custody cases. That's why we were all happy to have him take over your case," Cameron shared. Jason nodded. His reaction had been the same as well. Now he wasn't so sure.

"Maybe it wouldn't be a bad idea to have your investigators check on him," Cameron then suggested. To which he threw him a grin.

"I'm way ahead of you, couz. I called him up when I was in the car, and he sounded optimistic when we hung up. Hopefully we'll get some favorable news soon." Feeling overwhelmed by all his responsibilities, Jason leaned back into his chair. "God, I just want this to be over. I want a normal, peaceful life with April and the twins. And, maybe, more children if we are ever blessed to have them."

"I'm sure that'll happen. We have too much evidence against Carrie. Even your lawyers were sure of a repeal. It must be someone very powerful who could make the judge do their bidding and who can possibly take his position, maybe even license. We just have to figure out who would have such a hold," Cameron offered, his voice rich with speculation.

Someone powerful.

That rang a bell in Jason's mind. The judge was powerful in his own right. He came from a family that had roots in Chicago way back in the early days. With his family and his post, along with his fairly pristine reputation, how could anyone find anything to blackmail him?

"Maybe it's not him. Maybe they're threatening his family," Jason muttered, brows furrowed.

"You should let your investigators know to widen his search to include his family as well. It's worth a shot," Cameron offered, giving him a shrug when Jason shot him a startled look.

While he was on the phone, he thought might as well check in with April to see if there were any changes and to ease the ache he had. He missed her presence. He'd gotten used to having her beside him. Now, with all the turmoil in their lives, he foresaw their time together dwindling. So, he treasured any chance with her that he could get. Even if it was just a phone call.

"Hey, Jase," April said brightly. Jason breathed a sigh of relief.

"They woke up?" he asked, a slight squeeze of apprehension in his chest. As much as he'd like to believe in her, he needed concrete confirmation. He'd never felt as helpless as he'd been when they were at the hospital, seeing his children's stomach being pumped. Such an invasive treatment for such small bodies. And he hadn't been able to do anything but watch and wait.

"Yes. They're currently sleeping, still feeling the effects of the alcohol but the doctor said their vitals were fine," April related softly. "I sent you a photo of them when they were awake. Didn't you receive it?"

"Must have overlooked it. It's been such a hectic day." He hesitated. As much as he wanted to relate good news, he knew April needed to know about the judge's ruling.

"What? Why did he do that?" she asked angrily. He heard some whimpers in the backdrop and April soothing one of the babies. Hearing her move, he presumed she was moving away from the children. "Sorry. Tanner's quite sensitive to sound now. I had to move just outside their room so as to not disturb them. Now, about the judge."

"I believe someone powerful is forcing the ruling out of him. I've informed my investigators of the new angle. I'm sure we'll be getting some information soon."

"Most importantly, though, why our babies? Why not other cases? This is not random. Maybe it has something to do with you. Do you know anyone who'd want to target you?" Before he could answer, she rambled on. "And I've been thinking. The timing of the mole and the custody battle seems a bit too coincidental. They happened right after the other—first Carrie and then the mole. Maybe they're linked. Maybe it's the same person behind all of this," she shared.

Jason's mind was moving at lightning speed. April had verbalized what he had been feeling for a while now. But he hadn't been able to put what it was into words. Now, with April's words still reverberating in his brain, Jason felt he had a more solid road to travel on.

"Thank you, sweetheart. I know what I have to do now," he told her, sensing that everything is finally coming together. He just hoped none of his loved ones would be hurt while he settled everything.

"Well, let me know about it once you have something more certain," she said with a chuckle. Suddenly, he felt a change in her voice. "Why the heck is she here—Jason, I'll call you back."

"April? April!" Jason said into the phone but she'd already hung up. Shooting to his feet, with Cameron looking at him with concern, Jason was about to make his way to the hospital when his phone rang. It was his head of security. As much as he wanted to ignore it, he knew he couldn't.

Barking into the phone, a smile of satisfaction graced his face. Another breakthrough. "Thank you. I'll be there soon," he said.

"Who's that? What happened?" Cameron demanded. Before Jason could say anything, Harry walked in, looking decidedly concerned. What is it with him and getting interrupted today?

"Sorry. I didn't hear about the twins until this morning. I got here as soon as possible," he said.

"It's alright. You can accompany Cam to the hospital. Check on the twins. April says they've woken up," Jason said as he got ready to leave. Cameron narrowed his eyes.

"And what are you going to do while we go check on your kids?"

"I'm going to question a security guard."

CHAPTER 34

"What the hell are you doing here?" April growled as she stood in front of the closed door. She only had time to close it before Carrie descended upon her. How she wished she wasn't alone. Where were the bodyguards Jason had hired? They were supposed to make sure no one who wasn't on the list was allowed in the hall. That included crazy hoes like the one before her. In the face of her hostility, Carrie just looked at her, face impassive but eyes burning a hole in her.

"What do you think I'm doing? I'm visiting my children. Why didn't you tell me they were sick? I would have been here much faster," Carrie cried, face contorting to show sadness and worry. Puzzled, April looked around the hallway and noticed that everyone, those that were even from the other halls, were paying attention to them, both covertly and openly. When she saw the phones coming out, she made sure to stay calm and collected.

"Well, seeing as they got sick on your watch and by your hands, I don't see any reason for you to be here," April shot back angrily, gritting her teeth as she held back with all her strength. She didn't like how Carrie was always manipulating her image and the twins. She was frankly sick of it.

"What? How could you accuse me—"

"How was the Protective Services visit? I heard they were rather brutal," April taunted. Carrie didn't take it well, her face showing her anger before wrestling it back into submission. "And I heard you were in LA during the weekend. So, who was taking care of my babies while you were away?"

"LA? Why would I be at LA when I have my bundles of joy with me? Seriously, you have to get your ears checked," she retorted, showing the correct mixture of disbelief and happiness, making April's accusations sound ludicrous. April internally snorted. "Now, let me see my babies. They're waking up and will be calling for me soon."

"No. What I want to know is how you got their room number. Your name is not on the list of people who are allowed to see them. In fact, we've told the hospital to not let you within a ten-feet radius of *my* babies," April said as she folded her arms in front of her.

"They won't listen to you." She took a step forward, hissing those words right into her face.

"Jason has ordered them, witch." Taken aback from the sudden nearness, April forced herself to stand still. Moving back would only weaken her stance.

"What the hell are you doing here?" Joan demanded angrily when she returned from the cafeteria. She stood beside April, showing her support. "And what are you doing invading our personal space? Move back, you witch."

"Lookie here. Little April is hiding behind her mommy. If you're still in the leading strings, how can you take care of my babies properly?"

Before April could say anything else, one of the hospital officials came to them. This must be the reason this witch had gotten past the guards. Her eyes narrowing at her approach, April made a mental note to impress on the guards that her confirmation was needed before any Tom, Dick, and Harry could traipse down the hall.

"May I know what is going on here?" the official asked haughtily, looking down her nose at April. She was beautiful, wonderfully put together in an ensemble that was above her pay grade. Very far above. April looked from her to Carrie. "You are disturbing the other patient's recovery. Do let the mother visit her children."

"W-what? Jason specifically told *you* not to let *her* near his children," April sputtered, surprise replacing her suspicion. *What was this woman smoking?*

"I'm sorry. I don't have that in my files. Maybe it's a figment of your imagination. Like your perceived relationship with Mr. Halloway. Surely, he is surrounded by better and more beautiful women than you," the woman said, batting her eyes and sending a fake smile her way.

Disbelief filled her. She'd been there. She'd heard him. So why was this woman saying otherwise? And who was she to take pot shots at her relationship? Jason had proven, without a doubt that they were in an exclusive relationship. The media had accepted it—barely—but they'd stopped printing malicious things about her. And them. Mostly. So, what the hell was going on? Is she a friend of Carrie's? She does seem like she has friends in pretty high places. It's not that farfetched to believe she would have contacts in hospitals as well.

"You heard her, bitch. Move aside," Carrie said with a smug smile. April refused to. She had to be strong and assertive. Regardless of what happens, the twins needed her strength right now. She had to show that she was someone to be taken seriously even without Jason beside her.

"No. Jason told your boss that she is not allowed here. He gave her name and her picture with explicit instructions to keep her away from this wing. I suggest you consult your director before

216

throwing your nonexistent weight around," April said fiercely, glaring at the official who was now looking decidedly flustered.

"Don't make me call security," she warned but there was no strength behind her words which made April narrow her eyes even more. She was losing her confidence pretty fast.

"And don't make me call your director. Jason introduced us last night and he gave me his number. I won't hesitate to contact him and lodge a complaint against his rude staff. I'm sure he'd do anything to keep Jason's funds in this lovely establishment," April said, pulling out her phone and getting the contact ready. But the woman grabbed her hand before she could press 'Call'.

"No!" the woman fairly shouted before collecting herself. Everyone was staring at her. Even their eavesdroppers. She looked at the spectators then quickly collected herself. "I mean, that won't be necessary. I must have misunderstood the email sent out regarding this matter. I'll have to consult my supervisor. Please bear with me." With that, she walked away as fast as her legs could carry her, careful not to lose composure and break out into a run.

Looking at her, suspicion began to swirl in April's head. *Why did she feel so confident in the first place then?* Surely such emails would be straightforward and not too difficult to be misinterpreted. Heck, some of the nurses in the hallway had tried to stop Carrie but she walked by as if she knew she would be welcomed.

Turning to look at Carrie, she almost stepped back at the anger contorting her face. She looked ready to kill April. Hopefully the multitude of witnesses would stay her hand.

"You think you've won, bitch? Well, don't get too comfortable. I will be in your place soon enough. And you'll be fucking six feet under," she fairly growled.

"Is that a threat? Mom, did you get that? I'm sure the police will be very interested in this should I ever disappear," April mused, sending a bright grin to her nemesis when she saw the iPhone in Joan's hand. Seeing her take a step towards her mother, April added, "Don't even try. It's uploading on Cloud even as it's recording. And as further precaution, I have some other people recording this, too."

Knowing she was outgunned, Carrie sent her one last, fulminating glare before storming off. Everyone watched her leave. Once she was out of sight, Joan engulfed April in a tight hug.

"I'm so proud of you, baby. You stood up to her and didn't back down even once. Maybe next time she would think twice about messing with you," Joan said happily. Returning her hug, April gave her a weak smile before going into the room.

Luckily, the twins didn't fuss when they woke up. They'd heard her voice and was reassured that she wasn't far away. Playing with themselves and having, somehow, gotten their hands on the blocks placed on their bedside table, they gave her drooly smiles when they saw her.

Watching them entertain themselves, April sat by their cot, feeling relieved and exhausted. But, as much as she wanted to relax, her mind kept moving. Chugging out conjectures and hunches faster than she could process them.

It was just strange that Carrie had been so sure of entering. Maybe she had a plan or ploy. But approaching when knowing everyone was on high alert for her seemed a bit too brazen. And she also didn't have enough time to even loosely plan something. The duration between her recent appearance on television and her presence in the hospital was too small for her to have even contacted that female official, much less recruit her.

And that woman. April doubted she a friend of Carrie's. Much less an acquaintance. The speed at which she'd left—practically abandoning Carrie—made it clear there was no loyalty between them. It also brought into question whether they knew each other or not. And from the way she departed and her choice of final words, it indicated that she doesn't have much power in the hospital. Maybe more than those working on the floor but definitely not enough to override the director's, and thus Jason's instructions.

Which brought her to her last hunch. Maybe the twins weren't the target after all. Maybe it's all about Jason and his company. The twins could have only been the distractions, moving his attention away from the real focus. The fanfare and attention with regard to the custody battle was at odds with how they were treated when Carrie got part of her demands. Surely, she would know that they'd seen the marks on their skin? It's not as if they were hidden. They were right in plain sight. Which begs the question of why fight for them in the first place?

She felt that she was on the right track. Carrie was too confident, too full of herself. She didn't fear the authorities too much, looking quite assured of her claim. This indicated to someone powerful who had an interest in Jason's company.

Now, how could she confirm her suspicions?

~

Her heart raging at the humiliation, Carrie ignored the stares and got into the waiting car. Her ally, having been arranged by her employer, had abandoned her, leaving her in disgrace. And the ignominy of being recorded, she could never forgive that.

But why did that fool Connor have to be caught? Who was going to act as a middle man now? Even though she had been the one to bring him in, he was practically panting after that old coot. He had even been willing to chastise her—*the* Carrie Carter—upon her order. He was like a dog chasing a bitch in heat.

So, what am I going to do now?

With Child Protective Services chasing her, there was no room for any slip ups. She decided it was time to cut her losses. She had received enough from her employer, anyway. She was not going to take the fall or be caught up in this any further. Plus, she hadn't done anything to the twins apart from neglect. She had not touched them at all. That was all that stupid Chantal's doing.

Now that everyone was focused on the twins in the hospital, she had to distance herself as much as possible. Just then, she heard a commercial in the noisy and bothersome equipment in the vehicle: the radio. It was a certain celebrity praising the beauty of some island, punctuated with the accompaniment music to hula dance (which she found ridiculous because she knew this island wasn't in Hawaii). It ended with a government official inviting everyone to visit, bask, and enjoy their place this year.

She breathed out a sigh. *To Maldives, it is.*

CHAPTER 35

Jason looked at the person in what was usually the security break room and felt satisfaction fill him. He'd been wanting to have something against this man for the longest time ever. Ever since he'd first hit on April, in fact. Usually, he didn't take note of the men and women working in Security but he'd been keeping a close eye on this one. Maybe not close enough.

"What do you know about him?" Jason asked his head of security, Bradley Michaelson. He sneered.

"That he's a ladies' man and a fucking dick. No one likes him but he's never stepped out of line. Well, not that he's been caught, that is. Until now," he informed Jason, his voice echoing his own satisfaction.

"He's loaded, too," Bradley's second added. "He has this watch that's worth at least five grand. There are diamonds—*real* diamonds—around it. It fell out of his bag in the changing room once but he acted nonchalant about it. As if he could buy more if that watch stopped working. Which is weird, considering the pay for a security guard is quite low."

"Has he said anything?" Jason asked, crossing his arms. That provided further proof of his guilt. Someone must be paying him off. Someone as wealthy as Croesus.

"Not much. He just keeps repeating the same words. I think it's just a ploy to keep us off guard," Bradley said angrily.

Nodding, Jason turned back to the man who'd unknowingly kickstarted his relationship with April.

He didn't like how relaxed he was. From the glass by the door, Jason saw him whistling. *Didn't he know he'd been caught?* He was facing at least a lawsuit from his company. If the authorities found that anyone had arbitrarily profited from the released information, he'd be charged with insider trading and face jail time. So why was he so composed?

Not able to take it anymore, Jason decided to confront him.

Connor looked up when he heard the door open and just smiled, further inciting Jason's anger.

"Mr. Johnson, I hope you're aware of the severity of your situation. The only reason you're not with the cops is because we haven't called them yet. So, do you have anything to say that could possibly help you?" Jason asked coolly. As much as he wanted to punch his aloof face, Jason needed information more.

"I'm not going to jail," was his only response before he relaxed in his seat again.

"Mr. Johnson—"

"Save it, Mr. Halloway," Bradley interrupted by the door. Jason, leashing his anger, turned to him. "We've tried. He won't give it up." Curling his fingers into his palm, Jason stopped trying to get more out of him. It was clear that, even with his experienced head of security, *this man* wasn't going to spill anything.

"Then let's bring the cops here, shall we? Maybe a few nights would loosen his tongue."

~

"Are you sure this is a good idea?" Cameron asked warily as he accompanied April to the nurse's station on their floor. April barely suppressed the urge to roll her eyes, still riding the high of fiercely castigating the guards before making her way up. The guards had barely quelled their disrespect of her. Angered by their lack of attention, she had had to use some harsh words and threats to get them to take her seriously. Cameron's presence had helped as well but he'd been asking the same question for the past hour ever since she'd shared her suspicions with the men when they'd arrived.

"The answer is the same every time you ask me this question. It's not going to change. Not unless we find something good," April told him, hiding her smile by turning away. Luckily, by then, they'd reached the reception area. Approaching the receptionist, April greeted her. "Hi. Can I speak with the director?"

"Oh, yeah. Can I ask why?" the receptionist, Carla—as what her name tag stated—asked, apprehensive. "If this is about Pauline, you can be assured that the higher ups are dealing with her. She won't disturb you again."

"Pauline. That's the woman who tried to circumvent Jason's wishes, right?" April asked curiously. Finally, a name to put to the face. Carla nodded vigorously. She didn't like the anxiety she instilled but tried to use it for her own purposes. "May I know whether she does this on a regular basis? Assume an authority she doesn't have?"

At that, Carla rolled her eyes and snorted. Interesting. Sharing a look with Cameron, they both turned their heads to her. They knew it was going to be nuggets of gold.

"She's always been a bitch ever since her first day. I've been here for more than a decade and she's only been here for like a year but she's already got more promotions than me. She knows how to suck up...you know..."

"Dick," Cameron muttered which made the ladies laugh.

"Yeah, that. And she always knows how to hide that bitchiness in front of the higher ups, making the rest of us look like fools when we lodge a complaint. It helps that she helps *relieve* their stress from time to time. So, she gets away with a lot of things," Carla related, frustration leaking into her voice.

"But that doesn't explain why she deliberately tried to defy Jason's command," April said, looking intently at Carla. She needed answers and this woman was their best bet.

"It kind of does. Sometimes, she'd give an order that doesn't make sense or ones that don't come from the higher ups. She'd do that so as to make the life of whoever received it much more difficult. And our bosses would just close one eye. Maybe even both!'"

"But an order from the director? A simple direct order?"

"Maybe she got to him?" Cameron suggested then shrugged when April scowled at him.

"But Jason's their biggest benefactor. The director can't have such a loose cannon around which might possibly cause Jason to withdraw his support to this establishment."

"You're right. That's why I was so shocked when we heard about her actions. If...no, when the director hears about this, she'll most definitely be fired. And she needs the job. She has expensive taste. Like designer expensive. Like couture expensive. Hell, one of her outfits costs more than my six-month rent. And it has less material than my bed cover," Carla revealed, throwing her arms up into the air.

"She'd need to suck more cocks if she wants to keep this job and her outfits then," Cameron said crudely, making the gesture as well. April smacked his shoulder but smiled. He might not be as refined as Jason but his loyalty was true. She considered Carla's words and her mind made another connection—one that might give them a clearer idea of who was playing behind the strings.

"Or maybe she wouldn't need to do that. Maybe she doesn't need the job as much as we think she does," she muttered to herself before thanking Carla, much to the woman's bewilderment. Assuring her they weren't going to lodge a complaint, April grabbed Cameron and left. Before he could say anything else, she asked, "Can you call Jason's investigator please?"

~

Heading to his office, Jason wished he could just leave. He wanted April and his children in his arms. His children would probably be squirming away but April would stay with him and help him make sense of the mess that was his life. But it was exactly that mess that kept him away from them.

Passing by Joan's empty desk, he opened the door and was surprised to see Harry at his table using his desktop.

"I thought you were with April?" Jason asked as he dropped into his new couch; he'd replaced his used uncomfortable one with one that was cozier and friendlier to the twins. Of course, it might have something to do with his brief tryst but he wasn't going to admit to anything. April had given him a knowing look when they'd shopped for the couch.

"Yeah. But she sent me back to keep an eye on you when I told her who the spy is. While she and Cameron try to squeeze any new information out of anyone they meet," Harry told him, his eyes firmly glued to the screen.

"Why would she want to do that? The hospital has been very accommodating," Jason asked, sitting up, alarm filling him. When he last spoke to her, he got the impression that shso,his e was going to keep all her attention on their twins. Why would she leave them alone? And for a wild goose chase.

"Well, Carrie came by and wanted to see the twins—"

"What?! Didn't I inform the hospital to keep her away? I told them, emphatically, to not allow her within a ten-foot radius of their room." He took a sharp intake of breath. "Let me call them and get to the bottom of this—"

225

"There's no need to do that. April chased her away. But what got her mind racing, and subsequently mine, is why a hospital official tried to say otherwise," Harry said, sending Jason a scowl. He had to look away from the screen to effectively stop Jason's rash actions.

"That's why I need to talk to Ron," Jason said, irritated.

"No, you don't have to talk to the director of the hospital. What you need to do is let April do her own sleuthing. She's with Cameron in the hospital, trying to find more information. And I think she'll get far more information than you. People see her as less of a threat and more approachable than you. The same reason Cameron is with her and I'm here. With the advent of his kids, people see him in a friendlier light."

"Then, what am I supposed to do?" Jason dropped back into his couch, splaying out.

"Well, maybe I can help." Harry sat back in the chair, earning him an annoyed glare from Jason.

"You know that's *my* chair, right?"

"Is it? I think this chair suits me better."

Jason raised a brow. He hadn't expected Harry's teasing words. It's been years since Harry had teased anyone.

"You're different. Did something happen? With Elena?" He meant that to be a joke but realized there was some truth to his words when Harry sat up suddenly, causing the chair to topple backwards. Rushing to him in concern, he decided to shelf his line of query for now. "Man, are you, alright?"

"Yeah, yeah," Harry responded, not meeting his eyes. Jason noticed his cheeks looked quite red. He was definitely bringing it up on a later date. "As I was saying, I believe the guy you were interviewing knows Carrie."

"What? How? Carrie is definitely picky with who she associates herself with, from acquaintances to lovers. She'd never

226

lower herself to sleep with a security guard. No matter how hot he is. Don't tell anyone else," Jason quickly warned when Harry caught his description of Connor. Harry sent him a wicked smile but decided to let it go.

"I'm not sure how they met each other, but he was definitely the one who left with Carrie at the auction. I'd recognize that voice and hair anywhere."

"Maybe there *is* some connection between the leak and the custody battle after all," Jason mused, recalling April's words. He had been hard-pressed to believe her then, thinking there had been no obvious link between them. But he believed he owed his wonderful girlfriend an apology. "Let's go to the hospital. I have some groveling to do."

"I just came from there," Harry whined but got just the same. Jason just raised his brow. He had not heard that note on his voice for over a decade. Definitely worth bringing up on a later date. "You better grovel in a public setting and let me have some entertainment."

CHAPTER 36

"I'm sorry, baby," Jason suddenly said as April was about to lay her head on his chest. Sitting up, she sent him a puzzled look.

"What? Why?" she asked as she sent Daphne a smile. They were in their living room as, much to their delight, the twins were already released a few hours earlier. However, the twins hadn't been asleep when they were given the release papers, so, now, being in a familiar environment, it would be impossible to get them back to sleep. And with it being eleven, April resigned herself to a late night.

"I kind of brushed aside your comment about the leak and Carrie being linked. But when Harry told me that Connor was there at his auction, I immediately got my investigators on it," he rushed to assure her but, she just smiled.

"You don't have to tell me that. Sometimes, I, too, brush your dictates aside. That doesn't mean I love you any less," she told him, laughing at his bewildered expression. She knew he wanted to know what she brushed aside and saw him decide to let it go. For now.

"That's what Harry told me but I wanted honesty between us." He sent her an apologetic look, going to Daphne when she demanded he help her walk. "So, what did you learn at the hospital?" Slightly distracted when Jason started lifting Daphne with his fingers in her hands, she was startled when Tanner demanded the same from her.

"Well, the official is not really an official but a w-h-o-r-e," she said, spelling out the word in light of the presence of the twins. Ignoring Jason's laugh, she continued. "And she is an expensive escort. Very expensive. Suspiciously expensive."

"Money offered for her services?" Jason suggested as he helped Daphne kick Tanner, laughing with her when she scored a hit. "Be careful, baby."

"Jason," she scolded as she pulled Tanner away. Daphne cried out angrily but got distracted by her toy drum. Demanding to be released, she immediately started banging on it. April hoped their neighbors weren't home. It was going to be loud. She released Tanner, as he, too, wanted to play with his trucks, and she and Jason went back to the sofa.

"I'm thinking initially that was the case. But, that wouldn't really explain why she was so bold as to ignore your order this afternoon. She's definitely going to lose her job and her source of cash," April said, wrapping her arm around Jason. Looking up, she saw his brows adorably furrowed. "I believe she has another source that's going to open up very soon. A huge one if she's willing to take the risk. So, I had some of your investigators watch her bank accounts and trace any dubious inflows."

Getting used to his hugs, she wrapped her arms even tighter around him when he gave her such a hug. "That's brilliant, honey. Hopefully we'll hear something soon," he said, pressing his lips into her hair. A sense of accomplishment filled her. Finally, she was helping him protect their babies.

"What the heck is that noise? Don't you know that some people want to sleep?"

Joan suddenly marched into the room in her pajamas. April hid her face into Jason's side. She'd forgotten about her mother in the house and didn't want to be confronted by her just yet.

"Sorry. Daphne wanted to play with it and we can't say no considering what she'd gone through the last few days," Jason said in an apologetic tone. April felt Joan soften. Joan had been very affected by their hospitalization. It reminded her too much of when April had to stay there during her childhood.

"Well, don't let it happen again. As much as I love your kids, I love my sleep even more." With that, she stalked back to bed.

"How do you do it?" April demanded when she was sure her mother wasn't in earshot.

"My natural charm, I guess."

"More like natural smarminess," she teased. Before he could say anything, she picked Daphne up. "Come on, let's get them to bed. I think this little one is running on fumes as it is."

Still grousing at her jab, Jason picked a resisting Tanner and followed her to their room. Hearing him whine, April just smiled.

~

"You didn't have to come, baby," Jason said as they got out of his car. Throwing his keys to the valet, Jason sent April another worried look.

"Yes, I have to. Who's going to stop you from doing anything rash? No one but me." Getting past the security was easy; he was recognizable enough. However, getting past security without much scrutiny was impossible. Hiding his scowl, he let April get on the elevator in front of him.

"I'm not going to do anything rash. I'm just going to present the evidence and watch their reaction," he told her softly, seeing as they had an audience. She rolled her eyes.

"Yeah right. You have so much pent up anger I'm sure you're going to do something. Deliberately or not," she said with a snort. Deciding to keep his own counsel, Jason wrapped his arm around her, his other hand holding said evidence. "Don't worry. I'm sure it's going to fine."

"Clearly you don't know my parents," he muttered, ignoring the woman who was trying to take a photo of them. Luckily, April didn't see her.

People kept getting off at different levels. The numbers dwindled until, finally, they were alone. His heart sped up. He hadn't truly seen his parents, for the sake of seeing them, since he was twelve. It was going to be interesting how he'd feel and act once they met. Hopefully he wouldn't embarrass himself.

He hadn't been surprised when the investigators presented their findings. He was just surprised at the extent of their involvement. It had started from the beginning—from his first assistant up to Janice. They'd all been in his parents' pockets. Even the agency he used to get his assistants. All under their thumbs.

His other employees were legitimate and are all working solely for him. But his assistants, all of them handling sensitive company information, had been the spies and were all helping his parents to keep just ahead of him. Their revenues had always been more than his. He didn't mind because he knew their costs had often been much more, reducing their profit margins substantially.

Still, it hurt him to know the people who were a part of him would practice such underhanded tactics. If they'd asked, he knew he'd help. Maybe not expose all his plans and secrets but enough for them to make their own decisions in line with their own goals. But now, in light of all their trickery, he had no mercy.

Time for them to face the music.

CHAPTER 37

April tightened her hand around Jason's. Even though he showed an impassive face, she knew how much it must have hurt to realize such a betrayal. She already went through it when she realized her father was a mean drunk and started beating her mother. Even thinking about it now tied a knot around her heart. The hurt never really goes away.

They marched to his father's office, his eyes focused on the door. She tried to emulate him but her curiosity got the best of her. Her eyes roamed the floor and found it...lacking. The office looked devoid of life in color and personality.

Even though Jason's offices had the cubicles and such, at least the walls were painted in bright colors interspersed with soothing colors in the halls. Paintings or wall hangings helped brighten the place as well. The office she was walking through was a stark contrast to Jason's with its bland, empty grey walls, with only a sad plant placed in almost every corner. It was depressing just being there.

Even the workers exuded such mood. They were utterly focused on their work. No one overtly looked up but she could feel stares boring into her back when they passed by them so she knew they weren't that unaware of their presence. But their entire beings were turned to their desks and, thus, work. It unnerved her.

Finally, they reached the office—ignoring the assistant— and barged in. Well, Jason did. Since her hand was in his, she followed as well. When they entered the office, she had a brief impression that it was big before her eyes were drawn to the man sitting behind the desk.

Jason looked exactly like him, but instead of blond hair and green eyes, the man had brown hair sprinkled with gray ones and dark black eyes. He obviously kept in shape from the way he looked—healthy and with no obvious bulges. Combined with his height—being taller than Jason by an inch—he cut a commanding presence. Although, upon closure inspection, April might attribute the height difference to the soles of their shoes.

And he seemed to be delighted to see Jason. She didn't know how she knew that, but she believed it had something to do with her familiarity with Jason. His demeanor had brightened, somewhat when his eyes landed on his son. And it softened her impression of him.

Keep your head in the game, Saunders, she scolded herself and shook her head.

Keeping close to Jason, she waited for their first words.

"Jason," Mr. Halloway said, his voice a rich tenor.

"Father," was Jason's reply. Her head moved back and forth between them. It felt like a play in action, but the tension was getting to her.

"What can I do for you today? From my recollection, you've never been to my office before."

"I just want to tell you that I know what you're doing and I won't ever let it happen again. I'll press charges on the obvious players, that being my assistants, Carrie, and Connor. But I will stay my hand on you for now. If you press, though, I will press charges, parents or not. I have more than enough evidence to win," Jason fairly growled, his hand tightening on the file. April, knowing that he needed it, wrapped her arms around him. It couldn't have been easy telling your parent you'd throw them in jail. She believed it echoed that of parents who struggle with the decision to throw their own children out because of their faults. No one wants to be the reason their loved ones—or in this case, blood relations—suffered no matter how wrong they can be.

Thinking their deed done, she was surprised when she was greeted with Mr. Halloway's bewildered face. He was either a good actor or he truly didn't know what was going on. Which was preposterous as all evidence pointed to his company. Being the owner and CEO, it automatically proved his guilt.

"What are you talking about? I have not done anything that would throw me in jail. And why would I care about your assistants and this Carrie and Connor?"

"Stop the act. We know and have proof of their actions and the link to you. It's pretty damning to say the least. I'm sure the police will have a great time with the evidence I'll be giving them."

"I don't know what you're talking about. And I do not like having threats being bandied around my office," he said coolly. "So, either speak clearly or leave my building."

Jason and April shared a look. They both agreed that he sounded genuinely lost and apparently has not heard of Carrie nor Connor before. Hoping they weren't showing their trump card unnecessarily, April squeezed Jason's hand and nodded. Jason threw the file onto the table and they waited for Mr. Halloway's reaction.

He furrowed his brows, his features becoming more alarmed as he read more of the reports. Putting down the file before he even finished it, he looked paler and even more foreboding. Finally, he said, "I didn't do this. I didn't bribe your assistants nor the employment agency. I don't know who this Connor is and the only thing I know about Carrie Carter is that she is the mother of my grandchildren."

"Don't lie. We both know your company was in a precarious position. You were one step away from losing everything when you started stealing information and plans. Even now, you are barely in the black. So why don't you admit it? I've already told you I won't press charges against you. Even though we're not close, I still have my manners and I'm averse to sending my own parents to jail," Jason sneered, all his anger rushing out. His father acted in kind.

"That's why I was going to give you my company," he roared, glaring at him. "Do you think I don't know that I'm driving generations of hard work into the ground? You think I don't know of my failure as a leader? Because I do. But I can't let this company fail and, right now, you're the best Halloway for the job."

She was shocked. Knowing Jason, she knew it was hard especially for the Halloway men to admit to any failings. They were too proud. To see his father doing it and looking at his haggard face softened her heart even more.

"I'm old, Jason. I'm old and have nothing to show for the life I've led. I have no successes to call my own. My house is cold and empty. My company is on the brink of bankruptcy. In fact, I won't be able to last six months, never mind a year," he revealed softly.

"Maybe Jason can help—"

"No, I'm tired. The only thing I did right in my entire life was marrying your mother and having you. It's obvious you inherited the Halloway trait with your keen business acumen. It's only right that I give you the company. It's your birthright, something that you can hopefully pass on to your children," he offered as he dropped into his chair.

From the way Jason grew tense, April knew he was surprised and wanted to refuse. But she saw a sad and lonely old man who had nothing left to keep him in this life. As much as she

235

hated him for the way he treated Jason growing up, she couldn't hold her anger against him. He needed Jason right now.

"Jason will take it," she said before Jason could.

"No one is taking away my hard work from me," a voice said from the door just as they heard a gun being cocked.

~

They all turned to the door and Jason immediately pulled April to his back. His whole world was not making sense today. His father, who had always been proud and obnoxious, was giving him the one thing he hadn't known he'd wanted until today. The sense of belongingness had filled him when he realized his father was serious. Of course, April had interpreted it as him rejecting the offer and had to speak for him but he didn't mind.

Only now he had to deal with his mother who was shockingly holding a gun steadily in her hand. Even without the gun, there was a wildness about her that contrasted oddly with her cool and poise expression.

"What are you doing, Hannah?" Paul, his father, demanded, making a move to stand up. Hannah moved the gun over to him.

"Sit down!" she screamed, losing her cool facade. Her eyes had a ferociousness to it resembling that of a cornered wounded animal's. "You have always been a big baby. Weak! I don't know what I saw in you. If you weren't the heir to Halloway Corp., I'd have aborted that devil and you wouldn't have known."

Jason would like to say that he was surprised but he wasn't. He'd always known his parents had a shotgun wedding. He hadn't been wanted but had to be accepted to save face. That had been drilled into him the moment he understood anything. Even so, a child could hope that their parents would love them regardless.

"It doesn't matter. I have made my decision and changed my will. Jason will own this company whether I'm still alive next week or not," Paul declared through gritted teeth. Holding the file of evidence in his hand, he shook it in her direction. "I've been suspicious of you the moment you started paying attention to the workings of this corporation. But this…this is worse than I expected. Did you think you can get away with this?"

"Shut up, you fool! I'm the one who has been keeping this company together. I made the decisions that you're too scared to take, decisions that saved this pile of rocks—"

"Decisions that you *stole*," Paul corrected. Jason stayed as still as possible, hoping that they wouldn't grab Hannah's attention. He felt April tightening her hold on the back of his shirt. He brought his arm to the back, wrapping his hand around her. He hoped this wouldn't be the last time he held her.

Suddenly a shot rang out and Jason saw Paul jerk back, a spot of red staining his pristine white shirt, before falling over his table. Shocked, he turned his eyes on his mother and cursed under his breath. Hannah turned her attention to them.

"He has always been a sissy," she callously remarked.

"Mother, give me the gun. I'm sure we can get you to the hospital and get you checked out—"

"I don't care!" she shrieked, her hair starting to untangle from its neat chignon. "My life is over and I won't go down on my own!"

"Mother, you know that you will never get away with this," he began again, hoping to drive some sense into her, but she slashed her free hand in the air, dismissing his words.

"I don't care. I don't care. I don't care! Now, if you don't want to die, give me that bitch. The whore that just had to throw a wrench in my plans. If she hadn't come, Janice would still be working for you. My one source of information would still be there. Instead, jealousy got the best of her and I had to quickly replace her."

"Connor," Jason supplied as he slowly backed to Paul's desk, hoping that April could get help for both his father and them. He just had to keep his mother preoccupied. April was shaking slightly but didn't make a sound, following his every step without question. He was so proud of her.

"Yes, that stupid guard. Carrie got him for me, sleeping with him, making him love her. He was loyal. Stupidly loyal. And an opportunist. After years of discretion, he just had to sell the information to the next highest bidder making that damn information worthless!" she screeched, her eyes still locked on him. He was almost there. Just a bit more.

"But why did you come after my children?" he asked, muscles screaming from having to move at such a snail's pace.

"For distraction, of course." She sent him a smile. One that made his hair rise. This person was not sane. Not anymore. "You're weak, like your father. Swayed by your feelings. Your *responsibility*. Carrie was supposed to focus your attention away from your company, from any discrepancies that may occur from employing my new mole. Only she veered off course because of jealousy as well. Dumb woman. So, tell me, is your dick made of gold? What is it about you that makes you so desirable that all women want you? So much that they forget their objectives and their plans?"

"You'll have to ask them about it," he said, surprised at his cool expression.

"Enough chitchat," she said, stalking toward them. Luckily, they were already at the table and April was trying to unobtrusively get under it. But the she-devil saw her and began rushing forward, the gun trained on her.

Jason shot forward and grappled for her gun. For such a slight woman, she put up quite a fight. She wouldn't give in. He tried to push her hand away from his beloved but another shot rang

238

out. He didn't have the chance to check on April. Hannah was turning the gun to him next, her wrists turning.

Managing to keep the muzzle away from him, he was surprised when her weight was gone. He stumbled to a halt and braced himself for a shot but, instead, saw a police official prying the gun out of her hand while several others pinned her to the ground.

April must have managed to call them. Relief filled him, almost making him collapse. Paramedics rushed past him, heading for his father. He was glad that he would be able to spend more time with him. From the revelations today, he was sure they had some common ground—

Wait, why are there two stretchers?

Turning to the table, his heart almost stopped when he saw a pool of blood around April.

CHAPTER 38

Jason had never prayed so hard in his life as he did on the way to the hospital. April only had a grazed arm but she was still unconscious. In his alarm, he'd seen more blood than there actually was. The paramedics had treated her arm and were transporting her to the hospital for observation. They wouldn't allow him to ride with her because he wasn't a relative. He wanted to argue but it would only take away time needed to treat April. The ambulance with Paul had screeched out earlier.

Instead, he glared at them as they left. Then he jumped into his car, but he couldn't seem to start it. His hand was trembling and unable to hold still long enough to shift gears and his breathing became fast and choppy. Hoping to calm himself down, he chanted reassurances to himself regarding April, his children and even his—until recently estranged—father. He told himself no one in his family would ever be in danger again. The threat was gone. It was finally over.

Eventually, he stopped shaking and his breathing evened out. Driving out of the parking lot, he contacted everyone he could think of and headed to the hospital.

~

Sitting outside of the operating theater, he found that he had a harder time dealing with everything alone. He missed April and felt incomplete without her. After loudly demanding to see her, he was told by the doctor that she was fine even though she had still not woken up. They had moved her to a room but wouldn't allow him entry, though.

Unfortunately, for his father, it had been touch-and-go for a moment. He'd lost too much blood but they were able to replenish it, so he was much more stable now. Luckily, he'd rallied for Paul's recovery to be hastened and they were working on him now. They'd gotten the bullet—which had entered just shy of his left lung and heart—out and were patching up any internal injuries. He'd been informed that his father would be brought to another room within the hour. Relief coursed through him.

His relatives had trickled in throughout the operation. Joan wasn't able to make it because she had the twins to care for. With April not being there, they were very fractious and cranky. She would put them to bed, but no sooner than she went out of the room than the twins would wake up by even the slightest distance, not allowing her to leave. So, she transferred them to her room. Jason knew how worried she was for her daughter and as much as Joan wanted to see April to look in on her well-being, the needs of the twins overrode theirs. Even so, he made sure Joan was the first recipient of updates with any of April's progress.

Cameron and Sharon occupied a bench near him. Sharon was sleeping against Cameron's shoulder, refusing anyone who suggested she rest in her hotel room. Cameron had almost carried her out but she'd turned her teary eyes on him and he relented reluctantly, but only after extracting a promise from her that they'd leave if she ever felt too uncomfortable. It was an amusing sight that would have normally made Jason smile, but he could barely muster amusement now.

Meanwhile, Harry was pacing the hallway, probably the entire hospital. He kept appearing and disappearing from view. Sometimes, he'd carry bad coffee that everyone but Sharon forced down. Other times, he'd only scowl and move along. Jason knew

April and he were getting close, closer than she was with Cameron, and saw a glimmer of the boy he once knew when they were together. He hoped he'd stay.

When the police came, it was a surprise when they didn't require much of a statement from him. Apparently, April had already called them when his mother appeared and their operator had heard everything which helped since the cameras in and near that room had mysteriously stopped working at that time and all the employees had disappeared. She probably told them to leave, diminishing the possibility of witnesses to zero. It goes to show how intelligence and unfettered greed were a dangerous pair.

Jason had not been extremely surprised when his mother was revealed to be the mastermind behind such an extensive and convoluted plot. The investigations had pointed to his parents, or one of them, as he'd found out. He was just sad that it had to happen this way. He would have been happy to help them through any rough patches and give some pointers on how to navigate through this unstable economy. But she was too proud and hungry to admit to such failings and ask for help.

Anger was in the mix too as she had deliberately hurt his children. All the bruises and the alcohol. He was lucky his children were sturdy and able to withstand the effects until they had been checked by the doctors. If they'd been any more susceptible, he'd be planning their funeral already.

With his mother and Connor in custody, the police were now looking for Carrie. She's the final member in their sick triad. Everyone she's had a connection with, no matter how faint and distant, had been informed of her warrant of arrest. The media were blasting her images everywhere and all social media platforms were flooded with it. In this day and age, she had nowhere to run. He awaited her capture with savage pleasure. Even so, he'd posted guards around his penthouse and outside April's room as precaution. After all, Carrie had proven to be one fucking slippery eel.

"I just can't believe I didn't figure this out before," Harry said as he finally stopped pacing and slumped into a seat beside Jason. "I saw them more than you did and didn't even see the evil in that bitch's eyes. I could have stopped this and the twins would not have been hurt and traumatized. Your father would still be an ass but without a hole. And April would be fine, sitting beside you in your apartment and not lying in a hospital."

"No one saw it. We just thought she was being her usual bitchy self. No one thought she'd actually become a bitch," Cameron said, his voice echoing in the empty hall. Sharon stirred but fell back to sleep once he wrapped an arm around her.

"But still—"

"No. What's done is done," Jason said harshly. He couldn't stand Harry's guilt. He hadn't done anything. It wasn't his hand that hurt his children. It wasn't him who shot the gun. His only guilt was being blinded by a person's greed and pride. Something they were all guilty of. "We can just hope and pray that they all come out of this alive."

"Yeah," Cameron seconded and they all turned to Harry. Harry took his time to mull things over before he finally nodded.

"God, I hope everything will be fine."

Just as Jason was about to agree, a nurse came to them. Her face was free of any furrows and she had an air of unhesitating confidence. *Did that mean that everything was fine?* Jason, along with Cameron and Harry, looked to her in earnest.

She broke the ice. "Good news. Ms. Saunders' vitals are stable. She's currently in her room, resting, while the doctor—"

Jason was too happy to hear the rest of the nurse's report. Letting out a loud exhale of breath, all he could think about was that April was fine. The love of his life was fine.

~

The black cloud hovering over April suddenly lifted, forcing her to consciousness, pain, and suffering. Groaning, she admitted there was little suffering, but the pain was still there and ever growing. And it seemed to be coming from her arm.

Blearily opening her eyes and wondering why they were glued together, she saw white everything. Walls, ceiling, floor, bed sheets, pillows—everything—with the exception of her clothes, which were a hideous green. Grimacing in distaste, she saw her right hand hooked to an IV bag and her left upper arm bandaged. That must have been where the bullet had penetrated.

Refusing to picture that and worrying about her lapse in memory, she called for the nurse who entered barely a minute later. Surprised, April asked about Jason and became angry when the nurse answered, "He's not a family member so he's not allowed in for now. Only family members are permitted until the doctor says you are strong enough."

She was bewildered and wondered why such a rule was strictly enforced especially with someone as well-known and powerful as Jason. He could buy this hospital five times over and still have enough to buy another private jet. Her anger flared when the nurse refused to allow Jason in or even tried calling for April's doctor to check on her now that she was awake. This was ridiculous.

Just as she was about to explode, Jason entered, his back turned slightly away from her as he spoke to some people outside. The nurse tried to repeat her spiel but Jason ignored her and instead looked at April. Once he laid eyes on her, he quickly closed their distance and she found herself in his arms, with him being careful of her IV needle and wound. In the warmth of his embrace, something within her relaxed. She was safe.

~

244

April's room was soon filled. She didn't even have time to freshen up. Sharon had given her a tearful hug, refusing to let her go until Cameron spoke the magic words 'ice cream'. She was currently happily consuming an entire tub on a nearby chair. Cameron just gave her a smile and sat beside his wife.

She was most puzzled when Harry came to her. He looked troubled and there was a hint of guilt in his eyes. Without warning, he threw his arms around her and pulled her tight to his chest, murmuring, "I'm sorry," over and over again. April did not know what Harry was talking about. So, she just patted his back and occasionally stroked his hair. Suddenly, he was gone.

Looking up, she knew Jason had come to the end of his rope. Seeing her in another man's arms despite being related to him unleashed his possessive side; it was back with a vengeance. And with her being unconscious barely an hour ago, his protective side was out as well.

She scarcely had time to herself before Jason was there with a washcloth to help her wash some of the grime she felt. Beaming at him, she allowed him to wash her face but refused any other body part even though her limbs were protesting. While she washed her arms and legs, she asked about Hannah.

She recalled hurriedly calling the police while hiding behind Jason. As much as she hated using him as a shield, standing beside him would only distract him and make him vulnerable so she did the only thing she could. Luckily, the madwoman didn't notice.

Once she had reached under the desk, she only had time to check on Paul before Jason rushed to Hannah. In her attempt to check on Jason and find out what happened, April made the mistake of getting out from under the table. She had heard the shot but didn't know where it had been aimed until she felt a burning sensation on her arm. Her last thought, after seeing her blood

245

flowing in torrents down her arm, was how embarrassing it was that she was losing consciousness from it.

She smacked Jason's arm lightly when he laughed with Harry when she told them. Jason placed himself far from her reach, but her glare warned him she wouldn't forget this. Fortunately, Cameron and Sharon were leaning against each other, sleeping, so she only had to deal with the two insensitive baboons.

"Shouldn't they be in their room? Or at our house? I don't think it's safe for Sharon to be here with her being so pregnant," April inquired, concerned about Sharon's health. When he told her of Sharon's insistence, she frowned up at Jason and just shook her head. "She's stubborn but means well. I just hope her baby will be alright."

Suddenly, Jason sat on her bed and hugged her, burying his face into the crook of her neck. Surprised, she started to ask what was wrong but felt wetness where his head lay. Realizing it was an outpouring of his relief, she just wrapped her arms around him and absently watched Harry leave with a last look of what looked to be envy on his face.

A sudden coldness around her finger distracted her and brought her attention back to Jason. Looking down, all the breath left her lungs when she saw a ring on her fourth finger on her left hand. Her other hand came up to cover her mouth and she brought her ring-laden hand up to eye level, making sure she wasn't dreaming.

"J-Jason. What is this about?" she asked, unable to tear her eyes away from the shiny stone.

"This is a promise," Jason said, his hands taking hold of hers and his eyes looking at her. She was taken aback at the intensity in them. "April, when I thought I've lost you, I realized that we haven't done everything I wanted to do with you, like go out on a date. Our relationship is so topsy-turvy that we haven't spent time away for ourselves."

"Y-you don't have to give me a ring just for a date," she said softly, her mind still not processing what was going on. *A ring? Like an engagement ring? No, that couldn't be it. He's not even talking about an engagement, much less marriage.*

"It's not just for a date. I want all that time—all your time—for the rest of my life. Our lives. Just so you're aware, I come with two adorable baggage that won't let you have any time for yourself and will probably make you want to tear your hair off your head—"

"Stop," she admonished with a wet laugh. "They aren't that bad."

"I think you haven't seen their true colors yet," Jason returned with the same laugh. The two of them enjoyed the lightened atmosphere between them, a brief respite from the stress and strain of the past few days. But the glint from the ring pulled her attention back to the situation at hand.

"So, is this like a promise ring?" she asked uncertainly. "It's quite expensive to be a promise ring. Although I know you can afford it but still—"

"No. It's a promise that I will take care of you for the rest of our lives. It's a promise that I will love you from this day forward, for better, for worse, for richer, for poorer, in sickness and in health, until death do us part."

Her ears still ringing from his words, she hadn't realized she was crying and covering her face until he reclaimed her hands again.

"April, will you marry me?"

She looked at him, and then smiled.

"Yes!"

EPILOGUE

April opened her arms and Tanner and Daphne toddled into her, squealing in happiness. She wrapped her arms around them, hugging them close. They had grown so much since her week's stay in the hospital. They had visited, but, after learning that the hospital (with its risk of viral contamination) can be a dangerous place to expose small children to (with their low immunity), she insisted they just stay at home than jeopardize their health. Now, they were both able to walk on their own already. That saddened her a bit.

Paul had to have a longer stay. There had been a slight infection and they were still keeping him under observation. He and Jason had discussed about his care when he's released and decided on a live-in caretaker. But April was determined to change their minds—most importantly, Jason's. Paul needed family around him, people who cared for him. With the revelation of his wife's betrayal and the media's attention on him, he needed all the love and care he could get.

"You could have changed before greeting them," Joan said as she watched from the kitchen, softly admonishing her even as she smiled tearfully at her daughter. Knowing her mother's temperament, April knew not to be offended by her lack of welcome. She looked at her mother and saw through her façade. In her eyes were tears glistening of relief and love. Letting her bundle go, April went to greet her mother. *Just as reserved. Like mother, like daughter, so they say*, she thought. And if Joan felt a drop of what April did when the twins were in the hospital, April was sorry for inflicting such worry on her own mother.

"Hey, Mom. How are you?" she asked, picking Tanner up with her uninjured arm. He had been the most affected by her stay in the hospital; he would throw a tantrum every time they had to leave. They would then wait for him to exhaust himself and fall asleep before they could leave. Smoothing a hand over his hair and bouncing him, she whispered assurances to him as he laid his head on her shoulder. Daphne had also joined them but she preferred to stand beside them, wrapping her arms around April's leg.

"Alright. These are all your medicine," Jason said as he put down a bag on the counter before Joan could answer. "There's your vitamins, anti-nausea, iron, some supplements I picked up to help with the development. And yes, you have to eat it. It's non-negotiable—"

"Wait. Those sound like pregnancy medicine," Mrs. Salvador commented as she wiped her hand, having been busy cooking. Both she and Joan sent them puzzled looks and the couple shared excited ones. Joan was the first to figure it out.

"You're pregnant!" she shrieked, throwing her arms around April. Tanner whined at the disruption. Mrs. Salvador was beaming at them. Tanner cried. April turned to him, calming him, and let Jason answer for the both of them.

"Yes. Just shy of a month," he announced proudly, making April roll her eyes. He looked and sounded so proud but she knew it was only the calm before the storm. Before long, she knew he'd start going overboard with his overprotectiveness. But at least she knew the perfect way to change his mind.

Hiding her smile in Tanner's head, her eyes travelled around the room. Who'd have thought she'd find a family when she accepted the job? And that Jason would grow to be one of the

249

most important persons in her life? She had truly been blessed the minute she decided to go after the twins.

Her twins.

~

Jason sat back in his new office in his new house. Situated quite near to Cameron's, the estate took up close to twenty thousand square feet and he had the option of expanding. April had protested the "extravagant" and "unnecessary space" but he'd overruled her. He didn't have a hard time doing so when she saw the kitchen. It was the very reason he chose the house. Although it was not the main selling point, it was one he knew April would enjoy.

And the twins were enjoying the place especially the pool. They demanded to visit it *every day*. Be it just to splash around or actually swim. It helped that Cameron's children came by often as well. With Sharon giving birth just a month ago, their visits have also become a reprieve for April. However, since April visited her almost every afternoon, it fell upon him and Cameron to oversee the boisterous boys and the energetic babies.

Paul, his father, stayed with them now. He'd sold his home and moved in. Jason and April were happy with his decision. They'd noticed how melancholy he'd been when he stayed at the penthouse, recuperating. Hannah's betrayal and subsequent actions had weighed heavily on him, despite all their reassurances that he couldn't have known she'd go over the edge. The only person who could truly get through to him was Joan. They were able to talk about anything with each other, even about Hannah. Jason suspected there was something more going on between them but, as long as they kept their clothes on, he wouldn't clue April in on them. Yet.

With regard to Hannah, well, a lot had happened the past three months. Connor, seeing his claims of not going to the slammer becoming just wishful thinking, decided to confess everything he knew to the authorities which coincidentally implicated his mother.

They learned Hannah had blackmailed the judge. It seemed she was privy to some information from his youth that would hurt his family—something he didn't want to shine light on. But, with Hannah's madness hitting the headlines, he had no choice but to spill the beans. This was to both decrease her ammunition and rid himself of a liability. Jason didn't know what he had been so reluctant to tell, and he truly didn't care. As long as the judge no longer had anything to do with his family, he wouldn't pursue it.

The doctor who had made the report on Carrie's alleged claims of depression, on the other hand, was found out to have indeed falsified it. It seemed getting a few hundred thousand dollars made the risk of losing his license more bearable. Of course, his license was revoked and Jason was looking to find more dirt on him. This couldn't be his first time. He was just too convincing.

Unfortunately, Carrie was able to get off with a light sentence. She claimed she had not given the liquor to the twins. She might have contributed to the bruises but the main culprit was her nanny, Chantal. And, as much as Jason wanted to prove her wrong, the cameras his employee/spy had put around the house corroborated it. Even so, she was still obsessed with him, sending him messages and nudes to tempt him.

However, her pragmatism outweighed her obsession. She knew she had no chance with him, despite spamming him with unwanted pictures and videos. She was currently somewhere in the Bahamas, enjoying the money she received from Hannah. He was still keeping track of her, though, just in case.

Hannah's trial was still ongoing, but Jason refused to attend any of it. She was firmly in his past and not a part of his family. Not anymore.

Shaking his head to shake off thoughts about that woman, Jason smiled when he heard the twins laughing and shrieking from the pool. He decided to join them and went to change into his boxer trunks and ambled to the back. Surprisingly, April was there as well along with Sharon and her brood.

Sitting at the poolside table, April was talking animatedly with Sharon, holding on to Dawn, Cameron's and Sharon's latest addition. Dressed in a maxi dress to hide the slight roundness in her middle, she cooed at the sleeping Dawn before laughing with Sharon at the boys' antics. She caught sight of him at the door, though, and her smile turned into a pout.

Knowing about her mood swings, Jason made his way to their table. He took a seat beside her and slid his arm around her shoulder. He greeted Sharon and Dawn then he turned to April.

"Hey, sweetie. Why aren't you at Sharon's? I thought I heard you leave," he asked, looking warily for any tears. That's what his life had been like when they found out that she was pregnant. Of course, they were happy. Ecstatic even. And she didn't suffer from morning sickness, which was a blessing, but the one thing she was prone to was crying. One misspoken word and the waterworks would come out.

"I didn't feel like it," she said, still pouting. He rubbed her arm and smiled when she leaned against him, resting her head on his arm. "Anyway, there's still the twins' party tomorrow. I need all the rest I could get. We have so many people coming and I don't even know a quarter of them. When did the list include that many people?"

"I don't know but I'm sure the twins will love it," he whispered into her hair. "With the bounce castles, the ice cream, and the different sections for boys and girls, I'm also sure they wouldn't know their birthday had passed two months ago."

With all that had been going on then, they didn't have the energy or time to organize the momentous time for a baby. It was their first year, after all. So, they decided to do so when the dust had settled. They both agreed they wanted a small party with close friends. Only it now became a bigger production. Now, instead of the initial fifty people, they had over two hundred. He, himself, was puzzled how it ballooned to such proportions.

Blowing out a breath, letting him know she was letting the issue go for now, April laid Dawn down in her bassinet and hugged him. Feeling her belly pressing into him, he felt pride and happiness swell in him. He couldn't explain the pride but it was a primal thing. And the one time he'd tried to explain it to April, she'd let him know it was a guy thing. But Cameron understood it. It was the reason Sharon was pregnant all the time.

The happiness was simple to explain. He had the woman of his dreams and his children with one more on the way. They were all safe and happy, all their needs and wants satisfied. He could hear his children's laughter more often now. There was no more danger, hidden or otherwise. And they were all together.

What more could he ask for?

~

Gingerly lowering herself onto a sofa, April heaved a sigh of relief when her bottom finally touched the seat. Exhaustion demanded she go to bed but she was still high from the party. The twins had loved it obviously but for her to enjoy it was unexpected. Even Paul had made an appearance before Joan herded him back to his room, citing that he was still not well enough to stay long. April saw something more develop between them but decided to leave it aside for the twins.

She joined the twins in almost every game. Jason would also join for games that needed two adults. Of course, with her being hampered by the sudden shift in her center of gravity, they didn't win most games but they laughed a lot. And, during the times they'd win, she was a crying mess. Dang her hormones.

While her mind went back to the joys of the event earlier, the doorbell rang which she debated answering. She ran through the remaining people in the house who could answer the door. Joan and Mrs. Salvador were busy with the caterers and cleaning crew. Paul was already in bed, his energy still easily depleted. Jason was putting the twins to bed. While she was busy...resting. The doorbell kept ringing. It was starting to irritate her. *Why wouldn't they go away?*

Unable to bear the noise any longer, she sighed and got up, making her way to the door. She still couldn't believe what a difference a few extra pounds in front of her did to her gait and the way she brought herself and how the physical proof of the life inside of her brought out the tears even more. Generally, she just cried a lot.

"I'm coming," she called out over the incessant ringing of the doorbell. Still it rang. "Sheesh, give it a break." She opened the door and in front of her stood the last person she'd expected to see that day.

"Harry? Hey, where were you? The party's over, but you can still come in for some food if you're hungry." He only stood still in the doorway. April had to haul him inside. "Come on. Mom saved some, in case I get hungry. And you know her. She'd save enough for an army—"

"Elena's pregnant," Harry said woodenly, his face impassive and stricken. April had been in the middle of bringing him to the kitchen while rambling about everything and nothing when he'd made the announcement. She stopped and looked at him, surprised.

"Say what?" she said breathily. His face didn't change but his grip tightened.

254

"Elena's pregnant. And I'm going to be a father."

BOOK YOU MIGHT ENJOY

WORK FOR ME
RM Stones

"I hate you," I said.

Louise "Lou" Whitlock, a young college student, finds herself in debt with billionaire, Zachary Caldwell.

Willing to pay but didn't have any resources, she is forced to work for the enigmatic, hot-headed billionaire.

With both hating each other's presence, they are bound for a disaster.

But do they really hate each other or is hatred actually love in disguise?

Secrets are uncovered and revealed and there is something definitely more than what meets the eye.

Grab a copy and join Lou and Zach as they stumble and fight for what they think is right because after all, love can move mountains.

BOOK YOU MIGHT ENJOY

LIFE SUCKS IF YOU'RE MARRIED TO A BILLIONAIRE
Krystel Grace

Kei Forest, a stubborn young man, is living an ordinary college life until he receives a letter that will change his life forever.

Recently turned twenty-one, he is now faced with a decision that will shake the very foundation of his life.

His parents had left him an unimaginable wealth but under one condition: he must marry the arrogant business magnate Jace Langlois.

Will Kei put up with this ordeal? Or will he leave his husband after he gets his inheritance?

This is an LGBT book you shouldn't miss. Grab a copy now!

ACKNOWLEDGEMENTS

I would like to first thank my parents for allowing me to choose my own road in life and not limiting my creativity since I was young.

Secondly, I thank my siblings for all the nonsensical and ridiculous con-versations we had. That has helped me create my stories.

Lastly, I would like to thank all those who have read my book from when I first started. Through all your feedback and advice and support, I am able to be where I am today.

AUTHOR'S NOTE

Thank you so much for reading *Accidental Babies*! I can't express how grateful I am for reading something that was once just a thought inside my head.

Please feel free to send me an email. Just know that my publisher filters these emails. Good news is always welcome.
saiyidah_rahman@awesomeauthors.org

Sign up for my blog for updates and freebies!
saiyidah-rahman.awesomeauthors.org

One last thing: I'd love to hear your thoughts on the book. Please leave a review on Amazon or Goodreads because I just love reading your comments and getting to know you!

Can't wait to hear from you!

Saiyidah Rahman

ABOUT THE AUTHOR

Since she was young, Saiyidah loves to read. That is also why she needs to wear glasses, an ever constant headache to her parents. But it was her voracious reading that sparked her interest in writing. Having started at Wattpad, she began writing during her university years and have not stopped ever since.

When she is not writing, she is always eating. Living in the urban metropolis of Singapore, she has been exposed to food from many cultures. With so many cultures coming together in the melting pot that is Singapore, she is spoilt for choices and food is always in her mind.

www.ingramcontent.com/pod-product-compliance
Lightning Source LLC
Chambersburg PA
CBHW022155170626
46807CB00005B/2213